My Fa
Kidnapper

NEW YORK TIMES AND USA TODAY BESTSELLING AUTHOR
MELANIE MORELAND

My Favorite Kidnapper by Melanie Moreland
Copyright © 2023 Moreland Books Inc.
Copyright #1202009
ISBN Print 978-1-990803-58-1
All rights reserved

MORELAND
BOOKS INC.

Edited by Lisa Hollett of Silently Correcting Your Grammar
Proofreading by Sisters Get Lit.erary Author Services
Cover design by Feed Your Dreams Designs
Cover Art by Abby O. Sweet, Bigfoot Creative

Cover content is for illustrative purposes only and any persons
depicted on the cover is an illustration.

This book is a work of fiction.
The characters, events, and places portrayed in this book are

Readers with concerns about content or subjects depicted can check out the content advisory on my website:
https://melaniemoreland.com/extras/fan-suggestions/content-advisory/

This book is a romantic comedy. The content of this book is for entertainment purposes only.

I set out to write a darker themed, morally grey kidnapping story and the characters took it to someplace I never expected. This romantic comedy is not a parody or satire on the kidnapping trope nor to make light of human trafficking.

I hope you enjoy it in the intent it was written.

Contents

Dedication

For Karen
Who asked, pleaded, and begged.
Then laughed, loved, and encouraged.
This one is all yours.

And to my Matthew
My favorite one ever.
xxx

Chapter One

~~

DANTE

I pulled the car into a parking spot close to the doors of the venue, glancing around in curiosity. The building was large and spacious. Elegant, even from the outside—hardly a surprise knowing my sister-in-law, Amanda. There were other cars around, no doubt staff getting ready for the event. A van was parked around the side, and from what I had seen as I'd driven around the parking lot, it was a food-type vehicle, probably bringing in some outside catering for the wedding.

I stroked my fingers along my chin, frowning when I realized the scruff was longer than normal. I would have to trim it before returning later. But for now, I wanted to walk around and scope out the building.

"Looking for escape routes," my brother would mutter if he were around.

And he'd be right.

I was always completely aware of my surroundings. I knew the entrances and exits. The back doors and hidden spots staff was aware of for easy access. I familiarized myself every time. It was part of the game. Part of my life.

Inside, I strolled the halls, not surprised when I wasn't stopped or questioned by the occasional staff member I came across. A few looked at me with curiosity, but that was it. They recognized the fact that I wasn't to be bothered with inane questions about my visit. They simply nodded and kept doing their duties. My ego wanted to believe it was my menacing presence, but the truth was, my brother, Paolo, probably informed the venue I would be here looking around.

Either way, I was left alone.

I preferred it that way.

I paused, looking in the kitchen, located in the back part of the building and hidden from sight. It was a bustling, crowded area. The head chef barked out orders as they prepped for the elaborate dinner that would be served later tonight.

I saw the venue where my goddaughter would exchange vows with her soon-to-be husband. The ceilings soared, the roof mostly glass, and I imagined at sunset, the light was spectacular. Workers were draping boughs of flowers, carrying in arrangements, hanging tulle and tiny lights wrapped around branches. It would be lovely when finished, and I could appreciate the work behind the striking façade being created. Art didn't exist only on canvases or in stone. It existed everywhere if you chose to look for it.

And I was always looking.

I could already see the theme. Carolina, my niece and goddaughter, was a free spirit. Wild in some ways. She loved nature, the outdoors, and hated formality. Her mother, Amanda, was the exact opposite. She adored structure, haute couture, pomp and ceremony, and everything my brother's fortune could provide her. It appeared as though they had come to an agreement on the wedding, and a fancy woodland was being created everywhere. One that would never exist in nature, but extravagant enough to satisfy the mother and rustic enough to make the daughter content as well. It was a delicate balance.

I could only imagine the money my brother was spending to keep them both happy.

Not that he would care since he was crazy about both the women in his life.

I found the room for the reception and slipped inside. Easily holding three hundred guests, it was already set up for the evening. The tables were draped in linens—fine china, silverware, and crystal gleamed in the muted light. Fake trees, more flowers, lights, and moss-covered benches dotted the room. Material had been swathed overhead to look like a canopy of trees in the forest. The effect of the indoor woods was captivating, and I knew Carolina would love it. I walked the perimeter, mapping out the tables and pathways in my mind. I stopped and gazed in curiosity at the draped table in the corner and headed in that direction. The table held the wedding cake.

Except it was unlike any wedding cake I had ever seen. Rising from a fallen log, the cake appeared to be tiers of flowers, branches, and birch bark. So convincing I had to peer closely to ensure it wasn't real. Extending from the same log were additional cakes. They were nestled among entwined branches, each a work of art, spectacular down to the knots on the trees. I counted a dozen large cakes in addition to the six-tiered tower. A few were multiple layers; some were smaller. I realized cupcakes were also set along the log, each one its own piece of art. The moss-covered tabletop was actually hundreds of tiny, decorated cupcakes. I had never seen a display like it, and I wondered at the team that must have created it.

They were obviously still here in the building. Their supplies were sitting beside the display, waiting for their return. Curious, I looked at the materials.

A cart containing various icings. An airbrush machine and several containers of various-sized cupcakes. I had a sweet tooth I could never satisfy, and unable to resist, I reached in and took a small vanilla one, rolling it in the white buttercream and popping it into my mouth.

The cake was a flawless bite of vanilla. Rich, but light —exactly the way it should be. The buttercream was whipped, with a flavor I couldn't place but liked very much. I shut my eyes as I chewed and swallowed, almost groaning with delight over the utter perfection of the cake and frosting. It was the best I had ever tasted.

There was no choice. I had to have another one. I took a larger one, rolling it in the icing again and munching on it as I stared at the masterpiece. Brought to life with cake and frosting.

And talent.

One branch drooped a little, and I reached down to tuck it into position, shocked to realize it wasn't a twig, but edible. Inspecting it, I discovered most of the sculpture was real. The few flowers and branches woven in were for structure and to hide the inner supports. It was fabulous.

I leaned closer, continuing to scrutinize the work, when I heard a gasp behind me. I looked over my shoulder, freezing at the vision bearing down on me. The woman was like an explosion of rage as she rushed my way.

"What are you doing? Get away from that!"

I began to straighten, shocked as she slapped my hand like an errant schoolboy, causing the treat in my fingers to begin to fall. Luckily, she caught it, but she was incensed. "Oh my God, you're eating the cupcakes? I need those!"

I indicated the table. "It looked as if you were done. I didn't think one would be missed."

She cast her eyes over the trays. "You had two!" she spat, indignant. "I should have you arrested!"

"For stealing a cupcake? That's a bit over the top, I think."

"They aren't your cupcakes," she protested. "It's just rude."

"It was the best cupcake I have ever eaten."

That deflated her anger until she saw the icing and the obvious well I had left behind in the bucket. Her anger returned in a flash. She shoved the half-eaten cupcake at me and waved her hands as if shooing away a pesky bird.

"Take it and go. Don't touch my cake!"

Her cake?

She pushed at me ineffectually. "Get away!" she repeated. "What the h-e-double-hockey-sticks are you doing in here anyway?"

I blinked, not moving, finding myself enraptured by her fury.

H-e-double what?

She barely came to my chest. I outweighed her by eighty pounds easily. I could pick her up and carry her without breaking a sweat. Snap her neck like one of the twigs she was so angry over my touching. She was younger than me. A lot younger than my thirty-eight years. Dressed in yellow overalls with a black T-shirt underneath that had stripes on the arms, she resembled an angry bee, and I was obviously disturbing her little hive. Smears of icing decorated the bib of her overalls. Her brown hair was chaotic and messy, falling from a bun held haphazardly away from her face by chopsticks. Curls escaped and danced on her forehead and around her face like corkscrews. Her dark eyes were wide in fury, her cheeks flushed. I noticed more icing on her skin, and I was surprised to feel the urge to grab her face and lick it off.

Her anger brought me out of my odd thoughts.

"If you've made a mess of this, I will hunt you down and destroy you," she seethed. "If I'm short a cupcake, I will make sure they know it wasn't me. And don't touch it. I saw you poking at it."

"I merely touched a branch that was drooping."

"I merely touched a branch," she mimicked. "I'll barely touch you with my foot in your ass. Now, back away!"

I held up my hands in supplication, trying to hide my amusement. If it were anyone else speaking to me this way, they would face my wrath. But I found her misplaced ire oddly endearing. I liked her spark.

"You think this is funny?" she snarled. "I've been creating this for days. Weeks. And you come in and touch it? I have no idea who you are, but I will get you fired!" she threatened.

"I don't work here, Little Bee," I said, wanting to provoke her a little more. "Put away the stinger."

She reacted exactly the way I thought she would.

"Don't call me that. You're trespassing." She pointed to the door. "Get out, or I'll call the police."

I felt my lips quirk. She was so angry she was shaking. I found it adorable, which was odd.

I hated adorable.

"You don't know who I am, do you?" I asked. Obviously, Paolo's instructions hadn't included my speaking to her. She was fearless, standing in front of me, telling me off. It was captivating.

"A legend in your own mind, obviously. I don't give a flipping care who you are. The big bad wolf, for all I know. I'm here to finish this job, and I'm not going to let you stop me. Now, go away." She spun on her heel, picking up the airbrush and tilting her head, studying the cake sculpture and ignoring me.

I stepped closer. "You made this?" I asked quietly, breathing in the scent of vanilla, maple, chocolate, and spice. And something else. Something floral and feminine.

It was her. And once again, I liked it.

She paused, unsure of how to stay angry but still reply. "Yes. I did."

"All on your own?" I was shocked. It was such a massive undertaking I had assumed an entire group of people worked on it. Not one slip of a woman.

She turned her head, and I saw another smear of icing close to her ear, right next to a dimple I hadn't noticed. "Yes."

"Impressive. It is a work of art."

She blinked, looked at the display, sliding a cupcake into the right position. Her voice and expression softened. "It was meant to be."

"Did you design it?"

"Yes."

"And bake it?" I guessed.

She straightened her shoulders and turned to face me. "Yes, I did."

I lifted her hand, bent, and kissed the knuckles. "It is as beautiful and unique as you are. You should be proud."

Her mouth opened in surprise. I was shocked how much I wanted to kiss those lips. I had a feeling when not spewing angry words, they would be sweeter than the entire cake and icing sculpture behind her.

But I liked her spitting and enraged.

Keeping my eyes locked with hers, I reached around and grabbed another cupcake. Her eyes widened as I lifted it to my mouth and took a bite. Before she could explode, I pressed my lips to hers.

"Thank you for the snack."

Then I turned and walked away before I did something stupid like stay and kiss her until she begged me to fuck her right there.

Because I would.

Chapter Two

BRIANNA

The door shut behind the cupcake-stealing stranger, and I let out a muffled shriek of annoyance. I had no idea who he was, who *he* thought he was, but coming in here and touching the cake display?

Unacceptable.

I peered into the container, satisfied that I had more than enough cupcakes to complete the job. I had baked extra, but still. He'd eaten three. Without asking.

That was just plain rude.

If I saw him later, I would give him a piece of my mind.

I should probably tell him off for kissing me too. And touching my cake. But especially the stolen kiss. That was what I was the most pissed off about.

At least, I thought it was.

I shook my head. I was certain it was.

In the meantime, I needed to finish the cake display so I could drape it and keep it cool and safe.

I tucked some more cupcakes in place, adding icing and airbrushing them to look like the moss covering the table. Some of the larger ones became flowers that dotted the fallen tree stump. Then I positioned the edible pearls and glittering drops that looked like water, scattering them liberally.

I stood back, casting a critical eye over the table. It was magnificent. I clasped my hands together, grinning in delight. I had done it.

I had met Carolina Frost in university. She was in her last year, and I was in my first, although mine was an accelerated course. We were both taking design and had gone to sit at the same table one day when the cafeteria was extra busy and seats were scarce. We shared the table, introduced ourselves, and we became study partners and friends. Her advanced knowledge helped me with some of the classes I was struggling with, and I repaid her with cupcakes when I discovered her sweet tooth. We had two very different lifestyles. Her family was wealthy, she didn't work, she had a boyfriend, and she was carefree and a nature lover. She was naturally graceful and lovely. People were drawn to her warmth and outgoing personality.

I was broke all the time, worked two jobs to keep my head above water, hated the outdoors with a passion, and had no love life. I had neither the time nor the inclination for a relationship. I was too busy getting myself through school. I was shy and awkward, and crowds bothered me. She was younger than I was since I'd had to work and save up the money to go to school, but that never seemed to matter to her. She was mature and kind, and we liked each other, despite our differences.

And we got along well. She never made me feel less than her because of our different-sized bank accounts or our age gap. She was as happy to hang in a coffee shop around the corner from my little basement apartment as she was to laze around her massive bedroom at her parents' home. They were pleasant and welcoming the couple of times I'd gone there, but it made me uncomfortable, so we mostly hung at the coffee shop to study. We were schoolmates, friendly and happy to keep our relationship there. I didn't mix with her friends, and she didn't mix with mine.

Not that I had many.

After graduation, she got a job at a web design company owned by a relative. I finished my course, still worked part time at a graphics firm, and had added a pastry arts program, deciding that was where my real passion lay. It was my goal to open my own high-end bakery one day.

When she and Allan got engaged, she asked me to make her cake. I had been working at a bakery for years, and cake decorating was a passion of mine. I had a small side business that helped pay the bills, and I created fantasy wedding cakes—some of them taking me weeks to bake, decorate, and assemble. Part of the fee included my being at the wedding, setting up the cake, and making sure that it was perfect for the day. That it was cut and disassembled properly.

My reputation was building slowly. I didn't make much profit by the time I bought the ingredients, the hours I spent decorating and designing, plus the fact that the old witch I worked for overcharged me to store the cakes in her freezer, use the ovens, and borrow the delivery van on the day of the wedding. She did it grudgingly and only because it often brought customers into the store.

I longed for the day I didn't have to work for her. When I had my own bakery. But until I paid off some of my student loans and was in the position to open my own shop, it was my life.

For now.

I wondered what the stranger with the wandering lips would think of the cake now that it was done.

I tried not to think of his firm mouth pressed to mine. How tall he was. The heat and muscles I felt under his perfectly cut suit. The air of power and control he exuded. He looked stern and forbidding, yet he had teased me, his voice oddly placid when he spoke.

The way he smelled—like something exotic and decadent. Rich. How gentle his touch had been.

How I had almost wished he had kissed me again instead of stealing my cupcakes.

A squeal behind me brought me out of my musings. Carolina rushed forward, stopping in front of the table, her hand covering her mouth. Tears sprang to her eyes as she looked at the cake table.

"Bri," she murmured. "It's so incredible!"

Her mother strolled in, stopping in amazement. "I had no idea," she said. "How spectacular!"

Mrs. Frost had wanted a traditional cake. Ten tiers. Piped flowers. Bride and groom on top. Carolina had been adamant. *I agreed to an indoor wedding, Mom. But I want my woodland theme, and I want the cake Bri sketched for me.*

She had won the battle, and I could see from the pleased expression on her mother's face she was glad she had given in.

"It will be the talk of the crowd," Mrs. Frost said with a smile. "Young lady, you are exceedingly talented."

"She is going to own her own bakery one day," Carolina said as she slipped her arm around my waist, hugging me.

"You should do it soon," Mrs. Frost murmured.

I bit my tongue before I informed her it cost a lot of money to start up a business. Unless I had a sugar daddy, that wasn't happening right now.

Unbidden, the image of the man from earlier, the cupcake stealer, came to mind. I pushed that errant thought away but grabbed on to the flash of annoyance.

"Some old guy was in here earlier," I told Carolina. "Stole a few cupcakes. I had to tell him off."

"Oh no. Who was he?"

I shrugged. "A staff member showing up for work early, I assume." He'd said he didn't work here, but I thought he was lying to save his job.

"I'll investigate," Mrs. Frost assured me.

I shook my head. "I told him off, and he didn't do any harm. He was quite complimentary, aside from the cupcake stealing."

"Sounds like something Dad would do." Carolina smirked. "Or Uncle Dante."

Mrs. Frost laughed. "Yes, they both have a sweet tooth, which you inherited. But Dante isn't coming until later, and he isn't old." At my confused look, she smiled. "He is Paolo's older brother by two years and Carolina's godfather. He lives out of the country." She lifted her eyebrows. "He is rather high-handed."

"And grumpy as hell a lot of the time," Carolina added. "He speaks mostly in grunts and frowns."

I thought of the teasing way the stranger was with me. His smile as he ate the cupcakes. The fleeting feeling of his lips pressed to mine.

Not grumpy at all.

"Ah."

Mrs. Frost looked at her watch. "Come, Carolina, we need to get you ready. The wedding is in three hours."

Carolina hugged me again. "Thank you for the cake. It's breathtaking. And you'll be here, right?"

"Yep. Until it is cut and served."

"You're at table forty-one—close to the cake, the way you asked."

"Great. See you soon."

I watched them leave, feeling a little tug on my heart at their closeness. I had no family, my parents having died when I was younger. I'd bounced from foster home to foster home, and since I'd aged out, I had been on my own.

I had been my whole life, if I was honest.

I never knew the love of a mother or father. A sibling.

Anyone, really. The person I was closest to was Carolina, and even her, I held back. I didn't get involved in her life outside of school much, or with her family.

I didn't understand how to let someone in or get that close.

I shook my head and cleared my thoughts, doing a last once-over on the cake, adding some more touches. Finally done, I packed up the supplies. I would put them in the kitchen, then use the small room they'd given me to change and shower once I covered the cake table to stop dust and thieving fingers from touching it. I would come back after the ceremony and uncover it so when people came in, they saw it.

I was looking forward to seeing their reactions.

I got ready, slipping into the back of the altar room, watching from the shadows as Carolina and Allan said their vows. The twinkle lights and the wood arch wrapped with flowers were romantic. The room was filled with floral pieces and ferns. Leaves, branches, and fauna were woven together. Candles flickered. It was breathtaking.

Carolina was beautiful. Her gown was whimsical and suited her. The flowers she carried reflected the woodland theme—nothing symmetrical or hothouse about them. She said her vows in a loud, clear voice, smiling widely at her groom. I marveled at her obvious devotion to Allan and wondered what it would feel like to love someone that strongly.

More than once, I felt a shiver run up my neck and felt eyes on me, but when I looked around, I saw nothing. Everyone's attention was on the bride and groom—as it should be. Yet I couldn't rid myself of the feeling.

As they kissed, I slipped from the room and headed to the reception area. With the help of one of the servers, we uncovered the cake table, and I lit the tiny lights that flickered along the tree limb, highlighting some of the designs. I folded the cover and ran to the van, adding it to the extra cupcakes and supplies I had on hand. Before I could shut the door, a man appeared, startling me. I gasped, beginning to fall backward as I stumbled back in shock. He grabbed me, pulling me tight to his chest.

"Steady there, Little Bee."

Instantly, my hackles rose. It was the cupcake-kiss-stealing stranger.

"What are you doing? Are you stalking me?"

Just then, I noticed the cigar clamped between his lips. He stepped back, blowing a perfect smoke ring into the air. "I was taking a stroll between the nuptials and reception. I noticed the door to the van was open. I thought perhaps a robbery was happening." He peered around me. "I was wrong." Then he grinned, the action changing his entire demeanor. I'd thought he was handsome before. When he smiled, he was devastating. His deep brown hair was brushed high off his forehead. Heavy brows set off his eyes that were like liquid fire. Molten gold gleamed under thick lashes. Scruff framed his full lips. Two dimples high on his cheeks deepened when he smiled a certain way. They were little divots of sexy on his face. And he was in a tux. Tall, sensual, deadly.

And smiling.

Was he smiling at me?

I wasn't sure until I followed his gaze and realized where his attention landed and what made him smile.

"Don't even think about it, old man," I almost growled and grabbed the door to shut it.

He stopped me, his cigar discarded on the ground. He caught me around the waist, pulling me close again and overwhelming me with his rich scent. I had never encountered a cologne I wanted to roll in, but his was addictive. I blamed the fragrance for diverting my attention, and before I could do anything but bury my nose into his chest and inhale his essence, he popped the top off the container and grabbed more cupcakes. He stepped back, holding them high so I couldn't possibly take them away.

"Old man?" he questioned. "I'll address that later, but right now, I need icing."

"Has anyone ever told you that you are a rude, overbearing tyrant?" I frowned at him. "Stop stealing my cupcakes."

"I have been called all of those things," he acknowledged with a careless shrug. "High-handed, demanding, arrogant, bossy, to name a few others." He paused. "Not *old man*, though. That was rude, Little Bee."

I tried not to blush. It was a bit rude.

"So is Little Bee," I insisted.

"But you are one." He smiled. "All riled up and ready to attack. Defend your territory."

I lifted one eyebrow, not saying a word.

He smirked at me as if he knew my thoughts. "You're being rude again."

"I didn't say anything."

"You don't have to. You say it all with your eyes." He gestured impatiently to the van. "Now, icing," he repeated.

"I will have your job." I said haughtily. "For harassing me."

He chuckled and bent low, catching me by surprise as he kissed me again. Once. Then again. Harder, his lips lingering. He eased back, looking down at me, another smile pulling his lips upward.

Jesus, I suddenly wanted to smear icing on him and lick it off. Old man or not.

Everywhere.

He smiled wider, his dimples deepening.

"You are entertaining. I might let you do that one day. And I will disprove the old man theory," he vowed. "Thoroughly." He winked, turned, and walked away, stopping to pick up his discarded cigar. I shook my head, muttering to myself in embarrassment for speaking my thoughts out loud. I spun around, cursing when I realized he'd taken one entire container of icing, leaving the lid behind. The man was stealthy and fast. Like a ninja. I had to admit, I was impressed. For an old man, he moved quickly.

I counted six more missing cupcakes.

Six.

How the hell had he taken six?

His kisses weren't *that* intoxicating.

Were they?

I'd never know.

Since it was the last time that would happen, it would remain an unanswered question.

I was certain of it.

T made it through the long and painful dinner, on edge and slowly dying inside. I hated social functions. I was naturally shy, and being seated with a group of strangers was difficult for me, which was why I usually avoided social gatherings. I only made exceptions for weddings when one of my cakes was being served. Usually, the bride was only too happy for me to sit in the kitchen or elsewhere to keep an eye on the cake until it was time for me to make sure it was served properly, but Carolina had insisted I sit with the guests. I was used to much more casual attire, and my dress felt foreign against my skin, the material loose around my legs. My bare arms were cool and I wanted to tug at the neckline a hundred times, but I forced myself to sit still. I had thought it pretty when I got ready, but now it seemed plain compared to the glitter and shimmer of the dresses around me. Some of the necklines were cut so low you could almost see nipples, and some hems so short I wondered how they sat without exposing their butt cheeks or even something more private. My hem fell below my knees, the neckline modest, and the capped sleeves that seemed flirty in the store, now all felt old and frumpy. Even the pretty green seemed dull. I was mostly ignored at the table, the people around me drinking, laughing, and already knowing one another. I tugged my shawl around my shoulders, feeling invisible. I wanted to leave, but I watched the cake, ready to spring into action if anyone started touching it. But aside from admiring it, no one had approached it. As soon as it was cut, I was free to go. I counted the minutes.

I kept my eyes peeled for the cupcake stealer, but I didn't spot him. He had to be the event coordinator for the building, which explained his slightly haughty ways and how he kept appearing. I didn't say anything to Carolina about running into him again or the fact that he'd taken more cupcakes. I'd have to explain how he distracted me, and I really didn't want to do that.

I doubted I would get another gig here, so there was no point in ruining his career. And I had extra cupcakes, so no harm had really been done.

That was what I told myself.

It had nothing to do with his talented mouth.

Not at all.

After the speeches and first dance, I headed to the corner and watched as the staged photos were taken, the cake captured on film, then I helped the staff slice the cakes and slid cupcakes onto plates to go to tables and be shared. Once it was done, I sighed in relief and sadness. So much work to disappear so quickly. I heard the positive comments about the cakes, which made me smile, and I chatted with some people who came up to me to express their thoughts on my creation. I really hoped this display would lead to more jobs for me, and I gave my number to four couples and a few older mothers and fathers who had children being married or anniversary parties coming up.

The staff removed the last of the cakes and wheeled the table into the kitchen. They would clean up the cake, and I would take the last of the reusable supplies from the table and depart. I had to give them a short while to do so.

The band started up again, and I slipped to the balcony, enjoying the cool air and the quiet as I waited. I leaned on the rail overlooking the pond, the fountain's graceful arcs of water changing color as they cast ripples on the surface.

A song started, and I shut my eyes, tapping the gentle beat with my fingers on the iron rail. I began to hum, the lyrics and tune clear in my head. I sang softly, the notes coming easily. I loved to sing. When I was baking, I always had music playing, and I sang along all the time, grateful to be alone and able to do so. The tension in my shoulders loosened. I lost myself to the melody, my fingers and toes tapping out the rhythm.

There was no warning but the sudden sense of intensity behind me. The hairs on the back of my neck rose. My breathing picked up.

And then, he was there.

His chest pressed against my back, his enticing scent surrounding me.

"You should be dancing."

"I-I don't dance."

"You do now."

He spun me around, yanking me close. He wrapped a hand around my hair, tugging it until I was looking into his eyes. Under the light, the molten gold was rimmed in black. Unique. Like him.

"You dance with me."

He moved, and without thought, I followed. It was as if we'd danced together for a lifetime. My lack of height didn't matter. My inexperience didn't bother him. He led, and I went where he directed my body.

"Sing for me," he demanded. "Just for me."

Normally unable to sing in front of anyone, I opened my mouth and did exactly what he wanted. Low and soft, but loud enough he could hear. I sang the beautiful words as we moved around the deserted balcony, our footsteps never faltering, our bodies never separating. One song bled into another, and when I didn't know the words, I hummed. My head rested on his torso, and I felt the rumble of his chest as he sighed in pleasure. He kept me close, and for the first time in my life, I felt as if I was exactly where I belonged.

With him.

Which was all sorts of crazy.

I didn't know him.

I never would.

The song ended, the band taking a break, and he eased from me, staring down, his eyes locked on mine.

"Who are you?" he breathed.

"Nobody."

"Wrong answer, Little Bee."

"It's all I've ever been."

"Not anymore."

Then his mouth was on mine. Hard. Insistent. Passionate. I flung my arms around his neck as he lifted me into his arms, holding me tight to his body as he ravished my mouth. His tongue was velvet on mine as he explored me. I felt us move into the shadows, the cold, hard side of the building pressing into my back, a direct contrast to the heat of him. I wrapped my arms tighter around him, swimming in all he was. His warmth. His taste. The way he controlled the kiss. Controlled me. I was lost in a vortex of never-experienced emotions and sensations. My body was on fire, consumed by the desire pulsating through it. I wanted him.

It didn't matter who he was.

I wanted him.

He tore his mouth from mine, dropping his head to my neck, kissing and tonguing the skin, groaning curse words, wicked assurances, filthy promises of what he wanted to do to me. And I was going to let him.

Until the door opened, and I heard Carolina's voice. "I was sure I saw her come out here." The door shut again, but it broke the spell I was under.

I froze, the reality of what I was doing, what I was allowing to happen, hitting me. I didn't know this man. I hadn't even asked him his name.

I pushed at his chest, and he growled in displeasure but released me.

"We'll wait a moment and leave," he murmured.

"No," I snapped. "We won't."

And before he could react, I ran.

Away from him.

Away from that mouth.

That temptation.

I heard his shout of anger. His roar of fury.

I ran as if my life depended on escaping.

I had a feeling it did.

Chapter Three

DANTE

"*I'm nobody. It's all I've ever been.*"

I couldn't get those damn words out of my head. They were stuck in there on a loop, playing in the background constantly. I hated them. I hated the fact that I couldn't forget them.

Or her.

The little angry bee without a stinger. The one who tasted like honey.

The one whose memory I was trying to ignore.

She had run. One moment, she was in my arms, our mouths locked together, and the next, she was gone. Running away as fast as her little legs could move in the heels she wore.

I had to wait before I could follow, my erection making my movements restricted. Back inside the reception, I scanned the room for her, assuming she had returned to her cake. But it was gone, now simply a table containing pieces of the sweet treats ready to eat. I began to head to the kitchen to find her, when Carolina stepped in front of me.

"I haven't danced with my favorite godfather."

I laughed, unable to resist her teasing. I never had. I pulled her into my arms, and we began to move around the dance floor. "I am your only godfather."

"My belated, grumpy, yet still beloved one," she replied.

My younger brother Paolo had been a wild child his entire life, constantly into trouble. After our parents died, his behavior became worse. He drank too much, had a constant stream of girlfriends, and couldn't handle responsibilities or keep a job—even when I was his employer. I had almost given up on him, but on his twenty-second birthday, he met Amanda. She was seven years his senior and had an eight-year-old daughter she had raised as a single mother. He changed overnight, falling in love with both mother and daughter. He stopped his excessive drinking, became my right hand, a husband, and a father in a short span of time. Due to an accident in his early years, he was unable to father his own kids, and Carolina became his world. I became an uncle, and in short order, they asked me to be Carolina's godfather. She was a sweet, loving little girl I adored, and I accepted the honor quickly.

"Was the day everything you wanted, Pumpkin?" I asked, calling her by the nickname I'd given her years ago.

"That and more."

"You were, are, beautiful. I wish you every happiness."

She squeezed me.

"If that boy gives you trouble, you call me."

She laughed. "So chatty tonight, Uncle Dante."

I pressed a kiss to her forehead. I was a man of few words when it came to my family. To anything, really. People tended to take my silence for grumpiness. I didn't make an effort to change their opinion.

I spun her around the room, trying not to reflect on the fact that even though she was taller and more graceful than the angry bee I had danced with before, our movements earlier had been so in sync, it was as if I were dancing with the music itself. Carolina danced very well, but she didn't live the song. My little bee became part of the melody.

I finished the dance and handed her off to her impatiently waiting new husband, then stepped into the kitchen to find the woman who had run from me, only to discover she was gone from the premises entirely. The staff informed me she was an external contractor hired by the family. Outside, the van was gone, and I tried to recall the name I had seen etched on the side. Nothing came to mind, and I decided it was for the best. I was at least ten years her senior. I didn't live here. She was too innocent for someone like me. She needed a steady young man who would marry her, give her a family, and get fat from eating her cakes. It was a brief, unexpected encounter. That was all, I told myself sternly.

So, I returned to the wedding, determined to put her out of my mind.

Yet, she remained on the periphery, the images of her dancing in my arms, singing in her low, sultry voice, always present. I thought of her adorable anger, the way she told me off, not worried about who I was. I recalled her taste. How easily I could distract her and steal her decadent cupcakes.

But long after the wedding was over, I couldn't stop thinking about her, no matter what I did. I woke up each morning, hard and aching, my hand wrapped around my weeping dick, her already on my mind.

And I was tired of fighting it.

My brother's amused voice broke into my musings.

"What is eating you? Amanda says you're grumpier than usual."

I turned and met his teasing expression, accepting the glass of scotch from his hand.

"I beg to differ. Your wife is being overdramatic. I simply refused the vitamin-infused green smoothie she was trying to get me to drink." I shuddered. "I hate all that green shit." I lifted my glass, admiring the golden hue of the drink it contained. "This is what I need to stay healthy."

He laughed and sat at his desk, crossing his legs. "Amanda is constantly on a health kick of one kind or another. I gave up trying to stop her years ago. I just go along with it."

"You drink that shit?" I sat down across from him.

He grinned. "She thinks I do. I take it from her, kiss her, and dump it somewhere. Just like I scrape the kale salad off my plate into the garbage disposal or give the gluten-free shit to the staff."

"Good plan."

"She thinks she needs to try harder so our age difference isn't noticeable. She doesn't believe me when I tell her not only does it not matter at all to me what others think, but she looks younger than I do anyway. She looks younger than you."

"You certainly married up," I agreed. "She is much better-looking."

"Fuck you."

Then we began to laugh. Amanda was stunning. But she wasn't high-maintenance. I had no idea how Paolo managed to attract her or keep her, but I was grateful. She had saved him. I would drink her smoothies or eat her god-awful kale salad to make her happy.

Usually.

Today, I wasn't in the mood.

I crossed my leg over my knee, rubbing the ankle.

"So. The wedding cake."

Paolo paused. "What about it? I thought it was spectacular. And delicious. I snuck four pieces and even got the kitchen staff to give me a box of cupcakes."

I hid my smile. I'd eaten seven pieces at the reception, tasting every flavor, and I'd packed up a half dozen pieces in a box and brought it back to my condo. I had eaten them all and craved more.

I also craved information.

"The girl who made it doesn't work for the venue. I asked."

He shook his head. "No, she was a friend of Carolina's from university."

Elation flooded my chest, along with the realization she might be even younger than I thought.

"Her name," I demanded.

"Why?"

"I want to hire her company," I lied smoothly.

"She doesn't have one—yet anyway. She is working toward that."

"Her name," I repeated.

"Brianna."

Little Bee was Brianna. It suited her.

"Contact information. I need it."

"I don't have it."

"What? How did you pay her?"

"She requested cash. Amanda paid her."

"Give me her last name and address, then."

He stroked his chin. "I have no idea. I only met her twice, I think. Amanda maybe a couple more times. I have no recollection of her last name or any idea where she lives. She is Carolina's friend, and since she is an adult, I don't know the details of all her friends."

I pulled out my phone and texted Amanda, who had gone to have lunch with a friend. I sipped my scotch impatiently, waiting for her response. When it came, I snorted in disgust.

"She doesn't recall either. Paid Brianna cash."

"Well, you can ask Carolina when she is back from her honeymoon."

That was in two weeks, which was far too long. "I'll be back home. I'll text her now."

He lifted his eyebrows, shaking his head in reminder. "The resort you sent them to is cell-phone free. It's getting popular. No devices of any kind are allowed. We have an emergency email at the resort you so generously paid for, but no phones in the cabana or with them. Stops them from working on their honeymoon."

Inside, I raged, but I was good at keeping my emotions under wraps. I knew that. But my head was so full of this girl, I had forgotten that rule on the resort, but I could get around it.

"Well then, I'll get it later."

"I still have a couple of cupcakes I'll share."

I leaned back, pretending that was all I cared about. "Perfect."

"How much longer are you here for?"

I shrugged. I had planned on leaving tomorrow, but now I had other ideas. "A few more days. I have some things to take care of."

"How're the galleries?"

"Business is great. At all of them."

"And the, ah, other ventures?"

I tilted my head, not giving anything away. "Quiet. I am only needed on occasion."

"Good."

"Everything all right for you?"

He nodded. "Some new clients, fresh money. Lots of investing and no one has lost a cent."

I flashed him a grin. His clients would never lose a penny. My brother had a magic touch and, with my silent support, would beat the market, no matter what.

I raised my glass. "To another successful year."

He lifted his as well. "May we both get what we want."

I sipped my scotch.

I fully intended to.

"Uncle Dante?" Carolina's face was confused and shocked. Her confusion gave way to distress.

"Oh my God, what happened? Are Mom and Dad okay?"

I held up my hand, silencing her. "They're fine."

"How did you find me?"

"I gave you your honeymoon as a gift. I know where you are. I made the arrangements for the video call."

I didn't tell her that my initial plan had been to fly there to get the information I needed, but I decided it would take too long. Instead, I called the manager and arranged it.

Easily done when you owned the resort.

"What is so urgent, then?"

"I need the name of the lady who made your cake. And her contact information."

She frowned, looking exactly the way Amanda did when she was displeased with Paolo. I had seen that look often.

"And what could possibly be so urgent you need that contact info immediately? I'm only gone two weeks."

"I am hosting an event and need something spectacular. The cake I saw fits that bill. But I need to make sure she can do it in the time frame required, and I have to make a decision by Tuesday."

She pursed her lips, studying me. I was an expert liar. In my business, I had to be. I met her gaze calmly, my expression open, with no signs of nerves.

"I understand her name is Brianna," I prompted. "But your parents were unable to recall a last name. There was a sign on the side of the van she drove, but I admit I didn't take much note of it."

Because I was too busy kissing her and stealing her cupcakes.

I kept that part to myself.

"Are you the old guy she said bothered her?"

I winced at the words "old guy" and "bother." I preferred mature and charming. I would have to remind my little bee of that.

"I was admiring her work. She thought I was interfering."

Carolina snorted. "You—interfere? As if *that* ever happened."

"I can cancel the rest of your honeymoon, Pumpkin," I reminded her.

She grimaced. "Okay, just teasing. Brianna Michaels. She works at the Piece of Cake on Grating Street. She does her own stuff on the side."

"Phone number," I demanded, shocked to see my hand was shaking as I wrote down the information.

"It's in my cell phone, which I don't have with me, and I can't remember it."

"It's fine. I'll visit her at work."

"Do it quietly. The battle-ax she works for gives her a hard time. Although she charges her enough."

"Charges her?" I questioned.

"Bri uses the bakery's ovens and freezers to store the cakes she makes. And borrows the van for delivery. MaryJo charges her—way too much, in my opinion. It's hard for Bri to get ahead."

"I'll make sure she is well paid."

"Okay. I'd appreciate that."

"Thanks, Pumpkin. Sorry to have interrupted the, ah, honeymoon. Don't tell your father. He'll kill me."

"More champagne tonight would keep my lips sealed."

"I can do that."

"Do you have enough pull to get extra of the cookies they leave at night? I really love those."

The guests received a small plate of cookies each night for a snack. They were always a favorite. Given Carolina's sweet tooth, it didn't surprise me she liked that perk.

"I'll do my best."

I hung up and texted Jordan the manager, instructing him to increase the number of fresh-baked cookies at night. And to add cold milk to the tray. Carolina always loved milk with her cookies.

Given the information she'd provided, it was the least I could do.

Then I made another call, requesting the information I wanted.

"Twenty-four hours," I instructed.

"I'll try," Arnie replied. "Not much time."

"I'll pay double."

"Consider it done."

I hung up, pleased.

By tomorrow, I would know everything I needed to know about my little bee and how to find her.

I had a feeling she wouldn't be as pleased to see me as I was to see her.

Chapter Four

DANTE

I had the file in eighteen hours. When Arnie texted me at six a.m., I was already awake and working. I was always working. He came to my condo with the file and left, his wallet substantially heavier.

I poured another cup of coffee and opened the file, unable to wait another moment. My body was almost vibrating with anxiety, my fingers trembling as I opened the thin file. Arnie had grimaced when he'd handed it to me.

"Not much to report on, Dante. This woman lives a pretty simple life. Aside from drowning in debt, not much interesting about her."

That was where he was wrong. I found her fascinating.

I couldn't explain it. I didn't understand it.

I wasn't given to flights of fancy. I worked hard. I enjoyed the luxuries my world afforded me. Fast cars, nice houses. Good wine and rich food. The occasional companion to quench other needs. I fulfilled every desire.

But the intensity of what I felt for this small stranger was shocking. A craving I couldn't satisfy. It was constant. I needed more. I had to find her and figure it out. I was certain once I solved the mystery of her attraction, it would fade.

It always did.

I stared at the file, scanning the documents. Only four pages, it didn't take long.

Brianna Michaels was twenty-six. Twelve years younger than me. An orphan. An only child. Aged out of the foster system, having lived in at least a dozen homes.

She lived in a crummy basement apartment in a questionable area of Toronto. Worked an endless string of part-time jobs and was obviously not afraid of hard work. Her grades were excellent, indicating intelligence. From what I could gather, she had some business, graphic design, and culinary courses under her belt. She'd worked at Piece of Cake for years. Arnie was correct; her student debts were high. She'd worked full time for a few years to help put herself through school, but with the cost of living in Toronto on her own, she had still racked up a lot of debt. I ran a finger over my lips, pausing to take a sip of coffee. I didn't know for certain, but it looked as if she had been searching for her passion. Given the intricate cake art I had seen, I would say she'd found it. But that would be a niche market, and she would require a lot of money to start up and maintain her business while she built her reputation. I flipped through her finances again, noting the larger purchases were all supplies for her cake baking. I frowned at the bank deposits she made, wondering how she made ends meet. I ran a finger down a column, recalling Carolina's remarks about her boss charging her for usage of the oven and freezer. Her small pay deposits indicated how much she was charged if I was correlating the numbers properly.

I drained my coffee and turned to the last page. I had her address, her cell number, her credit history. Everything. But none of it gave me insight into her.

He'd included an envelope, and I opened it, my breath catching at the pictures Arnie had managed to take. He had obviously been to the bakery where she worked and had taken them without her noticing.

The first one, she was talking to a customer. She was smiling, and the shot was clear. The pretty curls I liked were hanging around her forehead and ears again. The color was interesting. A warm brown in its hue, her hair had traces of red and gold woven in. Her eyes were dark and heavily fringed in long lashes, set under delicate eyebrows. She had a straight, elegant nose and a generous, wide mouth I had enjoyed kissing. She had pierced ears, small studs in both of them. Simple. I studied another picture of her concentrating, a furrow between her brows. She was packing up something, the tip of her tongue peeking out. I recalled the feel of her tongue sliding with mine, however briefly. I wanted to feel it again. To taste her again.

There were two other pictures. One of her speaking with a woman I assumed was her boss. Brianna looked upset, her hands clutching a piece of paper. The older woman looked smug, and I instantly disliked her. She had an air of superiority about her. And I had a feeling she lorded it over Brianna often.

The last one made my breath catch. Arnie had zoomed in, showing me Brianna's face as the woman walked away. She looked exhausted. Defeated. Far older than her years. Far sadder than she should look.

I didn't like the defeated woman in the pictures. I preferred her riled up and snapping at me, her eyes bright with her fire as she told me off.

No one ever told me off. They didn't dare.

But she had. More than once. And I had liked it.

I studied the first picture again. My little bee wasn't a woman whose beauty and elegance screamed at you. Her prettiness was quieter. It showed in her smile, the wide set of her eyes, her lovely hair. She was small in stature, but big in heart. Somehow, I already knew that.

She had run from me. Disappeared. I had found her, and I wasn't going to let her run again.

She was a mystery. Why I needed more of her, I had no idea, but I was going to find out.

And it was going to happen today.

T walked into the bakery, the scent of bread and sweet goods hitting my nose. It was bustling, with staff helping the customers. A few tables sat to one side by the windows, but most of the business seemed to be pickup and to-go orders.

I waited patiently and ordered a breakfast roll and coffee, then carried them to the corner table. I wasn't sure if Brianna was in the bakery, but I wanted to see the place she toiled at so often.

I sipped the coffee, eating the sweet bun slowly. It was tasty, but not as good as the cake I had eaten the other day. I eyed the cakes in the display case, certain I knew which of them she had decorated. Her work was precise, imaginative, and different. The others were standard piped cakes. It was almost as if her personality was reflected in her art.

Movement by my table caused me to look up, and I met the gaze of an older woman. Recalling the photographs, I recognized the woman as Brianna's boss. I lifted my coffee, not speaking, letting her take the lead.

I assumed this would be interesting.

"Would you like a refill?" she asked.

"No, thank you," I replied politely.

"Can I get you anything?"

"I was admiring your cake display. You have some nice ones in the case."

She preened. Actually preened, patting her hair into place and smirking. "Thank you. I enjoy decorating."

I lifted my eyebrows. "You decorate them?"

She sat down without an invitation, and I slid my chair back away from her. I didn't like to be too close to strangers.

Unless they had dark eyes and icing smeared on their cheeks.

"Yes, I did."

"I was at a wedding not long ago," I improvised. "Beautiful woodland cake. I heard the name of this bakery mentioned."

"Yes," she lied. "It was mine."

"Really."

"Yes. I oversee all the specialty cakes. Would you like to order one?"

"Perhaps."

"I'll give you my card."

"What if I want something specific? Different?"

"Oh, I can help you. Contact me directly."

"Do you have pictures of your work?"

She looked uncomfortable. "I can send you some if you give me your email."

I tamped down my anger. She was taking credit for Brianna's work. Trying to steal business from her. Instead of saying she had a great chef and decorator, she wanted me to think it was all her. No doubt, she'd get Brianna to bake it and then sell it to me and take the money, cutting Brianna out entirely.

"I'll think about it. In the meantime, I'll take your card."

She handed it to me, and I took it, careful not to touch her fingers. I then pointedly picked up my phone, concentrating on the screen. She huffed an annoyed noise but stood and left. A few moments later, a young girl came over, offering me a refill. I shook my head.

"No, thanks. Actually, I wanted to talk to Brianna about a cake. Is she in?"

"Not until two," she replied brightly.

"Thanks."

I drained my coffee and stood. If she wasn't here, there was no point in staying.

I would return then.

I got busy with calls and emails, the time passing quickly. It was almost three when I walked back into the bakery. It was quieter, the display cases not as full, the tables mostly deserted. I bought another coffee and a couple of cookies and sat back in the corner where I could watch the counter.

I hadn't seen her, but I knew she was here. I felt her. It was the oddest sensation, a small tingle down my spine, but I sensed her close. I sipped the coffee, my body tightening when I heard her voice coming from behind the closed door leading to the kitchen.

"I said four dozen, Kenneth. Is it so hard to understand simple instructions?"

The door swung open, and she appeared, carrying a tray. She looked annoyed and pissed off—my favorite look on her. She was in another pair of overalls, these ones pink, with a white T-shirt underneath them. Her hair was bundled up, the rebellious curls spilling around her face. Without a trace of makeup or jewelry on, she still made my chest ache with her subtle beauty.

She was muttering to herself, checking the trays, wiping the counter, lifting the coffeepot. Since she was buzzing around like the little bee she was, I had a feeling her stinger was armed today. She looked ready for a fight, and I wanted to be the one to provoke her.

She came around the counter, offering refills to people, not noticing me yet. I watched her carefully, spying the weariness around her eyes, the bent slope of her shoulders. She had an apron tied around her waist, traces of various ingredients on it. As she came closer, I saw the dusting of flour on the tip of her elegant nose. She still hadn't seen me. She was busy filling a cup when she suddenly tensed, her shoulders drawing back. Her head snapped up, and our eyes met across the tables.

Her eyebrows flew up, her dark eyes widening to the point of hilarity. Her gaze bounced around the room, no doubt looking for an escape. She began to back up, but I raised my cup, shaking my head in silent refusal. She wasn't getting away from me. Not this time.

She tossed her head, stubborn and willful. Then she came over, a wide, false smile on her face.

"Would you like a refill, sir?" she asked as if she had never seen me before now.

"Yes," I replied, pushing my cup toward her. Her hand shook as she poured the coffee.

"Hello, my little bee," I murmured. "I've been waiting."

She dropped the pot.

BRIANNA

It had been a shit of a week since Carolina's wedding. Nothing went right. I had trouble sleeping. Visions of teasing golden eyes and a wickedly sinful mouth on mine kept me awake. When I did sleep, my dreams were filled with him. I'd wake up, desperate and wet, my hand between my legs, needing release. Never finding it.

I had returned the van, filled with gas, and washed, as per MaryJo's requirements. I had stopped arguing it was never clean or full when I picked it up. I needed it, and she knew it. She had informed me the extra mileage I was putting on it was driving up her insurance, and she wasn't happy about it. I hated it when she made her veiled threats and walked away. It left me on tenterhooks, not knowing what was coming next.

I found out yesterday when she'd given me the bill for the expenses she would be deducting from my salary. It left me basically nothing. I had gaped at the amount.

"This isn't what we agreed on," I argued.

"Expenses have gone up. You used the oven and electricity a lot for this job. Took up a lot of valuable freezer space."

"I already factored that in when we agreed. You can't do this, MaryJo. It leaves me with nothing to live on."

Even with what they'd paid me for the cake, by the time I deducted the cost of the ingredients and what I had to pay MaryJo, I barely made a dime. And I had put out all the money in advance, and I had to replace what I had spent. I wasn't going to be able to cover my rent since another payment was due on my student loans.

She had crossed her arms, not caring in the least. "Not my problem."

"Can you at least take it out over two checks? Please? I have to eat for the next couple of weeks and get to work. I have to buy another bus pass too."

"Fine."

"And can I get more hours? I'll take whatever you give me."

"I want a cut of your side gig."

"You already get a cut." I waved the bill. "More than I do."

"I want twenty percent on top, or forget using the equipment or the van."

"Twenty percent?" I repeated. "No."

"Forget it, then."

"I'll quit," I threatened. I was her best employee. We both knew it.

She laughed. "You need me much more than I need you. Think about it. I'm sure we can figure something out."

I'd been up all night, thinking, planning, budgeting. I was screwed, no matter what I did. The only way I could avoid it was to stop making my cakes and wait to build up my reputation once I finished school. I was taking a break right now to work more and save money. Another year and I would be finished with my culinary course and have the two degrees I wanted and needed to start my own business. Maybe I could find more hours at another bakery.

I would miss making my creations, and it would be hard to say no and halt the progress I had made, but I was used to having to fight for things.

I would just have to be patient a little longer.

Then this morning, I was laid off from my administrative assistant job. They were cutting back, and the department I worked in was the first to go. I was despondent. I had to find another job, perhaps a full-time one and give up on my dream—at least for a while. It might be my only choice. My cat had seemed ill, and I'd had to rush her to the vet, only to discover she had a major furball, which she barfed up on the examining table. Luckily, I had a great vet, but they still charged me for the visit. My bank account was growing smaller by the minute, it seemed.

I was distracted and in an off mood at work. Normally, baking soothed me. Not today. MaryJo was out this afternoon, so I didn't have to contend with her, which was a small blessing. But the entire front area was a mess, the schedule not organized, and the baking not going well. It never did when her two kids were working with me. I slammed around in the back, catching up, then headed out front, noticing the empty coffee cups on the tables and people waiting for refills.

It wasn't part of my job, but I grabbed the coffeepot and went around, filling mugs and trying to smile at people.

As I approached the last few tables, I felt it. That strange intensity I had sensed at Carolina's wedding. The one focused on me.

It wasn't possible.

But when I lifted my eyes and met the golden gaze of the man in the corner, my world shifted.

He didn't belong here. In the run-down shop with the chipped tables and paper napkin dispensers, he was a god. Another designer suit hugged his frame. Shiny black shoes covered his feet, not a speck of dust on them.

It wouldn't dare.

He oozed authority and power. Sex. His gaze was zeroed in. On me.

Heat flooded my body. My heart rate picked up. My breaths shortened. Instinctively, I began to back away, needing to flee his gaze. His aura.

But he shook his head, lifting his cup.

The chances he'd walked in here wanting coffee were nil.

He had come for me. I was certain of it. But I tried to bluff my way through and pretend I didn't remember who he was. The kisses we'd shared.

"Would you like a refill, sir?" I asked, keeping my voice neutral.

"Yes," he replied, pushing his cup toward me. I tried not to notice how my hand shook as I poured it. He didn't say anything, and I began to turn around when he spoke, but I knew I had failed in fooling him.

His next words confirmed it.

"Hello, my little bee," he murmured. "I've been waiting."

I had no control. My fingers loosened, and the pot slipped from my hand.

All I could do was watch it.

Chapter Five

DANTE

I lunged, grabbing the coffeepot by the handle before it hit the floor. I straightened, setting it on the edge of the table, and stepped closer to Brianna. I towered over her small frame, somehow liking that fact. I felt invincible.

"Not happy to see me?" I asked.

She opened her mouth to speak, then closed it. She looked at the coffeepot, then back at me.

Then she did the most extraordinary thing.

She began to cry. She flung herself into my arms, burying her face into my chest, wrapping her arms around my waist as she sobbed. I had little experience with comforting crying women since I was usually the one who made them weep, but instinctively, I pulled her close, pressing her face into my torso, surrounding her. Protecting her.

Looking around at the shocked expressions, I glared, making people look away. I had a feeling my appearance was the final straw for my little bee today. She had looked worried, tense, and exhausted as I watched her. Her smile was forced, and her voice pitch was wrong. She needed something, and I decided right then what she needed was me to help her.

I lifted her, my instincts confirmed when she didn't object and demand to be put down. I carried her into the kitchen, ignoring the looks of the patrons watching us covertly. At the back, the young man I had seen earlier was leaning against the counter, playing on his phone. A younger girl was hanging over his shoulder, watching, while another girl was filling cookie trays, ignoring them.

"You," I barked out, getting all their attention. I focused on the young man. "Your name," I demanded.

"Kenneth," he replied, slipping his phone into his pocket.

"Well, Kenneth, stop being such a lazy ass and get out front. Clear the tables, pour the coffee—do your job."

I indicated the girl who'd been hanging over him. "Fill the trays out front. Both of you need to show some initiative." I met the eyes of the girl who had been working. She had been the one to serve me earlier. "Make sure they do what they're supposed to."

"Is Bri okay?" she asked.

"She'll be fine. Give us a minute."

They left the kitchen, and I set Brianna down on the counter, standing between her legs. Her shoulders were still shaking with sobs, and I let her cry for a moment, still in shock at her reaction. I could hear the sounds of work happening out front, and I shook my head in frustration. Brianna didn't seem the type to let others slack off, so why she was allowing herself to be worked to the bone while they did nothing was a mystery. I leaned my hands on the counter, lowering my head to her ear and speaking quietly. "Enough now, Little Bee. I'm here, and everything is going to be fine."

She reacted to my voice, lifting her head. Her deep brown eyes glistened with tears, her rounded cheeks wet from the salty liquid. I ran my finger under her eye, staring at the wetness on the end of my finger. I slipped it into my mouth, tasting her sadness. She stilled as our eyes locked, her sobs ceasing, her shoulders drawing back.

"Even your tears are sweet," I murmured.

I didn't know who moved first. If I grabbed her or she reached for me. Our mouths melded together, and nothing else mattered.

The kitchen door opened, breaking us apart. Kenneth gaped at us.

"The front is cleaned. I was going to fill the trays."

"Good," Brianna stated, slipping from my embrace. She brushed under her eyes, her voice raspy from her tears. "I have two cakes to finish."

He nodded, stealing glances at me as he rolled a cart of trays out front.

"Make sure to load the cups into the dishwasher," she ordered.

"Yep."

I leaned against the counter, lazily wiping at my lips, still tasting her.

"I'm surprised you let them get away with idling around," I observed.

"When the owner is your mother, it's amazing what you can get away with," she replied. "I'm lucky to get any work out of them. Requests fall on deaf ears. Orders are laughed at. Complaining does nothing. Management only cares the money stays in the family." She met my look. "I've tried. Believe me, I've tried."

I nodded in understanding. I had met the woman, so the news she had her children working here and they chose not to do much wasn't a surprise. They acted as entitled as she did.

Brianna was quiet for a moment, then turned to look at me. The end of her nose was pink, her eyes still watery, but she had recovered her spunk.

"What are you doing here?"

"I came to see you."

"How did you find me?"

"Carolina."

"*Carolina?* How do you know Carolina?"

"I'm her godfather."

"You're Dante," she breathed out.

I bowed with a flourish, and I saw her lips quirk at my over-the-top gesture. "At your service, madam."

"When did she give you my information?" she demanded. "She never mentioned you asking."

"The other day."

"But..." she sputtered. "She's on her honeymoon."

"I called her."

She gaped at me. "You what? You called her on her *honeymoon* to find me? Are you insane?"

"She had left before I could inquire about you. Her father didn't know. And I dislike the word insane. I prefer determined."

"I'd prefer you leave."

"That's not what your lips were saying moments ago."

She tossed her hair, defiant. "I was overwhelmed. You can go now."

"Not happening until we talk."

She crossed her arms. "Talk, then."

"Not here, with Kenneth walking in at any moment and no doubt reporting whatever he overhears to his mother. Somewhere private. I'll pick you up at seven when you get off work."

"How do you know I get off at seven?" she asked.

"Like I said, determined."

"Pigheaded is more like it. I suppose when you're an old man, you have lots of time on your hands."

I crossed the room, slipping my fingers under her chin and forcing her to meet my eyes. "We are going to address the 'old man' comments later. For clarity, I am twelve years your senior, not forty. And nothing about me is old. You certainly react to my mouth on yours quickly enough."

She blushed, the heat of her skin warming the ends of my fingers.

"Rude," she muttered.

I leaned down. "You're going to react to my mouth everywhere soon enough, Little Bee. I'll show you how *not* old I am then when you're screaming my name."

I covered her gasp of shock with my lips, kissing her hard and deep. I stepped back, smirking as she blinked, a dazed look on her face.

"I'll be back by seven. No point in running. I know where you live."

And I walked away, not looking back.

It took everything in me to do so, but I knew if I didn't, I would haul her back into my arms, and Kenneth was going to get a show he hadn't bargained on.

BRIANNA

I felt the possession of his lips the rest of the afternoon. It was as if he imprinted his passion on me. He was the last person I had expected to see today. The reaction his presence caused shocked me. Simply sitting there, staring at me. I had felt intense relief course through me, all the bad things that had happened lately washing away. He was there.

For me.

I knew it as instinctively as I knew when I began to cry, he would help me. He wrapped me in his tight embrace and took control, allowing me five minutes to get out all the frustrations and worry. To burrow into his warmth and inhale his intoxicating scent.

Kenneth, Gwen, and Gretchen didn't question him. They knew better. He exuded power. Control. They did what he said. Gwen always worked, but the other two belonged to MaryJo and they couldn't care less. Nothing I did lit a fire under them. This was just a job to please Mommy and make some money. They had zero interest in the bakery or being good employees. I hated working with them but was never given a choice. I did ninety percent of the work and received a lot of disrespect and eye-rolling from the two of them. My pleas to hire other staff fell on deaf ears. By paying them, she could literally write off their allowance. She wasn't bothered if I or other staff had to work harder.

But they jumped to attention when Dante gave them directions. Kenneth walked into the kitchen after he'd left, looking unusually subdued. His phone was nowhere to be seen, and his apron was actually dirty.

"Is, ah, your boyfriend coming back?"

I was about to deny he was my boyfriend, but I caught the glimpse of worry in his eyes.

"Probably. He likes to stay close," I fibbed.

"Right. Okay, I'll stay out front."

He left, and I had to laugh a little. Apparently the power I felt Dante exude wasn't limited to me. He made Kenneth worried enough to actually work. That was a first.

Dante.

The name suited him. If he was Carolina's dad's brother, then he was Dante Frost.

Somehow it fit him perfectly.

I shook my head. Whatever his name was, he was crazy. Calling Carolina on her honeymoon, getting my name, coming here. I knew he lived elsewhere, so why he was still here, I had no idea.

And I refused to think of the reason.

As for dinner, Kenneth might be afraid of him, but I wasn't. And one thing I knew about Carolina, she might have told him where I worked, but she would never divulge my address. I wasn't going to dinner with him. And I wasn't scheduled here for another week, so by then, he would have grown tired of waiting for me and flown back to whatever part of the world he lived in.

I would leave early and avoid him.

Simple.

At six-thirty, I informed Kenneth I was heading home.

"You lock up this time," I said. "I always do it."

"I don't remember the passcode for the security system," he whined.

Feeling oddly brave, I shrugged. "Call your mother and ask."

I left via the back door, peeking around the corner.

The street was vacant except for a red SUV parked by the curb. No sign of any Lamborghinis or other fancy cars, which I was certain Mr. Dante Frost drove. I would be home before he arrived and be curled up on my favorite—and only—chair, eating ramen.

I had a feeling that would be my evenings for the foreseeable future.

I turned and began walking, hoping to catch the earlier bus. I arrived at the deserted stop, pulling my coat around my neck. It was cooler today, the wind strong. The weatherman forecast rain over the next two days, and it matched the mood I felt descending on me.

I refused to admit it was because I was heading home alone instead of eating with Dante.

I shut my eyes as I realized that even the thought of his name caused a shiver to run down my back.

His voice startled me. "Do you not understand English, Little Bee? Or do you like to try to test my patience?"

Again, that odd swell of relief flooded my chest. He was here.

I opened my eyes and met his gaze. He was behind the wheel of the red SUV, his head tilted, a deep frown on his face.

"I said I'd pick you up."

"I never agreed," I responded and turned my back. I knew I was acting like my cat. If I couldn't see him, he couldn't see me either. But maybe he'd go away.

I heard the sound of a door opening and measured footsteps. Then he was behind me.

"I didn't ask," he said, wrapping his arms around me and lifting me as if I weighed nothing.

I gasped in outrage as he swung around and took the few steps needed to place me in the vehicle. He carried me in much the same fashion as I used to carry my dolls. Legs hanging, pressed tight to my chest, not giving them the chance to fall. I couldn't move until he deposited me in the seat.

"You-you   high-handed,   cupcake-stealing...motherplucker!"

"Motherplucker? Oh, you wound me," he said with a laugh, leaning over me and snapping my seat belt closed. Our faces were so close, he could have kissed me. His gaze dropped to my lips, and then he met my eyes again. The intensity of his stare was overwhelming. He ran a finger down my cheek then tapped the end of my nose.

"Extraordinary," he whispered.

He stepped back, shutting the door and, with a smirk, engaging the locks. I glared as he unlocked his door and slid in.

"Comfy, Little Bee?"

I shivered, not responding.

He hit a button, and suddenly the heat surrounded me, wafting from the vents, the smooth leather I was sitting on warming me.

"Oh," I mumbled, instantly feeling better.

"Warmer?"

"Much."

"Good. Relax. We'll be at the restaurant in a few moments."

"I am not having dinner with you."

"Give me three good reasons why not, and I'll take you home," he said calmly, pulling away from the curb.

"First off, I don't know you."

"Dinner can help rectify that."

"Secondly, perhaps I already have plans."

He laughed. "You don't."

"And last, I am hardly dressed for *dinner*. I am sure the establishments you frequent could pay my rent for a month, so I cannot walk into one of those restaurants looking like this."

He pulled into a driveway, indicating the building. "Three strikes, you're out."

I looked at the sign, shocked. It was my favorite little family diner. Good food, inexpensive, and casual.

How had he chosen this restaurant? What were the odds? I was confused. Curious. Secretly pleased.

He parked the car and turned to look at me.

"I would take you anywhere and be proud to be seen with you. I think you're lovely, and frankly, my opinion is the only one that matters. But I know you like it here, so this is where we will eat."

"But—"

He held up his hand, silencing me. "Have dinner with me, Little Bee. I have a business proposition for you. I think you'll be interested."

I hesitated, and he leaned closer.

"Please."

"Okay," I agreed grudgingly. "But only because I'm hungry and I like it here."

He grinned. "Whatever you need to tell yourself. Stay there."

He slid from the car and came to my side, opening the door. He held out his hand, and I let him help me from my seat. I hated the urge to lean into him, to inhale his scent. He didn't seem to share my opinion, burying his face into my neck and breathing deeply.

"So fucking sweet," he muttered.

"It's the sugar."

"It's you," he replied. "Now, come. I don't want you cold again."

I hated that those words pleased me so much.

But I let him lead me into the restaurant.

Chapter Six

BRIANNA

He was out of place again. Too rich, too good-looking, too...*everything* to be inside this diner. But within five minutes, he'd charmed Gladys and Molly, and we sat in the back booth. The one usually reserved for family. He somehow managed to look as if he belonged there, even though I knew he clearly didn't. There were other diners, and the restaurant smelled delicious as always.

He asked for a cup of coffee and water. I got my usual cherry vanilla Coke. I loved it, and they were one of the few that had it in their fountain machine.

He took a sip of coffee and lifted his eyebrows. "This is delicious."

"They grind their own beans and make it fresh all day."

"Better than the bakery stuff."

I snorted. "MaryJo uses the cheapest of everything she can."

"Why do you work there?"

"It wasn't so bad when I started. Her brother ran the bakery, and he was a good boss. MaryJo was always in the background. He taught me a lot. When he died, she took over. By then, I had started my cake decorating and had some customers. He always let me use the equipment and the space for almost nothing."

"And that changed," he said.

"Yes. But the hours are flexible, it's close to my apartment, and although she is an awful boss, the place is busy and I get to try new things."

"While she takes all the credit."

"It is what it is for now. Other bakeries I have interviewed at said a flat no to my side business and wanted regular shifts. Some even pay lower than MaryJo, which I didn't think was possible. So, I'm putting in my time, paying off my debts, and learning what I can. Or mostly, learning how not to run a business."

Gladys came over, order pad in hand. "Ready?"

Dante leaned back. "What do you recommend?"

She pursed her lips. "Probably another restaurant."

Dante began to laugh. I stared at him in wonder. He was gorgeous when he laughed. His eyes crinkled, and the two deep dimples appeared high on his cheeks. His teeth were straight and white, shown off by his wide smile. His humor was infectious, and I found myself laughing with him.

He shut the menu. "Whatever she's having."

"Two hot beef sandwiches coming up," she replied without asking me. I always had the same thing.

She filled his cup and left.

"Is that what you have when you come here?"

"Yes. I love meat, but with my budget, I don't get it much. They make it all from scratch here, so it's awesome."

I shifted in my seat. "How did you know about this diner?"

"Carolina told me."

I shook my head. "She told you where I like to go and eat when you called her for my name?"

He smiled again. "No, when I spoke to her this afternoon."

I gaped at him. "You called her *again*? On her honeymoon? Are you crazy?"

He rubbed his chin, not looking sorry. "She wasn't as patient this time, but she gave me the name of this diner. Then an earful on privacy and leaving her alone."

I shook my head in disbelief. "I—you—I don't even know what to say. You have to stop calling her!"

"She said that. I assured her it was the last time. However, I wanted to take you somewhere you would be comfortable. She said you liked it here, called me some names, and told me I owed her another trip or she would tell Paolo, so I agreed."

"You are totally crazy."

"Determined, Little Bee. I'm determined."

"Determined to make me crazy."

He winked. "Only in the very best way."

Gladys arrived, sliding the full plates onto the table. I watched him survey the towering sandwich, the steam rising from the gravy. The little paper cup holding the horseradish. The mound of mashed potatoes with the pat of melting butter slipping over the top, and the mixed vegetables piled high. One eyebrow rose, and I expected him to push away the plate. Make some sarcastic remark. But instead, he picked up his utensils and waited until I had done the same.

He cut into his sandwich, and although he eyed it with trepidation, he placed the slice in his mouth and chewed it, looking thoughtful. He met my gaze. "It tastes like a dinner my mother would have made," he murmured. "When Paolo and I were kids."

"Is that a good thing?"

He smiled, the look on his face tender. "Very." He took another bite. "Delicious."

"I assumed you ate a lot of pasta with a name like Dante. Or Paolo."

He grinned. "Our mom was half Italian. She chose our names. I'm named after her father. My dad was

Canadian-Irish. We ate both. Pasta. Meat and potatoes. Mom was a good cook."

"I see."

"I like this. I see why you come here."

"Oh," I said.

"You look surprised."

"I assumed you were too rich to enjoy simple fare like this."

"We were just middle class growing up. My mom cooked meals every night. Good, simple food. My circumstances have changed now, but I can certainly appreciate good cooking. I'm not a snob, Brianna."

"Most rich people are."

"I'm not most rich people."

"That much is obvious. But you shouldn't be here. You don't belong here."

He looked thoughtful, then shrugged. "Perhaps not. But you're here, so I do belong. Now, eat your dinner."

Surprised by his words and the fact that he'd shared a little something of himself, I dug into my dinner, enjoying it. The meat fell apart in my mouth. The gravy was rich and thick. The potatoes were whipped and light and contained more butter and salt than I would normally eat in a week. He ate with impeccable manners, wiping his mouth, chewing leisurely, enjoying the modest meal.

He took a sip of water, watching me. "You eat slowly," he observed.

"Yes."

"You live alone?"

"You didn't ask Carolina that?" I retorted.

He grinned. "I forgot."

I had to laugh. He was effortlessly charming. Surprisingly good company. We only chatted about simple things. The weather. The wedding. My surprise he drove an SUV. A red one.

"Easier to find in a row of cars," he said.

Made sense.

"I live with my cat. Roomba."

"Excuse me? Roomba?"

I nodded. "She is a major grump. Hates everyone but me, and she only tolerates my presence because I feed her. I found her in a dumpster and brought her home. I named her Roomba because she was like a vacuum. Ate everything in sight for the first while. Still does, given half a chance."

Dante finished his meal, pushing away his empty plate. He chuckled at my explanation, then frowned as I set down my utensils. "Are you not going to eat more?"

"No, I'll take it with me and heat it up for dinner tomorrow."

"Are you full?"

"Um—"

He cut me off. "Finish it. I'll feed you tomorrow."

I began to protest, and he leaned close. "Eat it, or I will come sit beside you and feed it to you. You will not leave here hungry. You've had a long day, and you need the food."

"You're really bossy, you know that?"

"I'm aware."

I picked up my fork and began to eat again. I was still hungry, but his words echoed in my head.

"Why will you feed me?"

"Oh, Little Bee. I have a feeling that our negotiations will take a while. God knows I'll need to eat to keep up my strength." He winked.

"You're supposed to be grumpy. Everyone described you as grumpy," I said without thinking.

"I am grumpy most of the time. I don't like people much. I hate crowds, weddings, that sort of thing. I tend to tell people what to do, and they don't like that."

"Really," I replied sarcastically, indicating my plate.

"But you're eating. Your little sidekicks jumped to attention when I told them what to do. Most people want to be led, and I excel at it."

"Much of an ego?" I muttered around a mouthful, confident he couldn't hear me.

"My ego isn't the only large thing I have," he replied, draining his coffee and ignoring me as I sputtered.

"As for being grumpy with you, I find it difficult. You make me want to smile."

I finished all I could eat, pushing away my plate. He didn't argue with me and smiled at Gladys as she cleared off the table.

"More coffee?"

He nodded. "Excellent brew. Is your pie as good as your coffee?"

"Even better."

"Two pieces, then. You pick which kinds. I love them all."

She waddled off, happy.

"Do you make pies?" he asked.

"No, my hands ruin the pastry all the time. Cakes, yes. Pies, no."

"Not an issue. I prefer cakes."

"I assume you have a function or some other pressing matter you need a cake for? That is your business proposition?"

He waited until Gladys filled his cup, set down two large slices of pie in front of him and left. He tilted his head, studying me.

"Partially, but my proposal is more, ah, personal."

His voice was lower than before. Raspier. It sounded intimate. His eyes became intense again, his gaze heated.

I felt a shiver run down my spine that had nothing to do with cold and everything to do with him.

"P-personal?" I asked.

He nodded.

I felt my eyes widen. "I am not selling you my virginity."

It was his turn to sputter.

DANTE

Those were the last words I expected her to say. I choked on my coffee, wiping at my mouth.

"I beg your pardon."

"My virginity isn't for sale."

I had to ignore the way my body reacted to her saying the word virginity. I wasn't looking for a virgin. I wasn't looking for anyone—until I saw her. But now, knowing she was a virgin, I wanted her even more.

I cleared my throat. "I'm glad to hear that, but that is not what I want to discuss with you."

"What, then?"

"You mentioned you have a lot of debt."

"I am aware."

"You owed just under $27,000."

Then she narrowed her eyes. "How did you know that?"

"I made it my business to know."

"And what do you mean, owed? I still owe it."

"No. I paid it off."

She stared at me in shock, then recovered her voice. "What did you just say?"

"I paid off all your debts. You now owe it to me."

I let her process that information. I cut off a bite of pie and chewed it, swallowing the sweet dessert. It was good, but not as good as Brianna's cakes.

"What are you playing at?" she hissed. "You think you can pay off my debt, tell me I owe you, and expect me to do whatever you want?"

She looked around. "Is this a joke?"

"No."

"You show up at the bakery where I work and take over, you bring me to dinner, you have somehow found out detailed, personal information about me. And then you dare to pay off my debts, and tell me I now owe you?"

She sat back, her face pale. "Who the h-e-double-hockey-sticks are you?"

I bit back my amusement. Even upset, she didn't curse.

"I'm going to be your best customer. I want you to bake me some cakes."

She began to laugh.

"You're a lunatic," she said. "A complete lunatic."

"No, perfectly sane. I simply know what I want. And I want you."

She blinked. Looked around. Blinked again. Then once more, she did the most extraordinary thing.

She bolted.

She was up and racing away from the table as fast as she could possibly go. She even left her coat behind. I sighed in frustration. She would have to learn to stop running from me.

I finished the pie and coffee, giving her a head start and a false sense of victory. I knew where she lived. It was right behind the diner. She no doubt thought that she'd lock herself inside and would be safe from me. That I would forget about her, or she would try to convince herself she had misheard me.

She really had no idea who she was dealing with.

But she was about to find out.

BRIANNA

My entire body shook under the blanket, and I couldn't get warm.

It hadn't been a joke. He had paid off my debts. As soon as I got home, I checked my accounts. They all showed a zero balance.

How was this possible?

What was going on?

And the most important question—what did Dante really want?

I had no idea why I'd blurted out the comment about my virginity. I swore I was the oldest living virgin in the world—or at least in Toronto. Sex felt intimate and bonding. Lasting. I had never cared enough for anyone to have sex with them. The truth was, I had never met anyone I felt enough desire for to have sex with them.

I ignored the little voice in my head that said that was before I met Dante.

He was sexy. Insanely sexy.

But off-limits.

He was older, lived in another city, and obviously was crazy.

Who paid off a stranger's debts, then asked them to bake them some cakes in return?

I wondered if Carolina knew how crazy her godfather was. I glanced over at my purse then cursed when I realized my phone was in my coat pocket, along with my spare key. Which I'd left in the restaurant.

With Dante.

I dropped my head into my hands.

I wasn't very good at this escaping from him thing.

As if to solidify my thoughts, I heard a key slide into the lock, and my door opened. Dante walked in, carrying my coat. I stared at him, somehow not shocked to see him. He shut the door, hung my coat on the hook, then proceeded to remove his shoes and coat and come into the apartment.

"I didn't invite you in."

"Leaving me your keys suggested you expected me."

"I left them in a panic."

He pursed his lips. "Amazing what our subconscious does for us. You wanted me to come to you." He waved his hand. "Not that it mattered. I would have gotten in."

"Of course."

He sat down on the ottoman and looked around. "This is a god-awful place, isn't it?"

"Hey," I snapped. "Show some respect. It's my home."

He flashed his teeth. "Oh, you've made it charming, Little Bee, but you deserve so much better than a basement apartment. Is this even legal? Can you get out that window if there were a fire?"

"I have no idea."

He tutted.

"Why are you here?"

"We weren't finished our discussion," he replied, as if all of this was normal. Then he frowned. "You're shivering."

He stood and went to the tiny kitchen, opening my cupboards. He pulled out the can of Ovaltine and plugged in the kettle. He looked at ease, waiting patiently for the water to boil. He carried over the cup and handed it to me.

"Drink. The sugar will help."

"You're not having one?" I asked stupidly, as if he were a guest.

"I'm not the one in shock. I should have been a little more circumspect with my words." He tucked the blanket tighter around me. "Drink it," he repeated.

I did as he said, the hot drink warming me.

"That isn't a beverage I would associate with you," he remarked.

I shrugged, not wanting to explain. "I have one every night."

He ran a finger over his lips. "Interesting."

When I was calm again, I drew in a long breath and spoke.

"You paid off my debt, and now you want me to bake you some cakes," I said slowly. "To repay you."

"Yes."

I began to laugh. "Gold-filled ones?"

"No. Your usual kind. I will pay you for each cake. Five hundred dollars. You'll come out ahead."

I gaped at him. "Are you insane? Are you under medical supervision? No one pays that much for a cake!"

"Your customers do. Your fancy wedding cakes fetch a much higher price."

"So, you want me to make you—" I did some fast calculations in my head "—sixty wedding cakes? Planning a marriage-divorce spree, are you?"

"No, just regular cakes."

I shook my head. "Certifiable. You are completely certifiable. Do Carolina and her family know you're off your rocker?"

He ignored me. "There are stipulations."

"Which might be?"

"I will provide everything you need to make the cakes. However, they must be made in my kitchen."

"Your kitchen?"

"Yes. I want a cake every day."

I frowned. "For sixty days."

"Yes."

"Why can't I just make you all sixty and freeze them for you?"

"I want them fresh."

"So, where is your kitchen? Is it close enough I can take the bus?"

"No. You'll come with me."

"To where?"

"Italy."

He said it so matter-of-fact. As if it was no big deal.

I blinked. "Let me get this straight. You expect me to leave my life, travel with a stranger to Italy for sixty days, and bake you a cake every day?"

"Your life is not so great at the moment. You'll be perfectly safe with me, and yes."

The man was deranged. There was no doubt about it.

"Why?"

"I liked your cakes. Very much. I like you. I want to spend some time with you."

"And you've decided sixty days is the right amount of time?"

"Yes."

"I'm not for sale."

"I know that. But your cakes are. And I'm buying them. Your presence is the added bonus."

"No. I'll work off my debt somehow. Tell me your terms, and I'll figure something out."

He drew back his shoulders, his gaze becoming serious. It reminded me of the first time I saw him. Intense and focused. "I just did. Those are the only terms I'll accept."

"No."

"I'm not sure you have a choice."

"Then contact the bank and withdraw your payment."

"That isn't possible."

"Ask your brother to take it on. I'll work out terms with him."

"Not happening."

Suddenly, he was looming over me, his hands resting on the arms of my chair, trapping me.

"I want you. In my villa, baking me a cake every day. I want to watch you create your art. I want to smell the aroma of it. Taste it. I want to hear you sing as you bake. Then I want you in my bed, so I can taste you. Devour you. Get my fill. I need you to satisfy all my cravings."

My breathing picked up, and I had to swallow down my whimper. I shook my head.

"I won't sleep with you for money."

"No, you won't. You'll sleep with me because you want me as much as I want you. And I won't touch you until you ask. But you will ask, Little Bee. You'll give me what I want, including your body. Freely. I guarantee it."

"No," I managed to push out between my tightly clenched lips.

"It will happen."

"Leave. Now."

He straightened, tugging down his sleeves and smoothing back his hair. Then he moved so fast, I had no time to react. His mouth was on mine, his tongue sliding in, gliding and twisting, making me crazy instantly. I had no control over my own body. It bloomed like a rose under his touch, weeping for him, wanting him closer. Wanting his mouth harder, his tongue deeper.

Then as quickly as he was on me, he was gone.

Staring up at him, I touched my bruised lips.

"It will happen, Little Bee. The hard way or the easy way, it will happen."

He pulled a card from his pocket. "My number. You have twenty-four hours to decide."

He paused at the door. "Lock this behind me. You never know what sorts of weirdos are wandering around the neighborhood."

Then he was gone, and I heard his laughter echoing down the hall.

Chapter Seven

BRIANNA

I spent the first twenty-four hours after Dante left in a frenzy of worry. Then when the allotted time came and went, I realized I was overreacting.

What was he going to do? He couldn't force me to go to Italy with him. I had no passport, so I couldn't even leave the country.

He had been playing me. I was certain of it. Still, worry niggled at me, and I decided to leave the city for a few days. When I was out of sight and he didn't know where I was, he'd grow tired of waiting, and he would go back to whatever place he came from and leave me alone. I would speak to Carolina's father and arrange payments to Dante from afar.

The only thing that happened was a pizza arrived at my door at six. Hot and fragrant, it was laden with toppings and cheese and smelled incredible. The note attached was simple.

I said I would feed you.
Eat it. I'll know if you don't.
Dante

I was tempted to throw it out, but it came from a pizzeria I had been wanting to try and couldn't afford, and frankly, I was starving. It smelled too good to throw out, so once again, I found myself doing his bidding.

As I ate, I mulled over my options. I had no shifts until the weekend. No school. It was a rare break. Since I had no payment to make this week, I had a little extra cash. I decided to pack up Roomba and go to a small cottage up north. It was off-season, and the rate was cheap. I could take the bus, spend a few days by the water, and get a break. My cat traveled well and would sleep in her carrier on my lap. The bus ride was only four hours. The next morning, I walked to the bus terminal, keeping my eyes open, but I saw no trace of a red SUV or a tall, intense man watching me. Using my now debt-free Visa, I bought my ticket, then went to the store and bought some apples, crackers, and a jar of peanut butter. Great snacks for the bus and when I arrived.

My apartment was empty when I got home, and I breathed a sigh of relief. I noticed another small leak by the window and stuffed some wadded-up paper into the crack. I looked around with new eyes. It *was* a terrible little place. Dark and dingy. I had hung posters, had bright-colored blankets on the small futon bed that doubled as a couch if needed. The one armchair I had found at the side of the road and dragged home, using an old dress to recover it. I'd painted the arms and legs, and I had found the ottoman at a thrift store. The same with the faded rug on the floor. The kitchen consisted of a small stove that didn't work, a waist-high fridge, and a scarred countertop with an old sink and taps that rattled when I turned them on. The bathroom was minute. The front door of the apartment never locked properly, and the people above me wore clogs and liked to tap-dance in them late at night. Or at least, I swore it was clogs.

But the apartment was cheap and warm in the winter. Too warm most of the time. The window was legal, but grimy and old. It wasn't forever, and it was just me and Roomba.

However, it was, as Dante observed, god-awful.

I packed an overnight bag, keeping it simple. I loved overalls, the freedom and ease of them. I had several pairs in different colors, some short-length, others full. I paired them with T-shirts and sneakers. I put in a few pairs with some shirts, underwear, and sleeping attire. I didn't bother with makeup. I made sure I had enough food for Roomba and her kennel had her blanket and some treats at hand. She loved to roam outside when we went to the cabin. She never went far, but she enjoyed the outdoors while we were there.

I had a ticket for the ten-a.m. bus the next day. I got ready for bed early, glancing at the door. Dante had been full of it. I bet he was already gone, laughing over the fact that he'd wound me up. At least I got a couple of hot meals out of it.

I wasn't sure what I had expected. For him to break down my door and carry me off? Show up at the bus terminal and refuse to allow me to use my ticket? Whatever wild idea my imagination came up with was pure nonsense. It wasn't going to happen. Why he'd paid off my loan and told me he wanted some cakes was a mystery. Ultrarich people were known for their idiosyncrasies. Maybe he did this a lot. I refused to admit that I felt a small fraction of disappointment at his absence. That I wished I could have sparred with him one more time. Maybe kissed him.

I refused to think about that at all.

I reached into the cupboard for my tin of Ovaltine. I was almost out, and I would have to remember to get more when I got back. One foster home I had been in for a short while had been nice, and the lady had made me Ovaltine and talked to me every night before I went to bed. Sadly, I wasn't allowed to stay as she became ill, and I was only there for about a week. It was one of the few good memories I had growing up, and when I was on my own, I bought a tin and had a cup at night. It made me feel better somehow. Connected to something pleasant instead of all the awful memories I carried with me.

I lay on my futon, suddenly exhausted. I didn't bother to change, planning on doing so in the morning. The leggings and sweatshirt I wore were comfortable enough. Roomba climbed up beside me, stretching out behind me the way she always did. I reached back, stroking along her fur, and fell asleep quickly, welcoming the darkness.

Tomorrow would be a better day.

I woke, feeling sluggish. I burrowed back under the blanket, my bed feeling extraordinarily comfortable this morning and the room brighter than usual. My sleep had been filled with dreams. I had felt movement around me. My body being transported. Disjointed voices. Odd sounds. Dante had drifted through my mind more than once. I had felt his touch. Heard the timbre of his voice in my head.

"I'm sorry, Little Bee, but it has to happen."

"You'll love it."

"It's all right, we'll be there soon. I have you."

With my eyes still shut, I reached behind me, feeling the comforting warmth of Roomba as she slept. I stroked her fur, needing her presence to ground me. I wasn't sure why I felt so groggy this morning. I hadn't taken anything; in fact, I had fallen asleep fast. I reached for the glass I kept beside the bed and took a sip of the cool water. I frowned as I felt the weight of the goblet in my hand. Traced the heavy pattern cut into the edge. My usual cup was a small, cheap one I'd bought at the dollar store. I swallowed, setting it down on the table beside the futon, gripping the blanket. It was soft, light, warm. It smelled of sunshine and citrus. My blankets were old, rough, and always carried a trace of dampness. My futon felt different. Not hard and unforgiving. The mattress I was on cradled my body— like a cloud.

I sat up, forcing my tired eyes open. I stared around the unfamiliar room in shock. Cream-colored walls with pretty landscape pictures hanging on them greeted me. Large windows with curtains moving lazily in the soft breeze filled one wall. The bed I was in was plush, thick, and decadent. The blanket I was clutching felt puffy and soft gripped in my hand. Beside me, Roomba stretched, making a low noise in her throat as she rolled over. I relaxed, realizing I was having a dream. Within a dream. If I could feel Roomba, hear her, obviously, I was just dreaming. I slid from the bed, noting I was still in my sweatshirt and leggings. I huffed. I could have at least dreamed up some fancy jammies. The floor felt warm on my feet as I headed to the windows. I gasped at the scenery in front of me. Rolling hills, trees, vineyards, and green were all I could see for miles. I stepped onto the balcony, the stone still warm on my toes, and walked to the railing. Below me was a circular driveway with a fountain in the middle of it. The water splashed and danced in the sun, and the air was heavy with the scent of nature, the breeze clean and refreshing. I inhaled deeply, also catching the scent of coffee. I grinned. A good dream wouldn't be complete without coffee.

My stomach grumbled, and I recalled all I'd had for supper the night before was an apple and peanut butter crackers. I assumed if I was feeling hungry, that meant I was going to wake up soon and this pretty vista would vanish. I padded back into the room and took in its beauty again. The high ceilings. The light. The lovely tapestries I noticed for the first time. My suitcase, the cat carrier, and some boxes seemed out of place in this room, and I frowned.

Why would my suitcase, the carrier, and some boxes be in my dream?

I looked around again, my breathing picking up. I saw two doors on one of the walls, and I peeked in one, gaping. All my overalls were there, hanging neatly beside my worn T-shirts. The dress I had worn to Carolina's wedding was there too. On the opposite rail were more overalls in a variety of colors. New shirts made of cotton so soft it felt like silk under my touch. Never-worn sneakers were lined up on the floor.

My breathing came even faster, and I opened the other door, staring at the opulent bathroom. The huge tub and shower. The marble sink. I realized I had to pee.

That shouldn't happen in a dream, should it?

I used the facilities, trying to tamp down my panic. I washed my hands and face, studying it in the mirror as I brushed my teeth. My hair was wild around my pale face, my eyes wide as the reality of the situation became clear. I touched the cold glass.

I wasn't dreaming.

Everything I was feeling, everything I was seeing, was real.

I wasn't in my apartment in Toronto.

Where the heck was I?

I returned to the bedroom, spying another door on the opposite wall. I noticed Roomba was missing and saw that the door was ajar. She must have gone out that way.

I approached the door with caution and peeked out into the hallway. The floors were marble and pristine. I saw a staircase and tiptoed to the railing, glancing down. A huge foyer with the same marble on the floor was circular in shape. It had a massive wooden door, and I could see the entrances to some other rooms. I heard the faint notes of music playing.

The aroma of coffee was stronger, and I squared my shoulders.

I had a feeling I knew who was behind this change of scenery.

And we were about to discuss it.

DANTE

I heard her rushed footsteps coming down the stairs. I waited patiently for her to appear in the doorway. As I suspected, she headed for the front door first, and, unable to open it, she headed toward the brightness of this room, anticipating a way out. She stopped cold when she saw me sitting on the sofa, coffee cup in hand.

My God, she was a disaster. Her hair looked as if she'd been caught in a wind tunnel. Her clothing was stretched and wrinkled. She had lines on her face from her pillow. A small smudge of toothpaste by her bottom lip. She was fucking captivating.

But then I noticed the white pallor of her skin and the exhaustion that surrounded her.

Had I put too much sedative in her Ovaltine?

She had slept the entire way here, barely moving from me. Her head had rested on my lap once we were airborne, and she mumbled a lot in her sleep, nestling as close as she could to me, like a magnet. When I shifted, so did she. When I got up, she grimaced and whimpered but never woke up. She sighed a small sound of relief when I would return to her. I had carried her off the plane, to the car, and then into the villa without any commotion at all.

Perhaps my calculations had been off.

I was on my feet, heading toward her immediately.

"Are you all right?"

"Am I all right?" she repeated, her voice rising. "*Am I all right?* I went to bed last night in my apartment, and I woke up here! How do you think I am? I don't even know where here is!"

"You're at my villa. I brought you here."

"You brought me here," she repeated. She covered her mouth. "Oh my God, you're going to make me a sex slave and sell me."

I almost choked on my laughter. "No, that isn't my plan."

"Murder me, then. You're some kind of sicko. Your family had no idea." She suddenly crouched into a fighting stance. "Just try, old man. I can take you."

I held up my hands. "I am *not* coming at you. No harm will befall you while you are with me."

"Too late."

Satisfied she wasn't going to collapse, I returned to the sofa. I indicated the one opposite me, and after a brief hesitation, she came closer but didn't sit. Her cat jumped up on the sofa beside me, curling up and purring as I stroked her thick gray fur.

Brianna barely concealed her shock. "She hates everyone."

"She likes me. We became friends on the flight. She likes tuna."

"So you bribed your way into her affections."

"I gave her what she wanted, and she gave me what I needed. It was mutually beneficial."

"What did she do for you?"

I kept a straight face. "She didn't shit on the carpet."

"Shame," Brianna muttered, staring at Roomba. "Traitor," she hissed.

The cat ignored her, burying her head and resting one paw against my leg.

I poured a cup of coffee from the pot, added some cream, and held it out to Brianna. She looked at it and shook her head. "I don't think so."

I took a sip of it and set it on the table. "Nonsense. See? It's perfectly fine. I assumed you would need some caffeine to help wake up."

I knew she wanted it. She stared at it, refusing to move.

I poured more coffee into my cup. "Come on. I won't bite." I grinned. "Yet."

She came closer, edging slowly as if I was going to spring up and grab her. I supposed I couldn't blame her for thinking that way. "Relax, Little Bee. You're perfectly safe."

She snorted, the sound making me grin. "Yes, what else could happen?" she sneered. "You already kidnapped me."

"I told you. The hard way or the easy way. You were about to run—again. Since you so obviously wanted out of the city, I brought you here. Much nicer than that cabin you were going to hide in."

She looked startled that I knew where she was going, but she pushed on.

"Which is where, exactly?"

I took a sip of coffee. "On the coast of Italy."

She sat down, looking aghast. "I'm in Italy?"

"Yes." I held out a plate of fresh breakfast pastries. "You must be hungry."

"As if I would trust you not to drug those."

"Pick one. I'll take a bite and prove it's fine." I did want her to eat. And drink. She was still very pale.

"You could have drugged them all."

I frowned. "That would be a waste of these wonderful treats." I picked up one and took a bite, then chose another and did the same. I chewed and swallowed, then did it again. "Now, choose which of those you want. They are all fine."

"I am not eating one of those. They have your cooties on them."

"My *cooties*? Are we twelve?"

She snorted again. "You certainly aren't."

I narrowed my eyes. "Careful, Little Bee."

She stood, pacing around the room. I let her wander, drinking my coffee and taking one of the cootie-infested pastries and eating it. It was delicious.

She must have reached her limit because she came closer, snagging a pastry from the plate and taking the cup of coffee I had poured. She moved away, sipping and chewing. I heard her low moan of appreciation, and I hid my smile by taking a drink of my coffee.

"I want to go home."

"This is your home for the next while."

She finished her coffee and pastry, setting down the cup with a thump. "You can't keep me here."

"Where are you going to go?" I asked.

"To the police."

"I hope you speak Italian."

"I'll tell them you kidnapped me."

"Good luck with that. I'm a well-respected businessman who owns a great deal of the real estate and businesses in this small town. They won't believe you, even if you manage to make them understand."

"How did you get me here? I don't have a passport."

"I procured one for you."

"You-you have that sort of connection?"

"I have many connections, Little Bee. More than you can fathom."

"Why did you do this?" she cried. "What have I ever done to you?"

I stood, approaching her. She backed up, hitting the wall. I stood in front of her, close enough I could feel the warmth of her body. Sense the rapid breaths she was taking. "You bewitched me. You and your delicious cakes. Your sultry voice. Your sassy mouth. I can't get you out of my mind. I want you to bake for me. Sing for me. Dance with me. You will earn your freedom, one cake, one song, one dance at a time."

"You're crazy."

"Yes, I am. About you. You've gotten under my skin, Little Bee. In an instant. You're a craving I can't satisfy. So I am going to take all I can. Every bite. Every flavor. You are going to be mine for the next while. Once my craving is done, once my sweet tooth is satisfied, you'll go home."

"I don't believe you. You want more."

I wound one of her curls around my finger. It was silky and soft. I tugged it gently. "I do want more. And you'll give it to me. But it won't be a part of our agreement. It will be because you want it too."

"Please. Just let me go."

"I can't."

"I'll bake you as many cakes as you want. You must have a home in Toronto. I'll bake you a cake every day for a year," she bargained.

"I want you here."

"I don't understand," she whispered, her eyes wide.

"Neither do I," I admitted, gathering a handful of her tangled tresses into my fist. I stared down at her and felt the heat build between us as our eyes locked. Her cheeks were flushed now, from anger or passion, I didn't know. Her dark eyes glimmered in the light, and I ran my hand up her arm, stroking across her shoulder and exposed collarbone. Her skin was warm, soft, and tempting.

"Don't," she whispered.

"Then you need to stop looking at me like that."

Her gaze dropped to my mouth, then back up again. She licked her lips, and the need to taste them, to feel them move with mine, was paramount.

I lowered my head, our mouths almost touching. I felt the heat of her breath on my lips, but I didn't move. It was she who rose on her toes and pressed her mouth to mine.

One touch and I was lost. I yanked her tight to me and kissed her, sliding my tongue inside her mouth with a low groan. I tasted the sweet cheese and cherries from her pastry. The flavor of her coffee.

And her.

She was addictive.

And I was going to make her mine.

I pushed her into the wall, dropping my head to her neck and kissing the delicate skin. She gasped, her head falling back onto the hard surface.

Then she froze and pushed me away.

I stepped back, meeting her eyes.

They were wild and fearful.

"No," she said.

I held up my hands. She called the shots when it came to how much she was willing to give me. Always.

I already anticipated her next move, and I let her have it. Her gaze bounced around the room, settling on the open French doors that led to the large patio. She ducked under my arm and ran full tilt toward them. Toward what she saw as freedom.

I let her run. There was no place for her to go. The property was vast, surrounded by trees and a thick, high fence. Even if she managed to make it to the gate, she couldn't get over it. Smooth stone walls protected me. They would keep her safe as well. I would let her run and exhaust herself. Then I would fetch her, and once she calmed down, we would figure this out.

When I realized she was going to run to some horrendous little cabin out of the city to try to get away from me, I decided it was time to act. While she was out, I let myself into her tiny apartment, the lock easily picked. When I had been there the other night, she'd told me she had a cup of Ovaltine every night. The tin was almost empty, so adding a sedative was easy. I had a backup plan in case my theory was wrong.

But when I arrived that night, she was out cold. The two men I had with me made short work of packing up the boxes I had brought with us. I took her clothes and anything I thought she might want in the next while. Her already-packed case helped. Her cat proved surprisingly cooperative and let me put her in the carrier without a fuss. I carried an unconscious Brianna on to my private plane, and we were off the ground quickly. No one on board questioned the sleeping woman, and the customs man who came on board when we landed was someone I knew. The fast, false passport I'd had made was barely looked at, and we were on the way to the villa quickly. I had tucked her into bed, lying beside her for a while, then showered and went downstairs, deciding to let her sleep it off. I knew the sort of schedule she had, and I wasn't surprised she was tired all the time. She needed the rest.

I walked toward the patio doors to see what direction she had run off in, stopping by the sofa, and I began to laugh. She had been anxious to get away from me, but not so anxious that she hadn't snagged another cootie-infested pastry as she'd run past the table.

No doubt, she needed the energy.

We had a lot to discuss when I found her.

Chapter Eight

BRIANNA

I flopped down on the grass, barely inside the line of trees surrounding Dante's property. I was obviously out of shape, given how hard I was breathing. I looked back and shook my head. I hadn't gotten very far. It was probably due to the fact that the motherplucker had drugged me.

Drugged me.

Carolina was going to get an earful when she came home from her honeymoon. I certainly wasn't making any more cakes for her family get-togethers if this was how her relatives acted.

He kidnapped me.

Drugged me and kidnapped me and brought me to Italy.

Holy baby on a pogo stick, I was in Italy.

My situation could be worse. Dante could live in some small town in the Deep South where it was so hot you couldn't breathe. Or Alaska. I hated being cold. The climate here seemed...nice.

At least it was picturesque. It was pretty decent as far as being kidnapped went.

I took a bite of the sweet treat in my hand and chewed slowly.

And these pastries were awesome.

Still, he could have asked. I might have changed my mind.

I rolled my eyes, finding my anger again.

"*Not much of a life*," Dante had said, bluntly. "*This is a god-awful place, isn't it?*"

His observations were right. I hated so much of my daily life. The struggle. The apartment. I was constantly trying to keep my head above water financially, patch up leaks in the old window, chase bugs, keep warm, not lose my temper with MaryJo.

But it was my life, and he had no right to walk in and take it away.

I finished the pastry, wishing I'd been able to snag a bottle of water. I was thirsty. Maybe when I got to the police station, they would give me something to drink.

I stood and made my way through the trees, finally coming to a stone wall. I looked up, realizing there was no way to climb the wall. It was roughly ten feet high, smooth brick with no spots to grab to climb. For a moment, I was nonplussed, then I decided there had to be a gate to get into the estate. I would find that and climb over. I silently cursed Dante for being so wealthy and having such a large property as I tripped again, landing on my knee. I rubbed the sore joint, wishing I could scream profanities into the air, but I never swore, and I knew it would do me no good to do so anyway.

Still, I called him names under my breath as I wearily trudged to the front gates, wanting to cry as I stood in front of them. Soaring, thick metal spines were crafted into panels. As high as the stone walls, they were too close together to squeeze through, too smooth to climb, and, of course, locked.

"Dumbledore!" I yelled, wanting to stamp my feet.

So I did.

I heard a chuckle and spun on my heel to find Dante lounging on a blanket in the sun.

"Tantrums now? I was wondering when you'd get here," he said, looking unconcerned. "Took you a while. And the gates are not subject to magic spells."

"My pace is slower, thanks to you drugging me, you son of a monkey."

He looked startled, then began to laugh. "My mother was entirely human, Little Bee. I assure you." He beckoned to me. "I have cold water. And food. You must be thirsty and hungry."

I was both, but I refused to let him see. I headed his way slowly, and he stood. "Why are you limping?"

"I tripped," I began, then stopped. "Is this a flipping picnic?" I indicated the blanket and basket. The pillows that waited. "I'm trying to escape, and you make a picnic lunch? What the cuss?"

He laughed again. "You don't like to swear, do you?"

"No."

He startled me by cupping my face and kissing me again. I wanted to pull away and punch him, but I rather liked the feeling of his mouth on mine.

"Sit," he instructed.

It had to be his kisses that made me so compliant. I should be attacking him, using the knife I could see to hold him down in fear until he opened the gates.

Instead, I sat down. I was exhausted.

He sat next to me, handing me a cold water. I guzzled it down gratefully.

He tugged up my leggings, tutting over the bruises forming on my knees. He traced the small cut on one.

"Tore my flipping leggings, you jerk," I muttered. "Are there more of those pastries?"

He bent and kissed one knee, then the other. "I'm sorry you hurt yourself, Little Bee. I told you that you couldn't leave the grounds." My breath stuttered in my chest as he pressed his lips to my skin. I felt a shiver race down my spine at the feel of his mouth on me. I refused to think about where else his mouth could go.

"I'm going to get to the police," I insisted.

"I'll drive you in the morning."

I stopped halfway to reaching for one of the decadent pastries. "What?"

"I'll take you to the police. You can make your report."

"What's the catch?"

"Nothing. You can tell them your side of the story. I will tell mine. Whatever they decide to do, I will abide by."

I narrowed my eyes. Something was off about this offer.

"I don't trust you."

"You probably shouldn't. But you have no choice. Now, how about lunch?"

He unpacked the basket, and I eyed the food hungrily. Fresh bread, wonderful cheeses, and rich, pungent meat appeared in front of me. Small containers held olives, sliced cucumber, and tiny tomatoes. Another had more pastries.

Dante handed me a plate. "Eat, Little Bee. Please."

I was starving, and I filled my plate, then sat back and ate. The bread was crusty and delicious. The cheeses sharp and rich. The meat unlike anything I had tasted before.

"Why are these so sweet?" I asked, holding up a tomato.

"They are sweeter here. The soil, the climate," he explained.

I ate until I was full, including two more pastries. Dante ate, watching me closely. He filled my glass, first with water, then a sparking liquid that was tasty and refreshing.

I patted my lips with a napkin and sighed. "That was incredible. I almost forgot I was eating with a kidnapper."

"Your host, you mean."

"Not after tomorrow."

"We'll see. Maybe I drugged you again. You never had me check the food you ate."

I glared at him.

He began to laugh. "Teasing. God, your face is expressive. Maybe you won't tell me to fuck off, but your glare does. It's mesmerizing what you say with those dark eyes. You are so easy for me to read."

"Most people think I'm closed off."

"They aren't looking close enough."

I shook my head and shut my eyes, lifting my face to the sun. The warmth sank into my body. I was tired, the events of the last few days catching up with me. I startled at the feeling of Dante lifting my head and sliding a pillow under it. "Relax a little and let your food settle."

"Stop telling me what to do."

He pressed his lips to my head. "Okay, Little Bee. Whatever you say."

"I hope they put you in a cell with someone named Bubba and he likes the looks of you," I mumbled, turning onto my side. "Enjoy your last day of freedom, you son of a biscuit."

Gentle fingers stroked my head. Dante chuckled, the sound low and sexy. "Okay, Little Bee. Okay," he said again.

I woke to the sunshine again. I sat up in bed, blinking and confused. Beside me, Roomba slept, stretched out and enjoying the softness of the bed.

How had I gotten back into bed? The last thing I remembered was the picnic lunch with Dante after trying to find a way out of his estate. The wonderful food. His good company. Lying back in the sun. I must have fallen asleep, and Dante somehow brought me back and put me to bed.

I was shocked. I was usually a light sleeper. I had to be, given where I lived. More than once, someone had attempted to break in. A small fire in the hall one time. I had learned to sleep with one eye open, so to speak, in case I had to defend myself or get out fast. I never felt safe in that apartment, but it was all I could afford.

Here, though, I felt exactly that. Safe. Which was odd, considering the fact that I was here because Dante kidnapped me.

Except, it didn't really feel like a kidnapping. It felt as if I'd been given a reprieve of sorts. And I wasn't sure how to feel about that.

It was early morning, about eight, I judged. I pushed back the covers, noticing a bandage on one knee where I had scraped it. I recalled Dante kissing the injury. How his lips felt on me.

I shook my head. I couldn't think like that. I couldn't fall victim to his manipulative ways. I would develop

Stockholm syndrome and fall for my kidnapper. That wasn't happening. He'd promised to take me to the police today, and I was making him stick to that promise. I'd be home in a couple of days. He could go to jail.

I used the shower in my bathroom, delighting in the multiple jets. The steam rose around me as I used the fragrant shampoo and conditioner and lathered myself with the sweet-smelling soap. I wondered if I could sneak the products into my suitcase. They were luxury brands—way nicer than I could ever afford. I was sure he wouldn't miss them.

I changed into my pink overalls and a flowered T-shirt, ignoring the new ones hanging there. I added my pink sneakers and rolled up the cuffs on the pants. Taking a deep breath, I headed downstairs, following the scent of coffee to the dining room.

Dante sat at the table, holding a cup of coffee and the paper. Dressed casually in a Henley and jeans, he was devastatingly handsome. He had on simple black frames that highlighted his eyes. He peered at me over the top of his rims. "There you are, Little Bee. You've slept for hours. I trust you feel rested?"

I approached the table, shocked to see Roomba curled up on his lap. "What are you doing with my cat?"

He lifted his hands. "Nothing. She came to me. She likes me."

"Maybe you can get one when you get out of jail."

"Still want to take me to the police and report a crime?"

"Yes."

"Mind if we have breakfast first? The food in jail is bland, I'm told."

A woman walked in, holding two plates. My stomach grumbled at the scent of food. She smiled at me and spoke to Dante. He nodded in my direction, saying something.

"He kidnapped me," I said. "Can you help?"

There was no response, except she chuckled and patted his shoulder, then took the coffeepot and refilled his cup and poured another cup at the place beside him. She left the room, and he indicated the chair. I sat down, unable to resist the aroma.

"No help there," I mumbled.

"No English," he said mildly. "Eat your breakfast."

I picked up my fork, cutting off a mouthful of the fluffy omelet. "Delicious."

He smiled. "Not your usual Italian breakfast. But it is a carryover from living in Canada. I like eggs in the morning. I tend not to eat again until dinner, unless it is a snack."

"You ate a picnic lunch with me yesterday."

"You would be surprised what I would do for you, Little Bee."

"You carried me to my room."

He studied me over the rim of his coffee mug. "You were exhausted. No doubt from the travel and the walking miles to find your escape route."

"Don't forget the lingering drugs in my system."

He shook his head. "There are no side effects to them. They are very harmless, aside from knocking you out for a while. I think you were already exhausted and reacted to them more strongly than most people. You look more rested today, which I'm glad of. You can yell louder at the police."

I said nothing, sipping my coffee and eating my breakfast. I looked around the sun-filled room. It was charming. Simple, yet elegant and welcoming.

"You have a lovely home."

He nodded. "I like it here. It's quiet, and the vistas never fail to inspire me."

"What do you do exactly?"

He tilted his head, studying me. "Curious this morning, Brianna? Wondering about your abductor?"

"Yes."

"I'm an art dealer. I have a gallery here, larger ones in Naples and London, one in Toronto. I also collect art. I love it in every form." He took a sip of coffee. "Your cake was a complete work of art. The attention to detail. The shape and structure. The way you created it. I had never seen anything like it. And the fact that it tasted as good as it looked? That was—" he chuckled "—the icing on the cake, to coin a phrase. Blissful. You are very talented."

"You thought of my cake as art?"

"Yes. I see it everywhere. Art isn't just paintings or sculptures. I can see the beauty of something in the most rudimentary of items. You simply have to look and learn to appreciate the subtle splendor of an object." He paused. "Or a person."

I felt my cheeks flush. The way he looked at me when he said it, I had the feeling he was talking about me. I wasn't a great beauty; in fact, I considered myself to be quite plain. But somehow when he stared at me with that intensity, I felt different.

"So, you employ a lot of people?"

He nodded. "I also own several businesses in town and other cities. My holdings are quite vast, and I have a lot of people depending on me."

I felt an odd sense of guilt, which I immediately tamped down.

"You should have thought of them before you kidnapped me."

He smiled, shaking his head. "You don't understand, Little Bee. You captivated me, and I had no choice. I needed to have you here with me. You refused to listen, so I simply made it happen. It's what I do. I'll accept my punishment."

"And your businesses will suffer."

The smile never faded from his face. "It will have been worth it to share this short time with you."

I was nervous in the car. The town was about twenty minutes away, and Dante drove with the top down. The breeze stirred my hair and filled my head with the rich scent of the earth and sun. It was so beautiful here. In the town, he pointed out his gallery and some other shops. He pulled up to a small brick building, parking the car and unfastening his seat belt.

He handed me a passport, and I looked at it with curiosity. "That's me," I gasped.

"Yes. I had it made for you."

"Is it real?"

He didn't answer.

"Why are you giving it to me?"

"You will need it to get home," he said. "You'll have to get a flight and arrange to transport your things." He indicated the building. "I'll be in jail."

I swallowed. "Right."

"Can you drive a stick?"

"Um, no."

"You'll have to figure out how to get back to the estate. I'm sure one of the officers will escort you."

"Oh."

He scratched his chin. "You should have enough money in your account to cover the flight. You have a credit card you can use," he mused out loud. "You'll need a car to get to Naples. It's less than two hours away. We flew into the airport there with my private jet, but my assets will be seized once I'm locked up, so I can't help you. The language barrier will be an issue, but you'll figure it out. You're a smart woman."

My heartbeat picked up, and sweat broke out along the back of my neck. I hadn't thought about any of that.

He leaned his elbow on the door of the car, pursing his lips thoughtfully. "Now, your cat. That could be a problem. I sort of smuggled her in, and I doubt you have papers with you. You may have to leave her. I'll arrange to ship her back once I'm free." He laughed suddenly. "Shit, I should call my legal team. They'll need to get on this."

The sweat beaded on my forehead. I had no idea how to hire a car. The limit on my credit card was five hundred dollars. I wasn't sure that would cover a flight home. And I didn't want to leave Roomba. Would it be totally rude to ask my kidnapper for the money?

A police officer came out of the building, walking toward us, and Dante climbed out of the car, shaking his hand. He indicated me in the passenger seat, and the officer frowned. They spoke in fast Italian, and I caught only a word or two. *Bellissima* was one. *Infuriata,* which I knew meant angry. The officer rubbed his chin, looking unhappy. "Kidnap?" he questioned in heavily accented English, looking at me.

This was my chance. I jumped from the car, running toward him. "Yes. I have been kidnapped."

The officer looked between Dante and me. "What is ransom?" he asked.

"Oh." I waved my hand. "He isn't asking for a ransom."

"She is priceless," Dante murmured. "Look at her."

"You have been, ah, mistreated?"

"Um, no. I have a lovely room, and he has been very kind. We had a picnic."

The officer frowned as Dante translated. "You brought by force? Smuggled?"

I huffed out a long breath. "No, he brought me on his private jet. I slept the whole way—because he drugged me. He even brought my cat and has made friends with it!" My voice rose a little, and the officer looked confused. Dante handed him my passport, saying something. He studied it and tapped it on his palm as he questioned me.

"No hurt? No ransom? No force?"

"No. But he is using me! Abusing his power. Like a sex slave—but no sex," I added. "We agreed. He wants me to bake him cakes plus sing and dance! He's like a demented Phantom of the Opera with a sweet tooth. Using me!"

Dante bowed his head, covering his mouth. The officer said something, and Dante answered. There was more rapid-fire Italian, and the officer had the audacity to smile.

"Cakes?" he questioned.

Dante kissed his fingers. "Delicious. And a voice like an angel." He smiled indulgently at me.

I tried not to blush at his words. *Why was he being so sweet?*

Dante said something else, using his hands, gesturing a lot. Then he held out his arms, wrists up, as if offering to allow the man to arrest him. The officer reached behind him, producing a pair of handcuffs. Dante looked resigned but stayed silent.

The uncomfortable feeling I had been fighting blossomed. My chest became tight.

He was actually going to let them arrest him? Take him away and put him in jail?

What had I done?

"Wait!" I yelled.

They glanced at me.

"Mistake. Error. I didn't mean it. No arresting!" I said, squeezing between them. "I'm here. Happy to be here. It's beautiful. No jail. No." I shook my head. "My mistake."

Dante wrapped his arm around my waist, drawing me back to his torso. He pressed a kiss to my head, and I awkwardly patted his arm. "All good."

The officer looked down at me, then smiled.

"Not kidnapped?"

"No. Here of my own free will."

"Not angry now?"

"Um, no."

He said something to Dante, who laughed and responded to the other man. The officer held out my passport, and I took it. They shook hands, and the officer turned to go.

"Last chance," Dante breathed.

I said nothing. The officer returned to the building, and Dante led me to the car. He got in and pulled away from the building. He said nothing until we arrived and stopped in front of a small café.

"I need coffee and something sweet," he said, glancing my way. "Coming, Little Bee? The lattes here are incredible."

I followed him, silent, sitting at a table he indicated before going inside and returning with a tray. Some pastries and two steaming lattes were on it, and he slid the tray between us.

Nothing was said as we sipped and chewed. I looked around at the street that was getting busier as time went by. Shops opened, locals called to one another, and tourists began to filter in. Many people greeted Dante. He acknowledged them all with the tilt of his chin, standing to shake hands with a few men. But he didn't speak until the tray was empty.

"What changed your mind?"

"You have people depending on you. I know what it's like not to have that, and I didn't want to take that away from them. Plus, I'm not sure Carolina would forgive me if I got her favorite uncle arrested. Even if he deserved it."

"I'm her godfather."

"That makes this even funnier. Kidnapped by a godfather. It sounds like a movie."

"We could give it a happy ending."

I met his eyes. "How?"

"You accept my offer. Stay. Bake me my cakes. Enjoy some freedom from the drudgery of your life as you know it now. Bask in the sun. Swim. Rest. Let me spoil you a little."

"I won't sleep with you."

He tilted his head. "I told you that doesn't come into play."

"What do you get out of this? It's just cake. You can't tell me there aren't a hundred different delicious cakes here you could eat."

"They aren't *your* cakes. I want a piece of art every day. I want to hear you sing in my kitchen and dance with me on the patio at night."

"If I refuse?"

He rubbed his eyes. "Don't."

I finished my coffee.

"It's beautiful here. You said so yourself. No worries or stress for a while. You can sleep, rest, bake. Enjoy the country. I'll show you whatever you want to see. Does that sound like such a terrible way to spend a few weeks?"

I stood. "Can we go?"

He nodded, looking grim. He put some money on the table and took my elbow, escorting me to the car. We were silent on the drive to the villa, and I stared at the incredible views.

When we arrived, he opened my door and helped me out.

"You won't let me go."

"I don't want to, no."

"Why me?"

He looked down at me, then crowded me against the car. He leaned in, his arms forming a cage I couldn't escape from. His mouth descended on mine, hard and blistering. I tried to resist, but I couldn't. My body acted of its own free will, and I wrapped my arms around his neck, whimpering as he ravished me. He yanked me tight to his chest, lifting me off the ground as if I weighed nothing. He fisted my hair, holding me close. I gripped the back of his neck, wanting more. Wanting him. Terrified of that fact.

Then he stopped, set me on my feet, and stared down at me. We were breathing hard, each of us still holding on to the other.

He slid his hand to my face and kissed me again. "That's why."

Then he walked away.

Chapter Nine

DANTE

I drifted in the pool, the water cool against my overheated skin. I had worked awhile in my office, watched Brianna ramble around the grounds from the chair at my desk. Wondered a hundred times what she was thinking. Then I hit my gym and worked out until I was a sweating mess. I did my laps in the pool and pulled myself onto a floating lounger, enjoying the late-afternoon sun and the gentle breeze as it wafted over me.

I silently willed her to me. I wanted her to talk to me. I wanted to convince her to stay of her own accord. I wasn't letting her go, but things would go better if she decided she had made the choice on her own terms.

Finally, she approached the pool, her hair piled high on her head, messy and chaotic, her overalls grass-stained and her feet bare. The tip of her pretty nose was pink from the sun, and I wondered if freckles would appear on her pale skin. She was so incredibly appealing to me, and she had no idea. I had never reacted to another woman the way I reacted to her.

"Wanna come in? Water's great."

"I don't have a suit."

"I can get rid of mine, and we can skinny-dip."

She looked startled, then shook her head. "No, thank you," she replied primly.

I bit back my laughter. I loved teasing her.

"Enjoy your tour?"

"It's lovely here," she admitted.

"Great spot to unwind."

"Be a prisoner, you mean."

I slipped off the lounger, moving closer to the edge. "You aren't a prisoner. I'll take you anywhere you want to go. Get you anything you want or need. You only have to ask."

Roomba wandered out of the house and onto the stone patio, lying in the sun. She stretched out, rolling over, looking content.

"Your cat likes it here. Admit it, you do too."

"I said it was pretty."

I reached the side of the pool. "You're being petulant now. You're hot. You need to cool down."

"And how—"

She was cut off as I grabbed her ankle and tugged. She fell into the pool with a muffled scream, coming up, her hair streaming around her. She wiped her face, planting her feet on the bottom of the pool, and glared.

"Ah, there's the fire I like," I said.

"Fudgsicle! You're such a jerk. I could have drowned."

"I would have rescued you. Given you mouth-to-mouth. In fact, if you're feeling faint..." I arched an eyebrow at her.

"No, thank you. I am not interested."

"Liar," I teased. As soon as I said "mouth," her gaze went to my lips. She was interested, all right.

"What did you say to that police officer?" she demanded, crossing her arms.

I didn't lie. "I told him I had brought you here as a guest and you were angry with me and wanted to go home. He asked why you were angry."

"And you said?"

"I told him I hadn't disclosed where I was taking you, and you hadn't brought the right clothes and were pissed at me. That you were saying I had kidnapped you and wanted me arrested. I asked him to put the cuffs on me to shut you up. He thought it was amusing that I would indulge you."

She gasped in outrage. "That was all a setup?"

I edged closer. "You told him you were kidnapped. Then you backpedaled."

"You helped. He thought I was crazy."

"A little," I admitted. "I told him you came with me on my plane and that you slept because you were tired. That *I* was the one who made you tired." I quirked my eyebrows suggestively.

"You...*motherducker*! I was drugged!"

Motherducker? That was a new one. Where did she come up with these? I had to hide my amusement. She was getting angry again.

"He didn't believe that. He said he saw the way you looked at me. He heard how I praised you. You told your version, I told mine. You changed your mind because you know, deep down, you want to stay here and be with me. You couldn't tell him a lie and say you wanted to leave."

"I never said that," she sputtered.

I stopped in front of her. "But you feel it. I know you do."

She was spectacular. Her cheeks were flushed, her eyes snapping fury at me. She had her hands clenched into fists, ready for a fight. Her full mouth was tempting.

"I hate you," she whispered.

I grabbed the shoulder straps of her overalls and pulled her upward, the water causing me no resistance. I kissed her, letting her feel the passion and desire I had for her. I hauled her close, bending her to my will. She kissed me back, feeling the same passion I did.

I pulled back, leaving her floundering.

161

"I know you do. That's why this works."

I left her in the pool.

S
he refused to have dinner with me, staying in her room. I ate in the dining room, asking my housekeeper to take her a plate. Gia informed me that Brianna hadn't eaten much, and against my own judgment, I left her alone.

I passed her room later in the evening, noticing the light spilling out under the door. It stood ajar, and I looked in. Brianna was sitting on her bed, wearing a T-shirt and shorts. Her hair was loose, and she had a notebook on her bent knees. She was writing furiously. Roomba was next to her, asleep.

I tapped and entered her room. She looked up, her eyes wide in her face.

"Writing to your government for rescue?" I asked lightly.

"No."

I sat on the edge of the bed, studying her. She looked calm. Serious. She had a pencil tucked behind her ear.

"Plotting your escape? Planning on messages in a bottle? Ideas on how to murder me in my sleep?"

"Making my list of demands."

Her words surprised me. "I see. Negotiations, then." I paused. "So, you will stay, Little Bee?"

"If you meet my conditions."

I lifted my hand and tucked a curl behind her ear, pausing to stroke the lobe gently. "Haven't you figured out you only have to ask and you can have it?"

"So if I asked nicely, you would let me go home?"

I shut my eyes at the rush of sadness her words caused. I couldn't let her go. I wanted her too much. But I could make a huge concession.

"I will take you home. You will stay with me in my condo and bake me my cakes until your debt is paid."

She pursed her lips. "I'd rather stay here."

Her confession was unexpected. I felt how wide my smile grew. "Yeah?"

"It's pretty. And sunny. But not stifling. Toronto in the summer is ghastly."

"Okay. What else?"

"In the morning. I want an appointment."

"An appointment?"

"Your housekeeper, who does speak English, by the way, says you are a very busy man of business. Lots of appointments. I want your undivided attention. So, I would like an appointment."

I withheld my smile. Of course she figured out Gia spoke English. Broken and halting, but she spoke it. I nodded and stood. "Ten o'clock. My office is on the third floor. Gia will show you how to access it."

"Fine."

I indicated the plate of cheeses and bread Gia had brought up after Brianna's dinner had been returned, barely touched.

"Eat, please. I don't want you getting sick."

I crossed to the door, pausing. "And, Brianna…"

She looked up.

"You always have my full attention when you're in the room."

I left her.

BRIANNA

I stared after Dante, listening to his fading footsteps and the click of his door shutting. His words were simple but honest. And they were profound. To someone so used to being invisible, what he said meant so much.

"You always have my full attention when you're in the room."

I had no idea what to make of them. Or him at times.

I had spent the afternoon walking the grounds. Enjoying the breeze and the sun. Being honest with myself.

I liked it here.

I was still angry that he had taken me. Drugged and kidnapped me. It was illegal and highly inappropriate. But the bottom line was, he was charming, sweet, and funny. He was also correct in his views on what I had left behind. Not much of it was good.

I could spend sixty days baking him cakes. Basking in the sunshine, resting. Being looked after. I hadn't been looked after my entire life. By agreeing to his odd request, I would be debt-free, and when I went back to Toronto, I could find a new job and get away from MaryJo. Maybe I could get Dante to give me a reference. I'd be like a private pastry chef of sorts. That would look good on a résumé.

I sat in the sun for hours, mulling over my options. Not that I had many. Something had shifted when I saw him talking to the police officer. When I heard my own explanation to the officer, I felt almost silly. What Dante did was wrong. So wrong. But he hadn't hurt me in any way. He made me angry, but he hadn't hurt me. I had a feeling there were lots of women who wouldn't mind if he spirited them away to a villa in Italy.

And his kisses. I wasn't sure what to make of my reactions to him. He was so sexy. Older, experienced, and sure of himself. He touched me, and I melted, all my resistance gone. As I'd never felt desire for a man, it was heady. Overwhelming. And I liked it.

Leaning back on my elbows, I contemplated a different sort of relationship with Dante. Giving him what he so clearly wanted. I had no idea what he found so attractive about me, aside from his love of my cakes. But there had to be something. Maybe he liked younger, curvy girls. It could be as simple as that. All men had a type.

I rolled over, feeling the heat of the sun on my back soak through my overalls and shirt. Maybe I should give him what he wanted. It would be a reckless decision, but I had played it safe my whole life, and where had it gotten me? I was in debt, alone, in a dead-end job, and still a virgin at twenty-six. Dante was happy to change all those things.

I could only imagine what a physical relationship with him would entail. It would be intense, I was certain. Yet I knew he would be gentle with me when needed. What better way to discover my sexuality than with someone experienced who could teach me?

Simply thinking about it made me shiver.

All my thoughts came back to me as I sat on my bed, writing my lists. I had done my usual pro and con list, shaking my head as the pros became a great deal longer than the cons. And almost every single one had to do with Dante.

The countryside was incredible—and I had barely explored it. I wanted to see more. Feel the sun. Enjoy the days. The thought of not returning to that cramped little apartment made me feel lighter. Not having to listen to MaryJo and her spoiled, entitled kids. Work seven days a week just to keep my head above water—all of those were pros. And the list grew. The food. A chance to see a bit of Italy—something I'd never thought possible, given my resources and life.

My cons seemed fairly weak. The *Kidnapped me!* stood out, but I was having a hard time holding on to my anger. I chewed the end of the pen, wondering if I was suffering from Stockholm syndrome. Or, more accurately, Dante Delusion. Either way, it was bothersome.

Giving up control to Dante was a major point. I'd had only myself to rely on my entire life. I decided where, when, what I was doing. Now, he would be in charge. Deciding when I could leave the estate, who I interacted with, when I slept or ate. Yet somehow, I knew it would all be done with my best interests in mind. And he would want me to be happy.

Baking a cake a day seemed a petty point since I was used to working much harder than that. Even adding in decorating time, it was a pretty light schedule.

I left it there anyway. It made the list look balanced.

I couldn't put missing Roomba. The cock-a-doodle-doo had catnapped her too. I mean, what kind of cray cray thought of that? The Dante kind, I decided. Anyway, she seemed all in favor of remaining.

I looked at the other lists I had written. What I needed. My own lists of demands.

I put the pad of paper on the nightstand and slid under the light covers. I wondered what he would counter with.

I could only imagine.

I guessed I would discover that soon enough.

I curled up, falling asleep quickly.

I needed to add this comfy bed to the list of pros.

I'd do that in the morning.

Chapter Ten

DANTE

I leaned in the doorway, watching Brianna sleep. In the early morning light, she looked like an angel, though I knew she was anything but. Sassy, proud, strong, and independent, she tried my patience like no other woman before her. Perhaps that was what attracted me to her so strongly. Why I was acting this way. Like some degenerate. Staring at her as she slept. Worrying about her eating.

Kidnapping her and bringing her here.

Despite her beliefs that I did this all the time, I had never behaved in this fashion. I was high-handed. Focused and determined. But usually with women, they came to me. I was always honest with them, and we used each other until we were no longer interested

—often me breaking it off first. I had never taken someone without their consent, with the intent of my own pleasure.

But with Brianna, all the rules were out the window. The thought of leaving her behind had been unacceptable. The certainty she would tell me to go stuff myself or some other polite expression was high. I couldn't take that chance.

I spied her notebook on the nightstand, and the urge to peek into her notes was strong. Gia had told me Brianna had sought her out, asking in slow, carefully mimed actions for a pen and paper. She had given Brianna what she requested, and I had assured Gia it wasn't an issue, although my curiosity burned hot, wondering what my little bee was writing.

"Speak English to her if you can," I instructed. "She will be here a while."

"So pretty," Gia said.

"Yes. She'll be baking a lot. She'll need some instruction on how to use the ovens."

"Okay," she agreed with a surprised look on her face. But she knew better than to ask questions.

I tore my gaze from the paper and the mysteries it held and pushed away from the door. I had to leave before the lure of Brianna's wild hair and the outline of her supple body drew me closer. Simply the glimpse of her bare leg and shapely calf peeking out of the blankets drew my attention. I wanted to crawl into that bed with her and wake her up in a fashion she'd never experienced. Since learning she was a virgin, I'd found my mind filled with all the things I wanted to be her first with. I was like some overgrown frat boy with one thing on his mind.

Getting the girl.

Thoughts of the other day drifted through my head. After giving in and eating the picnic I had brought out, she had fallen asleep on the blanket, still exhausted. I watched her for a while, wondering why she fascinated me so. Nothing about her screamed spectacular, yet I found her endlessly engaging. I enjoyed her reactions. The way her dark eyes emoted her inner feelings. How her cheeks flushed when she was angry. Her use of odd expressions to relay her feelings, never swearing, but her anger raging.

I had packed up the food, then stooped and carried her to the golf cart I used to get around the estate quickly. She made a small sound in her throat, burrowing into me. I hated to set her in the passenger seat but did so, and I drove carefully down the winding drive to the house. I carried her up the stairs, marveling at the fact that she didn't wake or stir, instead nestling close again, her hand fisting my shirt. She showed so much trust to me in her sleep. Trust, I hoped, that would extend to her waking hours soon enough.

Once again, I shook my head as I headed down to the kitchen for coffee. What was it about this girl that brought out all these foreign feelings and desires? Without a clue as to the whys, I could only hope once I sated them, and sent her away, I could go back to my life before Brianna.

I ignored the laughter in my head.

Gia showed her into my office promptly at ten. Brianna was wearing another set of her overalls—these lime green with a yellow T-shirt underneath it. Both looked worn, and I wondered why she hadn't picked one of the new sets I'd made sure to purchase for her.

Brianna looked around in curiosity. My office took up a large section of the third floor. The view outside the windows was spectacular. I had opened the walls so the office ran the full length of the house, and you could see both vistas clearly, the rolling hills, vineyards, and trees an endless source of beauty for the eyes.

I had a lot of art on display. My favorite pieces I had collected. Sculptures, paintings, pottery. Whatever I truly loved was in this room, for my eyes only and those few I allowed into this space. If I was receiving other visitors, I met them at the gallery, or downstairs in a smaller office I used mostly for show. This was my private sanctuary.

I watched her wander. Studied *her* studying the paintings. Tracing the sculptures with her eyes. Her hand rose more than once as she copied the lines of a piece midair, a delicate rendering she was committing to memory. She was a joy to observe, taking it all in.

Then I cleared my throat, and she spun on her heel, coming over to the desk.

"Sorry," she muttered. "So many lovely things."

"I'm glad you like them. Do you enjoy art?"

She smiled, looking self-conscious. "I don't know anything about it. I couldn't tell you something real from something fake. Or who an artist was by the brushstrokes or subject. I only know what I like."

"That means something."

"I used to go to the galleries on free nights or weekends. Look at the paintings. I'd hear people discuss them, but I never understood it. I only enjoyed what I saw."

"You create art with your cakes. You elevate them."

She frowned. "I never thought about it that way."

"It's true."

She peered around again, still curious. "You own an art gallery, you said?"

"A few, yes."

"You pointed one out in the town we were in. Could I see it one day?"

I sat back, crossing my legs. "Are you staying, Little Bee?"

She sat up straighter, all business now. I withheld my smile at her sudden fierceness. Good God, she was delightful.

"If you meet my demands."

I folded my fingers together, keeping my voice neutral. "Let's hear them."

"Sixty cakes, sixty days."

I nodded.

"I might need a day off from baking."

"We can adjust."

"I don't know if I can get the same ingredients as in Canada. The cakes might not taste the same, and you won't be happy. Do they even have cream cheese in Italy?"

"Give me a list of what you need, and I will have it flown in if necessary."

She handed me a list, and I scanned it. I was impressed. It was very thorough. The list even included the types of pans and decorating equipment she required.

"I need to know your favorites. I don't know if I can come up with sixty different kinds of cake, but I can vary the flavors."

"I love spiced cakes. Carrot. That one you had on the tree with pecans on the top."

"Hummingbird."

"Yes. And vanilla is a favorite. Pineapple upside-down cake is one as well."

"Do you like mousse, jelly, jam fillings? Lemon? Pound cake?"

"I'll make this easy, Little Bee. You make it, I'll love it. I don't care if you make the same one a few times. Especially the hummingbird one. I liked it. Except coconut. I cannot stomach the stuff."

"You will really eat a cake every single day?"

I laughed. "A piece at least, probably two. Or more. I have a tremendous sweet tooth. Gia and Mario will have a slice. You too. Can the rest be wrapped and frozen?"

"Most of them."

"Okay. Next."

"I need my phone for music. I always have music playing."

I opened the drawer and slid a brand-new phone her way. "Your phone was ancient and barely functional. I copied all your music to this one. My number is programmed, along with all your contacts. Consider it a gift."

She picked it up and studied it, her eyes wide. Then she set it down, surprising me by not arguing.

"I need aprons."

"I'll take you into town, and you can pick what you like. There is a large kitchen store. Perhaps you can find some of your things there."

She had a few other small items that were easily agreed on. Her demands were hardly that at all. More like requests or needs. The women I'd had in my life before demanded many more things. Expensive things.

"I want a bicycle."

"A bicycle?" I asked, confused. "I have a fully equipped gym for exercise."

"No, not to exercise. To explore a little. If I need something, I could go into town and get it without bothering anyone."

"I'll get you a car."

"I don't know how to drive."

"I'll teach you," I said, surprised.

She saw my reaction and shrugged. "I could never afford a car in Toronto, so there was no point in learning then or now. I would really rather have a bike. With a basket."

"Then I will get you one."

She came to another item, and she grew uncomfortable. She squirmed a little, unsure how to address it.

"Tell me what you need," I encouraged her.

"My apartment in Toronto," she began, and I knew what she was worried about.

"I broke your lease. It was cleared out of all your personal things after we left and your landlord contacted and paid. Your belongings are safe in storage. When you leave, I have a great little studio apartment in a safe neighborhood where you can live. Don't think about it again."

She gaped at me, and I continued.

"And I let MaryJo know you are no longer her employee. I may have also informed her that her kids are entitled brats and her business is about to die a slow death without your talent to keep it going."

Brianna blinked. Opened her mouth. Closed it. Tried to look affronted. Failed. She only looked relieved. Almost grateful. Then she frowned, digging in and finding her anger. "You had no right to do that. That was my home and my job, and you just took them away from me."

"Is that right?"

"Yes, Captain Oblivious, and you know it!"

"Your so-called home was a deathtrap and a health hazard. You will have a much better apartment to live in later. And your job was sucking you dry. I will help you get a better one, or if need be, I will buy you a bakery. So put away the bottom lip and move on."

"Are you sure you shouldn't be on medication?"

I held back my amusement. "I'm bossy and direct. And rich enough to be able to be both. Get used to it. Next demand."

She looked away and cleared her throat. She spoke so quietly, I had to strain to hear her. "I know you have paid off my debt, but I have no money. I don't know how to access my bank account in Canada, and I need, ah, things." She met my eyes briefly. "Personal things."

I felt a tug in my chest at her carefully chosen words. She was proud, and having to ask me for anything was difficult for her. I was once again hit with a wave of tenderness for her. An overwhelming desire to ease her embarrassment and worry.

I took an envelope from the desk and leaned forward, extending it to her.

"For you."

She opened it, her eyes growing huge at the bundle of cash and the black card inside it.

"What is this?"

"You are my responsibility while you are here. The cash is for whatever you want, and the card is for you to use. You will need some more clothes and things. And whatever personal items you require. When you run out of cash, let me know and I will give you more." I met her shocked stare. "This is not up for negotiation."

"So I'll be like your mistress while I'm here? You're going to pay me to have sex with you?"

I laughed and stood, walking around the desk to sit next to her. I took her hand. "This is me trying to make up for messing up your life, Little Bee. I shouldn't have kidnapped you, but I couldn't help it. I want you to enjoy the next while. Relax and find a little peace."

"And the other part of what you want..." She trailed off.

"Will happen. Or won't. It has nothing to do with this. You call the shots here, Brianna. Your choice. I want you. I want to have you in my bed. I want to watch you learn all the pleasure I can give you."

"But you won't make me."

"No. I think you want me just as much, but you have to decide." I touched her cheek. "Do you want me to be completely honest?"

"Yes."

"I want you more than I have ever wanted another woman. But the bottom line is, I'm not forever. I never will be. As fascinating as you are, as much as I want you, it will end. And if you say no, I'll have some great desserts and, once you leave, move on."

"In sixty days."

"Or before. I have no idea. I'm not built for forever. I'm for the moment." I sighed and sat back, forcing myself not to touch her. "If you want that, can accept that, I promise you I will make whatever time we have amazing for you. But it is your decision. If you bake for me, sing while you're doing it, and spend some time with me, I'll be happy."

"But not as happy as you would be if we slept with each other."

I smiled, trying to lighten the atmosphere. "I doubt there will be much sleep involved, Little Bee. I have too many plans for you."

Her cheeks flushed.

"I'll order your supplies. And take you into town for your aprons, a bike, and whatever else you need."

"I'd like a swimsuit. I don't know how to swim, but I'd like to use the pool."

It was my turn to gape. "Jesus. You don't know how to swim?" I'd pulled her into the pool. It was the shallow end, but I hadn't thought of the possibility she couldn't swim. It must have scared her, but she never showed it. "I'm sorry. I shouldn't have pulled you in that way. I didn't know."

She shrugged. "You were there, so I wasn't scared. But maybe I could practice."

"I'll teach you," I offered again, pleased at her trust.

"Okay."

I stood. "We'll go into town after lunch, and you can get a suit and whatever else you need. You can wander a bit if you want while I check in at the gallery."

She stood in front of me, a small smile on her face. "Aren't you worried I'll try to run? Or tell people I've been kidnapped?"

I touched the end of her nose affectionately. "I think we're past that now, Little Bee. I'm trusting you."

She grinned. "Careful, old man. Maybe I'm lulling you into a false sense of security."

I pulled her close. "One of these days, I am going to disprove that old man theory."

She giggled and ducked under my arm, heading to the door. "Only if I say yes."

"When you say yes," I corrected.

I watched her go, a feeling of relief and an odd sadness in my chest. She was staying. This was good. She knew the rules, and she hadn't seemed upset. When we went ahead in our relationship, because I knew it would happen sooner or later, she understood it would end.

It always did for me.

Why the thought of something ending that hadn't even begun made me sad, I had no idea.

It made no sense, yet I felt it.

Chapter Eleven

DANTE

We drove back into town, and I took Brianna to a shop that Gia's daughter owned. It had lots of women's fashions in the window, and I knew Simona would take care of Brianna.

Simona was pleased to see me, and we greeted each other in normal fashion, bussing each other's cheeks. I noticed the sparkle of discontent in Brianna's eyes when I drew back, and I wondered if she felt jealous seeing me kiss another woman. I stored that information away for later. I introduced them, faltering slightly as I tried to put a label on Brianna. I settled for guest, and Simona shook her hand, saying her mother had said I had a lady friend staying for a while.

In Italian, I told Simona to make sure Brianna got everything she wanted. "Don't let her look at prices. If she asks, lie and cut it in half at least, or tell her I get a discount." I knew her shop was expensive. "She needs a bathing suit and some personal items. Maybe a dress or some other light wear. Anything she smiles at, tries and likes, or even catches her eye—it's hers. I'll be back later and settle."

"No problem."

I turned to Brianna. She was looking over my shoulder, and I followed her gaze. A pretty sundress hung on the end of a rack, diaphanous and light. It was yellow and feminine. "Try it on," I encouraged her. "You'll need a couple of nice dresses. I'm going to go and tend to a few things at the gallery. Will an hour be enough?"

"More than enough."

"The shoe store is next door. The pharmacy is across the street. Use the card or the cash. Someone can help you with the language."

"I can go with her," Simona assured me. "You attend to your business."

"I'll meet you back here."

Brianna nodded, looking nervous. I bent and kissed her, wanting her to relax and enjoy herself. "I'm trusting you," I whispered.

"I know."

"Get back at me and spend a lot of money," I replied. "Get some more of those sexy overalls you wear. They drive me crazy."

She scoffed. "That's a pretty short drive."

I was laughing as I left.

T sorted through what needed to be done at the gallery quickly. It was a small space, selling mid-level pieces. Not the larger, more elite galleries I had in other locations. But it was a great cover for living so close, and I liked being able to employ the locals. I handed my manager some paperwork on acquisitions coming in and checked on the new inventory. There were a couple of nice paintings and one particularly fine piece of sculpture I'd located from an estate sale. They would fetch a good price and look appealing in the gallery for a while.

I spoke to some clients via phone and sent some emails, then strolled back to the shop. I'd been gone a little longer than I expected, and I wondered how much money Brianna had spent.

Except when I arrived, Simona informed me Brianna had only stayed for a short time and bought hardly anything. "A swimsuit and a cover-up. That was all."

"What about the dress?"

"She tried it and one other on, and they look beautiful on her, but she said no. She said no to everything, and she left."

I was confused. "The shoe store?"

"She left alone, Dante. She insisted she was fine. She paid cash for her purchase."

"I'll be back soon," I promised. Outside, I glanced up and down the street. I hadn't seen her walking this way, and the other direction led to the less populated business section. And the area the bus went. Confusion gave way to anger.

She had played me. She had cash and a credit card. I'd been gone long enough to give her time. A bus went through here every day, heading to Naples. I racked my brain, trying to recall if I had her passport or she did.

She was running.

Fury beat through me. She was like every other woman out there. I had fallen for her seeming capitulation. She had no plans to stay. She had used the goddamn phone I gave her last night and looked up the information she needed. Planned all this out.

Disappointment hit me like a tidal wave. I was sure she was different. Honest.

But she was...

My thoughts ended as if I had slammed on the brakes, and my mind came to a jarring halt.

Sitting at a table in the shade, at the small café we'd been to yesterday, was Brianna. The chair beside her held a few small bags. A latte was in front of her.

She was here. She hadn't run. Relief tore through me. The disappointment vanished.

But she wasn't alone. Standing to one side was the police officer from the other day and seated next to her was Ramon Winters. A former client, an undeclared enemy, and the man I loathed over all others.

Sitting beside my little bee.

At first glance, they seemed to be simply chatting, but as I drew closer, I saw the tight set of Brianna's shoulders. The tension around her mouth. Her sunglasses covered her eyes, but I knew even without seeing them, they would be upset.

"*Amore*," I called out.

Her head turned quickly, and she stood. "Darling!" she replied. "I have been waiting forever!" she scolded.

Her words and the effusive way she flung her arms around my neck surprised me, but I caught on quickly, dropping a kiss to her neck, then her mouth as she eased back. "You left me alone so long, I was famished."

I chuckled and kissed her again, knowing we had a rapt audience. "I was caught up in paperwork, my love." I lifted her hand to my mouth and kissed her knuckles. "Forgive me." Then I glanced up. "But you have such charming company."

Officer Rossi smiled at me. "I saw your little prisoner sitting here and came to check on her. I thought perhaps she had run to Mr. Winters for help. Maybe you had angered her again."

Winters frowned, glancing between us. "Prisoner?"

Brianna laughed. "Inside joke."

"I am the one in prison," I inserted. "Her prisoner of love."

"Oh hush, you," she laughed and slapped my chest playfully.

Officer Rossi laughed. "So funny. I am glad all is good." He touched his hat. "Until we meet again."

He strolled away, and Winters and I stared at each other. Brianna stayed beside me, and I looped an arm around her waist. "You did not do much shopping, my love," I murmured to her, watching the way he looked at her.

"Later," she responded.

"We were having a nice coffee together," Winters spoke. "I saw the lovely lady alone and was persuaded to join her."

I felt Brianna tense up. His words were carefully chosen to upset me. I knew Brianna would never ask a stranger to have coffee with her. A male one, anyway. I pressed a kiss to her temple. "Maybe you shouldn't be listening to the voices in your own head, Winters. They're often misleading."

His glare intensified, and Brianna tugged me to the table, sitting down across from him and patting the chair next to her.

He scowled at me. "How's the gallery?"

"Business is excellent, thank you."

Brianna looked between us. "Dante is going to show me around this afternoon. Such a lovely little town."

Her words defused the situation, and he leaned back. "Have you been here long?"

"No, only a few days."

"You are from America?"

"Canada, actually. We met while Dante was there, and he brought me back with him."

"How lovely for you," Winters said, his tone and gaze saying it was anything but lovely.

"Oh, it is," Brianna replied, not responding to his tone. "Such a wonderful surprise. I couldn't bear for him to leave me behind." She grasped my hand clenched on my knee, lifting it to her mouth and kissing my knuckles in such a sweet fashion it caught me off guard. Her lips lingered, and I had to smile at her.

"Ah, my little bee, I couldn't have left you if I tried."

"Why did Officer Rossi call you a prisoner?"

Brianna spoke before I could. "Oh." She laughed lightly. "That was my doing. Dante said no to me, and I was shocked. He never says no. The officer was standing there, and I demanded he arrest Dante for such cheek. Told him to take him to jail." She shrugged. "As I said, it was an inside joke."

"I thought he referred to you as the prisoner."

She waved off his words. "I think some things got lost in translation. Now tell me, Mr. Winters, are you married? Any children?"

He couldn't lie to her, not with me sitting there. "Yes. To both."

"Ah."

Her one word said it all. He shouldn't have sat at her table.

"What do you do for a living? Are you an art dealer as well, like my Dante?"

My Dante.

She was brilliant. She spoke to him as if he were a colleague of mine and highlighted the relationship she wanted him to think we had. Someone she had no personal interest in but, instead, a polite one. He didn't like it, and he stood. "Perhaps another day, we can chat again. I must leave you now." He nodded and walked away.

Brianna sighed and sat back. She pulled off her glasses and rubbed her eyes. "I did not invite him to sit at my table."

"I surmised that."

"You looked ready to murder him when you walked over here."

I stood. "I need a coffee for this."

"May I have a fresh one? I think he touched my cup."

"I will dispose of it."

I returned with two fresh lattes and pastries. We sipped the coffee, the sun warm.

"You bought very little. Simona said you left quickly." I glanced at the few bags. "What else did you purchase?"

"A few toiletries. A pair of flip-flops." She paused. "I saw you come out of the shop and head this way. You looked furious even then."

I sat back, resting my arm along the back of my chair. "I thought you had run," I said honestly.

She shook her head, looking outraged, and I regretted my first instinct of distrust. "What? How? Walk to Naples?"

"There is a bus every afternoon."

"Good to know for when I do decide to make my escape," she scoffed. "Why would you think that?"

"I thought perhaps you planned it."

"Yes, because we both know I'm so good at planning things like escapes or evading kidnapping art dealers who like to drive me mental. Fricking frack, you annoy me."

I had to chuckle. "Stinger down, Little Bee."

"I said I wouldn't run, and I won't."

"Okay. Got it. What have you been doing?"

"I've been wandering around, looking at things."

"Why didn't you buy more?"

"Everything is so expensive, Dante. I only bought a suit at her shop because I liked it. I'm sure I can find somewhere less expensive to buy a few items."

"Were there other things you liked?"

She hesitated.

"Were there?" I pressed, already knowing the answer.

"Yes."

"Finish your coffee."

I piled the bags into the back of the car, ignoring Brianna's protests. Both dresses she'd looked at and tried on, plus one I had liked, were hung in garment bags. Some casual clothes were in the bags in case she wanted to wear something other than her overalls, although I did like the convenience of the straps for yanking her close.

Better shoes than flip-flops were purchased. I opened an account for her at the kitchen store, and we got some items she needed that I wouldn't have to have shipped, including a decorating set, pans, bowls, and other baking implements she requested.

She found a bicycle she loved—bright red with a basket, as per her request. It would be delivered tomorrow. She wasn't overly happy with the helmet, but I lied and told her it was law here, so she accepted it. I didn't want to think of her on the country roads without one. I also got her a reflective vest, which *was* law, although I had no plans on allowing her to ride after dark.

We ran into Officer Rossi a couple of times, and he smiled indulgently at us, taking in the way our hands were clasped and the smiles on our faces. It was good for him to see us together. It gave credence to our relationship and chased away any doubts. He did think she was a little crazy with the arresting thing, but it did no harm.

In the car, I glanced at Brianna. "You were very good with Winters."

"He just sat down and started talking to me. Crowding me. I disliked him immediately. I could see the white line where his wedding ring should be. How slimy."

"He is that."

We were quiet for a moment. "You have a talent."

"Decorating cakes, I know."

"No, another one. You defused the situation with Rossi. Told off Winters without insulting him. You are amazing."

"Oh. Well, thanks."

We pulled up to the villa's gates.

"Why does Winters hate you so much?"

I drove up the driveway. "He thinks I had something to do with a missing piece of art he had."

I parked, and we got out of the car. "Why would he think that?" she asked.

I handed her some bags and winked.

"Because I did."

Chapter Twelve

BRIANNA

I put away the clothes Dante had bought me, running my hand over the yellow sundress. It was so pretty and girly. Not what I usually wore, but mostly because overalls were cheap, lasted a long time, and washed easily. Something like this required care. The only other dress I owned was the one I'd worn to Carolina's wedding, and I had bought it at the thrift store. Most of my clothing came from secondhand stores. Now I had a whole bunch of new items to choose from. It felt odd to have clothes hanging in my closet that hadn't been worn by someone else.

My closet.

I shook my head. I was brainwashed. This wasn't *my* closet. These weren't *my* things. It all belonged to Dante.

Except, somehow, they all felt like mine. Dante had given them to me freely. Insisted on them. He'd even had a quiet conversation with Simona, stepping out of the shop, and I now owned lingerie that would have paid my rent for a month. My ratty Fruit of the Loom cotton underwear and serviceable bras were relegated to the bottom drawer, and soft, lacy undergarments filled the top one. Pretty, but not uncomfortable. Simona had explained I had been wearing the incorrect size bra, and the one I left the store in felt like a second skin to me. When I explained I wasn't much for fancy, she helped me choose pieces that were pretty and feminine without making me feel like a trussed-up piece of meat.

I stared at the clothes. The lingerie. I thought about how upset Dante had looked when he was headed down the street toward the café. How his face changed when he spotted me. His smile had been full of relief. He looked so happy to see me. He was protective, scaring Winters off. He was generous to a fault, insisting on purchasing all these items. He was a mystery to me—one I couldn't explain. Carolina had always described him as stern and grumpy. *"I'm exceedingly fond of him, and him me, but there is always a line,"* she told me. *"He isn't one for hugs or touchy stuff. But he's always been there for me and always will be."*

His brother and sister-in-law described him as aloof. He himself said he was cold.

There was no doubt he was intense. Scary when angry. Determined and bossy. Extremely high-handed and demanding. Had a propensity for doing as he pleased, even if it meant taking control of someone else's life by kidnapping them.

Yet with me, he showed a gentler side. He smiled. Laughed. Teased. Asked for little in return, to be honest. My company. My cakes.

And my body.

He made no secret of the fact that he wanted me. And the bottom line was, the longer I was in his presence, the more I wanted to give it to him. I wasn't sure how much longer I could resist. How much I really wanted to resist. Sixty days with a sexy man who wanted to spoil me, teach me about sex, and shower me with gifts? It would be a lovely memory to think back on when I was old and gray. A fun story to shock my children with. I had to make sure the only thing I lost to him was my virginity.

I wasn't sure I would survive losing my heart as well.

I walked into the kitchen, surprised to see Dante cooking. I took a minute to stare. I had seen him in a suit. He wore dress shirts every day that showed off his broad shoulders and form. In the pool, I'd felt his wall of muscles, seen how his biceps rippled, but somehow in a casual Henley and jeans, the sleeves of his shirt pushed up, a towel flung over his shoulder, and barefoot, he was sexier than ever.

"Good. There you are. Dinner is almost ready."

"Where is Gia?" I asked.

He frowned as he tasted the sauce simmering on the stove. "Little Bee, I have two villas, condos in London, Naples, and Toronto. Do you really think I employ full-time housekeepers in all of them? This is my primary residence, and even here, Gia works only part time. She and her husband, Mario, look after the villa and the grounds and hire the right people to maintain it."

"I see."

"Gia often cooks me breakfast, but I am perfectly capable of cooking for myself. My mother taught me when I was younger." He added some pepper into the sauce. "I fend for myself a great deal of the time."

"Ah. So all the containers of sauce in the freezer that Gia showed me..." I trailed off.

He narrowed his eyes. "You saw that, did you?"

I laughed. "Yes. But Gia told me you cook as well."

"I prefer to grill, but I was hungry and pasta is fast." He dropped some noodles into the boiling water. "Three minutes, dinner will be ready. You like shrimp, right?"

"Love it."

"Okay. I thought we'd eat on the patio. It was supposed to rain but looks as if it passed us. We'll eat there."

"What can I do?"

"Take the wine and salad outside. I'll bring the pasta."

"No garlic bread?"

He shook his head. "That is such an Americanized thing. I have some focaccia Gia made earlier if you want."

"Please."

I carried the tray outside, setting it on the table. The sky was dull, but it was still pleasant. Roomba lay on the warm stone, looking content. I bent and rubbed her tummy. She opened one eye and rolled over, ignoring me. Typical. I returned inside and got the focaccia from Dante, and he followed me with the steaming bowls. I sat down, eyeing the shrimp and fettuccine with admiration. It smelled divine.

"Lemon cream and white wine sauce," Dante offered. "One of Gia's specialties. I love it with the shrimp and some fresh cheese on top."

I took a bite, unable to hold in my groan. It was incredible. Dante's hand froze as he poured the wine, and he shook his head slightly as if to clear it, then he finished filling the glasses and began to eat. We were mostly quiet as we chewed, although I complimented him on the food. He finished first, sitting back and sipping his wine.

"What you said in the car earlier, about why Winters hates you."

"It's a long story. Another time." His tone brooked no argument. I was burning with curiosity, but I knew not to push it. I tried his favorite subject.

"Is there anything you like aside from cakes?" I asked.

"I love all sweets. Cakes are my favorite, but I like pies. Cookies."

"What kinds of cookies?" I wiped my mouth. "I don't see you as a chocolate chip kind of guy."

"They're fine. But I like peanut butter. My favorite is a kind my mom used to make when I was little. I haven't had them for a long time."

"What kind?"

"I don't remember the name. They were really simple. Just a good cookie. Soft and chewy. They had cinnamon on them."

"Snickerdoodles?"

"Yes!" he exclaimed, smacking the table. "I used to eat them by the handful with milk. My mom kept raw dough in the freezer to bake all the time when I was young."

"Ah. So you were crazy for desserts even then?" I kept a straight face. "They had ovens in the old days? Did those exist in prehistoric times?"

He narrowed his eyes. "You think you're funny?"

"Yes."

"One day," he threatened. "One day, I won't let that pass."

I picked up the dishes and stacked them on the tray. "So you keep saying."

He caught me in the kitchen, pressing against me, his chest to my back. "As soon as you beg, I'll show you, Little Bee. I'll take you so good and so hard, you won't remember your name. And every time you call me old man, I'll fuck you again. Until you're screaming my name. And I'll keep going. I'll fuck you until one of us passes out from exhaustion." He bit down on my earlobe, brushing my nipples with his thumbs as he cupped my breasts. "And my stamina is strong, little girl. So strong." He bent and ghosted his lips over my neck.

I whimpered.

"You keep it up," he added.

"Isn't that your job?" I quipped.

"Don't worry, baby. It's up every time you're around. And one day, you'll tip me over the edge, and I won't be able to wait."

He spun me in his arms, our faces so close together our breath mingled. "That time gets shorter every time you mouth off and call me an old man. Revenge is going to be sweet—for both of us."

He cupped my face and bit my bottom lip, running his tongue over it. Then he stood back, releasing me. I stumbled a little, and he caught me, making sure I was steady before letting me go.

Our eyes locked.

"Soon," he said. "Very soon."

Unable to relax, I dug through the cupboards, finding everything I needed. I had heard Dante climb the steps to the third floor, and I knew he'd be in his office for a while. Gia had shown me how to use the oven, and I turned it on to heat and got busy. I measured and mixed, hoping I recalled the recipe correctly. Roomba came in, wound around my ankles, then headed back outside. She loved being able to roam in and out. She stayed in the area around the pool, wandering to the grass and among the bushes, but seemed content to stay close.

I slid the first tray of cookies in and prepped the second. If they turned out, I could make more, but I wanted to be sure. I had tidied up the kitchen after Dante had stormed away. I shouldn't tease him, but I did like his reactions when I called him old man. He was anything but old; however, his responses to my words were always intense. I shivered as I recalled his sexual threats tonight. My own reaction had been physical. My underwear grew damp, my nipples hardened, and I ached for something. I just wasn't sure what that something was, although I was sure Dante would know and happily give it to me.

The timer went off, and I pulled out the tray. My snickerdoodles were golden, smelled delicious, and looked perfect. I slid in the other tray and, after a few moments, transferred the cookies to a plate, humming to keep the silence at bay. I was contemplating carrying them upstairs when I heard Dante's heavy tread coming toward the kitchen.

"What am I..."

He inhaled again. "Are those *cookies*?"

I held out the plate. "Yes."

DANTE

I couldn't work, no matter how I tried. None of the messages were important, and the emails weren't urgent. Even one about a piece I'd been trying to purchase from an estate didn't hold my interest.

My interest was somewhere in this house, just out of my reach.

Brianna had crawled under my skin and stayed there. She invaded my thoughts, slipped into my dreams, wove her way into every aspect of my world.

And she was downstairs, doing God knew what, in my house. I felt bad that I had stormed away from her, leaving her in a messy kitchen, but I had no choice. If I hadn't forced myself back, I would have taken her right then. I felt how she reacted to me. The hard tips of her nipples as I cupped her breasts. The way she arched her back to get closer to my touch. The low, needy whimper that escaped her lips as I kissed her neck. I had to get away. Leave her.

But it did no good. I could smell her on my hands. The fragrance from her hair, the scent of her skin, was still in my nose. Her laughter echoed in my head. Her teasing words and the way her eyes danced as she said them. No one spoke to me the way she did. No other woman ever had. She was unique.

I stood, giving up. I would go find her and see what she was doing.

But when I opened my door, another scent hit me. Sweet, heavy with sugar and cinnamon. And I heard humming. I inhaled again, my mouth watering.

My little bee was baking.

I raced down the steps and into the kitchen. "What am I..."

I stopped at the sight of the plate Brianna held. Another sniff and I knew. "Are those *cookies*?"

She had barely said yes before I grabbed one, biting down. Soft and chewy. Rich and dense. Cinnamon, sugar, and the perfect cookie, all rolled into one. I groaned at the taste. Chewed and swallowed. Reached for another one.

Brianna set down the plate as I devoured the next piece of perfection, and she slid a glass of milk in front of me. I lost count of the number of cookies I ate, opening my eyes to look at Brianna. She seemed shocked, and I realized I had eaten a lot of cookies. Probably more than I thought. "Tell me there were a dozen on that plate."

"Sixteen."

I had eaten six cookies. In a row.

"That was impressive," she muttered.

"Those were amazing."

The timer went off, and she pulled another tray out of the oven. "Hopefully these will last you until tomorrow."

I took another one, biting down. "You let me relive a little piece of my childhood," I told her. "Thank you."

She picked one up, studying it, then bit down, chewing slowly. "Thirty seconds less next time. I have to get used to your oven."

"They're perfect to me."

She smiled. "Good. I can practice until the cake supplies come in."

"Yes. Yes, you can."

I watched her efficiently put the cookies into a container, wash the cookie sheet and slide it back into the oven to dry. The rest of the kitchen was spotless. She smiled at me. "Don't eat them all, Dante. You'll be sick."

"Wouldn't dream of it."

She walked past me. "I'm going to bed."

I caught her hand. "Thank you, Little Bee. I mean it. They're great."

"Do they count as one of the sixty?"

I felt a flutter of something at her question, but I nodded. "Yes, if you want."

A strange look passed over her face. "Good night, Dante."

I pulled her close and kissed her forehead. "Good night, Little Bee."

I watched her walk away, feeling strangely morose. Her cookies no longer held any appeal for me, and I put on the lid and locked up the patio doors. I noted the clouds gathering and wondered if the rain would fall in the night.

We needed a good storm to clear the air.

And I wasn't sure I was just talking about the weather.

Chapter Thirteen

BRIANNA

I woke up, startled. It took me a moment to realize a storm was raging outside and my patio door had opened and was banging in the wind. I jumped out of bed and grabbed the door handle, shutting and locking it. I peered outside. It was raining hard, the thunder rolling low and angry, the lightning illuminating the sky in jagged shards of electricity.

My heart was beating fast from the scare, and I turned back to the bed and frowned. Roomba wasn't on the mattress. Storms didn't usually bother her, but perhaps the sound of the door hitting the frame had startled her. I turned on the light, peering under the bed, but she wasn't there. I looked everywhere in the room but couldn't find her. She always slept beside me at night. I sat down, racking my brain, suddenly worried. Had she been beside me when I went to bed? My mind had been so consumed with Dante, the way he made me feel, and what was happening between us, I hadn't noticed.

I had a horrible thought. What if she was still outside? Had Dante shut the patio doors, not knowing she wasn't in the house?

I jumped off the bed and headed downstairs, the marble cold under my feet. I checked the living area and the kitchen, looking everywhere, but she never appeared. I opened the patio doors, peering into the darkness and rain, and called for Roomba, raising my voice to be heard over the rain. If she was outside, she would be wet and cold. Probably scared. Perhaps too scared to come to the sound of my voice.

I went outside, immediately soaked by the pelting rain. I called loudly and searched, panicked. What if she had run? Would she be lost? Were there any wild animals here? I had never asked Dante that. I felt the tears fill my eyes, and I called again, my imagination working overtime.

I was so upset I didn't watch where I was going. One minute, I was running, looking for Roomba, the next, I was airborne, grasping at nothing and hitting the surface of the pool. I went under, frozen in shock. I kicked my way up, splashing and gasping for air, going under once again. I had landed in the deep end of the pool this time. I couldn't see where the surface was, the dark engulfing me. I inhaled some water, terrified. I tried to fight my way up again, but my arms and legs felt like dead weights. I began to panic, thrashing harder when there was a disruption of the water around me, and strong arms grabbed hold of me, pulling me up fast.

"Jesus Christ!" Dante yelled. "What the hell?"

I gasped for air, clinging to him. I sobbed in relief, and he held me tighter. "I've got you, Brianna. You're safe."

"Dante," I cried, unable to think clearly.

He cradled me in his arms, carrying us to the steps. The rain beat down on us, the storm making me shiver.

"What the hell are you doing out here?" he asked as he climbed from the water.

"Roomba," I gasped as the air hit us. "I can't find her. I think she's lost."

"Your damn cat is asleep on my bed. Where she is every night," he snarled. "No matter how often I put her out of the room, she comes back."

Relief filled me, even as disbelief set in. "On your bed? But she's with me when I go to sleep and wake up!"

"Well, she visits as soon as you're out."

"If you hate it so much, then shut your door," I said snidely.

He held me closer. "I leave it open for you, Little Bee."

He set me on my feet inside the villa, shutting and locking the doors behind me. I was shaking from the cold, the shock, and the entire situation. Dante cursed again, scooping me into his arms and racing for the stairs.

"Water," I protested. "We're getting everything wet."

"Fuck that," he snapped.

He headed to his room, setting me on the floor again. I was shaking so hard, my legs barely held me up. He muttered something, going to the bathroom, snapping on a light, and returning with a towel. He stripped off my shorts and shirt, and I was too tired to protest as he briskly ran the towel over my body, his actions bringing some much-needed warmth to my skin. He towel-dried my hair, frowning as my body continued to quake. He wrapped his arm around my waist, lifting me as if I weighed nothing, and deposited me on his bed, throwing the covers over me. I shook, my teeth chattering, watching with wide eyes as he yanked off his sleep pants, dried off his chest, and crawled into bed with me.

"What-what are you doing?" I asked.

He pulled me into his arms, holding me tightly. "Warming you up."

Our damp skin molded together. He ran his hands up and down my back. Entwined our legs. Pressed my head to his chest. Murmured soft words. My shaking began to ease, the cold draining away as his heat dispelled it. My body began to relax. He pulled me closer, his strokes becoming different. No longer practical. More caressing. Intimate. He stroked longer, slower, drifting his hands over my buttocks and thighs. My shivering now had nothing to do with cold.

It had everything to do with his touch.

"You scared the fuck out of me," he said.

"I'm sorry," I whispered. "I panicked."

"You should have come to get me. I don't know why the sensor lights didn't come on outside," he grunted. "Jesus, if I hadn't come out—I can't even think."

"I'm sorry," I repeated, stifling a gasp as he wrapped his hand around my thigh, tugging me tight to his form. So tight, I could feel him. His desire.

He gazed down at me, the dim light from the lamp in the corner letting me see his eyes. Deep, intense, and focused. On me. He rolled so he was hovering over me, his torso pressing me into the pillowy mattress. His scent was full and rich on his sheets, surrounding us. *He* surrounded me. He slid between my legs, fitting there as if that was where he belonged. His breathing was labored, his chest moving rapidly, matching the rhythm of mine.

"I'm getting your pillow wet," I whispered. "My hair..."

"...will dry," he finished, his eyes never leaving my face. A question was swirling in the depths of his eyes. His voice was low, rough, needy.

"Dante," I whimpered, feeling his muscles under my fingers as I clutched at his shoulders, emotions overtaking me. Need. Want. Desire. All of it. I needed to be closer to him. I wanted his weight on me. I desired it all. Especially him.

"Say it," he murmured. "You have to say it."

"Please."

"Please, what?" he asked, drifting a finger over my cheek, tracing the outline of my lips.

"Make me yours."

"Thank God," he replied and covered my mouth with his.

DANTE

I kissed Brianna with everything in me. The relief, the desire, the raging inferno of lust she had stirred up within me from the moment I saw her.

I had heard her heading downstairs, and I wondered if the storm was bothering her. I had my windows open, enjoying the cool air and the sound of the rain and the storm. The thunder eased off, and the next thing I knew I heard her voice outside, calling for her infernal cat. Who was lying on my bed, not caring that her owner thought her missing. I flung back the covers, causing the cat to jump down and sashay its way to the door in front of me. I hurried downstairs, my heart going into my throat when I saw Brianna stumble and fall into the pool.

The damn storm must have knocked out some of the outside lights, and she hadn't realized how close she was to the pool as she looked for Roomba. I rushed outside, diving in and grabbing her, yanking her up as she gasped for air. I pulled us to the shallow end, hauling her into my arms, horrified to think of what could have happened if I hadn't heard her.

Bringing her to my room, I only meant to warm her, to offer her comfort. To give it to myself that she was okay. Safe. Not dead at the bottom of my pool, but here with me.

But as her shivering stopped and her body began to tremble with a different emotion, my desire overtook everything else in my head. My cock was hard and aching for her. My mouth yearned for hers. I was desperate, barely hanging on, when she finally said the words I needed to hear.

Everything else but her, but us, ceased to exist or matter. She was here. In my arms. My bed. She wanted me as much as I wanted her. I kissed her deeply, stroking my tongue along hers, exploring her mouth and encouraging her to do the same. Her first tentative slides against my tongue grew bolder, and soon, she was as lost as I was. She clutched at my shoulders, moving her hands restlessly along my back, pressing me down to her. I slid my hands under her shapely ass, cupping and kneading the flesh, wrapping her legs around me. My cock was nestled into her warm, wet center. She gasped into my mouth at the feeling of me. I kissed her neck, ghosted along her collarbone, and sucked her tight, hard nipples into my mouth, tonguing them and making her writhe under me. I rolled so she straddled me, staring down at me in confusion.

"Explore me, Little Bee. Discover everything you want."

I'd been with many women. Bedded the most experienced lovers. None of their touches ever affected me the way hers did. The feel of her fingers on my skin, the way her mouth felt as she kissed and tasted me, teased me with her tongue, growing bolder as my groans grew louder and longer, was perfect. She liked to be kissed, and I brought her face to mine, doing exactly that as she stretched over my torso, her hair a dark curtain around us. I slid my hand between her legs, touching her. She was wet. Hot. She whimpered, her legs widening as I stroked her. Played with her tight little clit as she moved with me. I slipped a finger inside her, shutting my eyes as she gripped me. "You are so tight, Brianna. So fucking tight, you'll strangle my cock."

"I can't—"

"You can. But we'll make sure you're satisfied first."

"I—"

I cut her off again, this time with my mouth. I rolled us again and kept kissing her. I touched her clit, strumming it as she undulated with my hand. Seeking, wanting more. Wanting everything I could give her. I slid my finger back in, thrusting—gently at first, then picking up speed as her body began to take over. I added another finger, stretching her, and she moaned in pleasure. I kept my thumb on her clit, making sure to keep the pressure right, and she grabbed at me, her back arching, my name falling from her lips. "Dante!"

"Yes, beautiful. Come for me," I encouraged. "Come all over my hand, then I'll give you what you really want."

She was incredible in her release. Her eyes wide, a small gasping cry coming from her mouth. She gripped my arm, caught in a wave of pleasure, and I let her ride it out, capturing her mouth with mine and swallowing her scream.

Her orgasm passed, and I gentled my touch again. Kissing her softly. Affectionately. Moving between her legs, I rubbed myself against her, coating my cock in her release. "Are you sure?" I asked quietly. I would stop now if that was what she wanted. I would give her anything.

"Please," she replied. "I want to feel you."

I knew she was on birth control pills. I had packed them myself. Still, I asked, "Condom?"

"No. You."

I bent her leg, bringing my mouth back to hers. "It will hurt for a moment. But it will pass. I'll make it up."

"I know."

I pushed in, inch by inch. Going slowly so she got used to my size. Until I couldn't. Until the desire to claim, to possess, became too strong. The heat and wetness of her overcame all my instincts to be gentle and instead roared in their desire to have her. *Now.*

I snapped my hips and buried myself to the hilt.

Brianna cried out. I groaned at the feel of her. I was overwhelmed at the sensation of being joined with her. It was like nothing I had ever experienced.

I had to move. Ached with need to thrust into her. When she tilted her hips under me, I withdrew and pushed forward.

I heard her moan. It wasn't in pain.

We fell into a rhythm quickly. Long, steady strokes. She moved with me, slowly at first, then it was as if we'd done this a hundred times. She was perfect around me. The ecstasy of being inside her was incredible. My body thrummed in pleasure. She made noises of delight, clutching at me. Our mouths fused together, our breath mingling. She gripped at my back and shoulders. I grasped the headboard, beginning to move harder, faster. Needing deeper. Needing everything she could give me. I took and took until she shattered. Crying out in her release, the timbre of her voice low and raspy. Choked with desire.

And I came. Hard, cursing, sweating. Thrusting until I couldn't move anymore. Coming harder than I had ever done in my life. Grunting her name, praising her, whispering how beautiful she was.

And then, I collapsed in her arms.

For a moment, the room was quiet except for our harsh breathing. I lifted my head and kissed her, adoring her with my mouth. "All right, Little Bee?"

She hummed, tugging on my head so I lay on her chest. "I'm good. That was...incredible. Is it always like that?"

"No. But for us, yes."

Silence descended. I shifted and lay on my back, drawing her to my chest. "Sleep now. I have you."

She tightened her grip on my torso. "I have you right back."

Her words made me smile as I drifted off.

Chapter Fourteen

BRIANNA

Wrapped in Dante's arms, I was still processing what had occurred. Nothing had prepared me for sex. Sex with Dante. He was like the thunderstorm outside, consuming me. The clouds and power coming together to envelop me. I had no idea orgasms could feel so intense. The few I'd given myself had been fleeting and weak, leaving me wholly unsatisfied. But with him, it was as if my body had come alive for the first time. Everywhere he touched blossomed and expanded. Everything he did brought me pleasure. Even that first moment of discomfort had a special meaning, because it was him. It was us.

He sighed, the sound rumbling in his chest. I tilted up my head, looking at him. His hair was in disarray, his scruff heavy. I thought of how it felt brushing against my skin. Rough, yet soft. His lips pursed as he slept, and I recalled the possession of his mouth on mine. How those lips sucked at my breasts, nipped at my neck, and devoured mine. Like a man starving and I was his last meal.

For the first time in my life, I felt sexy. Desirable. He woke something in me I didn't know existed.

I wanted more.

I carefully eased off his chest, studying him. The soft light behind me enabled me to see his muscles and sculpted chest. His arms were thick and strong, his neck corded. He was handsome in an unusual way. His brother, Carolina's dad, was good-looking in a softer way. Dante was all angles and shadows, with a high forehead, strong nose and chin, and a long face. I still caught a flash of the dimples high on his cheeks when he smiled a certain way.

I laid my hand on his chest, feeling the strength beneath my fingers. He was solid and vibrant. Gently, I traced a finger along his sternum, feeling his muscles shift under my touch. I paused where the blanket lay draped over his stomach. Glancing up, I froze when I realized his eyes were open, his intense gaze focused on me. "If you keep going, I won't be responsible for my actions."

I glanced down, not surprised to see the blanket tenting. I slipped my hand under the covers, wrapping it around him. He was surprisingly soft to touch. Steel under velvet. He groaned as I stroked him, a low hiss escaping his mouth.

"Little Bee, you are playing with fire."

"Maybe I want to get burned." I shifted upward so our mouths were close. "If I asked, would you do that again?"

"Do what again?" he asked with a small smile.

"Take me?"

He cupped the back of my head, his large hand warm on my scalp. "Say it, Brianna. Tell me what you want."

"I want you inside me again."

He groaned, and I smiled as I pressed my mouth to his, knowing exactly how to get him going. "If you think you can possibly do that, old man."

In a second, I was under him, his mouth ravishing mine.

I got him going, all right.

T traced his chest, our legs entwined. I rubbed my calf along his, and he chuckled. "Careful, little girl. You must be sore, and I have no self-control around you."

Dawn was breaking, the sunlight beginning to glimmer. It was supposed to be a better day today, weather-wise. I planned on baking more cookies, wanting to stay busy until the cake supplies arrived.

I began to pull away, and he tightened his grip. "No, stay. Just try not to tempt me with your sexy ways."

It was my turn to chuckle. "I'm not sexy."

"Yes, you are. The way you move, the artless mannerisms you have. Your curves. They drive me to distraction."

"My curves," I repeated. "How polite."

"What are you talking about?"

"I'm aware because I'm short, I'm chubby. Some would say fat. It's not attractive to most men."

"I'm not most men. And you're not fat."

I shrugged.

He was quiet for a moment. "Is that why you only bought one swimsuit? You're self-conscious?"

"That was the only one I was comfortable in, yes."

He flung back the covers and stood. I tried not to ogle him, but I failed. With the sun behind him, he looked like a god. A sexy, intense god.

He pulled me with him and crossed the room, sitting on a wide chair. He pulled me to his lap, so my back was to his chest, and he looped his calves around mine. "Look," he said.

I directed my gaze to where he pointed, and I grimaced, attempting to turn my head. He grasped my chin. "No. Look, Little Bee. Look with me."

I met his eyes in the full-length mirror, not wanting to focus on the image of us. He tutted. "Look."

With a huff of air, I did. He sat behind me, a statue of muscle and power. I was a powder puff.

He put his arm around me, spreading his hand wide on my stomach. "Look how soft you are. How pale and delicate."

I was pale. He was tanned from years in the sun, a golden hue that set him apart from those who lived in the city. He was healthy and strong.

"You look better."

"I look different. Not better. I love how you look. Pretty, feminine, your skin like ivory. Except here." He turned my head and kissed the end of my nose. "The sun got you there. And the longer you're here, you will be kissed all over by the sun. I look forward to discovering the freckles."

He turned my head back, entwining our hands and lifting my foot up with his. "All of you is tiny. One of your little hands fits into my palm, yet they are strong and create such delicious art. Your feet are half the size of mine, but I bet they outwalk me every day. Your body suits you perfectly, and whoever says differently is an idiot. Your size doesn't indicate the strength you carry in here." He touched my chest. "Bees are small, but they are one of the most industrious creatures on earth. Remember that."

He moved his hands to my hips. "I love your curves. The roundness here. I can hold you, feel you moving. You have a beautiful shape. Perfect for children. Men stare at you, and you don't even know it. I love watching you walk toward me, the way your breasts sway slightly, tempting me. When you leave, I watch your hips, imagine them between my hands. I wanted to bite your ass the first time I saw it." He paused. "In fact, I still do."

He pushed me forward, lifting me, and bent, biting one cheek. I gasped and started to giggle, and he did the same to the other. The giggles turned into laughter, and he straightened, pulling me back to his chest again.

"You are irresistible. Perfectly curvy. Any man who thinks less, is not the man for you." He rested his chin on my shoulder. "A real man likes having something to hold when he makes love to a woman. I like your softness. How you feel when I hold you. How you move with me. Not a flat board, but a real woman."

"Ah," I whispered.

"I love that you're short. I feel like a protector beside you. Your petiteness, everything about you makes me feel taller. Bigger. Stronger."

His words healed something inside me, and I had trouble speaking. "Ah," I repeated.

"You need to look at yourself and see all the good, Brianna. You are beautiful."

"Thank you," I murmured.

His intense gaze became sharper. Focused. He slid his hand down, using his legs to part mine, stroking my upper thighs.

"What-what are you doing?"

"I want you to see what I see when you come. How beautiful and sexy you are in that moment."

He slid his hands higher and widened his legs, exposing me fully. "Watch."

Mesmerized, I did as he instructed. He gathered my hair with one hand, holding my neck to the side as he kissed the skin, his lips teasing and tasting me. He used his other hand, gently teasing me, sliding a finger along my folds and touching my clit with light passes. He met my eyes. "Already wet for me. I love that."

My eyes fluttered shut as he tapped my clit, slowly circling it. "Open your eyes. Watch. I'm going to make you come quickly, then I'm taking you back to bed and I'm going to fuck you." He slid a finger inside me, and I watched as he withdrew it, seeing the glistening digit. "Like hot, silken honey," he whispered. "I love seeing your desire on my skin. I love feeling it." He added another finger. "Still so tight, Brianna. I can't tell you how fucking incredible it feels when my cock is inside you. It's a vise, squeezing me, sucking my come from me."

His dirty words did something to me. He used his thumb on my clit, swirling it in maddeningly slow circles. He began to move his fingers faster, pushing them in deep, making me cry out as I felt my orgasm beginning to mount.

"Look at us," he rasped in my ear, going back to my neck. I stared at our reflection. He was a dark shadow hovering over me. I was small compared to him, but I didn't see myself the way I usually did. I saw what he saw. A woman caught in the throes of passion as he ravished my neck like a bloodthirsty vampire. I was caught up in the moment. My face was flushed, the pink racing down my neck and chest. My back was arched as I tried to ride his hand. He gripped one breast in his large hand, teasing the hard nipple. His other hand played me like a violin, knowing exactly how to touch me and when. "Let go," he hummed. "Then I'm going to give you my cock. And you're going to take all of me until I've had my fill."

His words pushed me over the edge, and my orgasm crested. I was unable to look away, our eyes locked in the reflection, his golden stare hypnotic. My mouth hung open, and I cried out his name, bending and pushing to get closer. Higher and higher I rose until I couldn't take it anymore and I succumbed. I was free-falling from fifty thousand feet, and I didn't care if I survived the plummet. He turned my head, covering my mouth and kissing me so hard, I was breathless. Lost.

Then he found me. His touch gentled, his arms came around me, and his mouth became adoring. Soft touches, whispered words. He carried me to the bed, laying me out and hovering over me.

"One more, Little Bee. You're going to give me one more."

"What if I can't?"

He slid inside me, and I gasped. He was big, hard, and he felt so good.

"You can."

He was right.

Chapter Fifteen

BRIANNA

The world the next morning was filled with bright sunshine. The rain had cleared the air, and the sky was blue with only a handful of fluffy white clouds scattered around. I was in Dante's bed, the blankets pulled up around me. His room was bigger than mine, the bed king-sized and the room masculine. His en suite was massive, with both a bath and a walk-in shower. I could only imagine how large the closet was. His balcony overlooked the back of the house where the pool and garden were located. The room smelled like him, a manly, clean scent with citrus undertones.

I shivered thinking about the pool and what had happened last night. How he'd saved me. Then made love to me. Or had sex. I wasn't sure which it was for him. I knew how it felt for me. There had been more than passion. There had been underlying emotion—for both of us. Dante was an incredible lover, and I was glad he'd been my first. What happened in front of the mirror... I had no words. Erotic. Educational. So deeply intimate. I saw myself differently. I saw myself the way Dante saw me. I would try to carry that with me.

Beside me, Roomba snoozed, and I stroked her heavy fur. "It all happened because of you," I muttered. I bent over and kissed her furry head. "Thank you."

I slid from the bed, a few muscles protesting as I moved. I felt an ache inside, but it wasn't painful. Simply a reminder of what had transpired last night. A large part of me hoped it would happen again tonight.

I headed to my room and showered, the hot water easing a few aches. I was surprised to see how late it was —I never slept in. Not that I'd had much sleep in the night. Dante had been all over me. And this morning in front of the mirror had been unexpected. Hearing how he saw me was an eye-opener. I pulled on my purple overalls, turning up the cuffs, and picked one of the new shirts. It was flowery and pretty, and I put my hair in pigtails since I was going to be baking. I'd checked last night, and he had all the ingredients I needed to make him peanut butter cookies as long as I substituted the brown sugar with demerara. I would grind it to make it finer.

I looked in the mirror. I looked like me. My lips were a little swollen and I had a few marks on my neck, but otherwise, I looked the same. I still wasn't sure what Dante had seen when he met me, but I knew he truly believed I was beautiful. He wanted me to remember that. I straightened my shoulders. I would try —for him.

I went downstairs, my nerves suddenly kicking in. How should I act around him? How would he act? Like nothing had happened? My steps faltered as a thought occurred to me. Now that he'd gotten what he'd wanted, maybe he wouldn't want anything from me now but some cakes. He might even decide to let me bake a bunch and send me home.

My heart plummeted. I didn't want to go home. It was strange, but this villa, being here with him, already felt more like home than anywhere had my entire life. He felt like home. Being in his arms was the first time I didn't wonder where I belonged in the world. It felt as if I belonged with him.

"Little Bee?"

I looked up, seeing Dante standing at the bottom of the stairs, watching me. "Are you all right?"

"Um, yeah, I'm fine."

He climbed the steps, stopping below me. He searched my gaze and reached up to tuck a stray piece of hair behind my ear. "You look adorable today. And I like the pigtails. But you also looked upset. Worried."

"I was, ah, thinking of a recipe."

He smiled and cupped the back of my neck, bringing my face to his for a kiss. It was warm, affectionate, and quickly became heated. He was breathing hard as he drew back. "Now, it's a good morning. I've been waiting for you to have breakfast with me."

"You should have woken me up," I replied, relief racing through me.

"I kept you up most of the night. You needed your sleep."

"Oh," I squeaked.

"You were incredible, Little Bee. Thank you for your gift. I'm honored," he murmured, lifting my hand and kissing it. "Last night was..." He trailed off. "It just was. I have no words."

I could only nod. He entwined our fingers. "Now, come and eat. Your supplies will arrive this morning, and I want a cake tonight. Plus, I think we should have an early night." He winked at me, looking handsome and sexy. His eyes were heated and intense. I loved it when he looked at me that way.

I followed him, my heart suddenly lighter. He still wanted me. Wanted this.

"My sixty days of cakes begins today, then," I said.

He squeezed my hand. "I look forward to them."

Strangely enough, sixty unexpectedly seemed like too small a number, but I forced a smile. "Me too."

It felt odd having breakfast like normal, when nothing felt normal to me. Mario came into the kitchen to tell Dante the crew would be coming to fix the lights outside and add the features they discussed. At my quizzical look, Dante shrugged.

"Last night will never happen again. Extra lights and backups are being added and more motion sensors. And I'm looking at a fence for the pool."

"I doubt what happened last night will ever occur again. You don't need a fence."

He leaned forward and kissed the end of my nose. "Not taking a chance."

He was affectionate and sweet during breakfast. Relaxed. He touched me often, tutting when I didn't finish my food, sliding his chair closer and hand-feeding me bites of omelet and adding jam to my croissant to tempt me. I felt his eyes on me, and every time I looked at him, his focus was on me.

"Do you regret last night?" he asked, breaking the silence.

"Not at all."

"You're uncomfortable with me this morning. No lip, no smiles." He sat straighter. "Did I hurt you? Was it too much? You're so small, and I got carried away—"

I cut him off. "No. I'm fine." I sighed. "I feel different this morning. Last night was...intense. I'm not sure what it meant or if I should act differently. If you want it again..." I trailed off at the shocked look on his face.

He shifted closer, taking my hands. "Listen to me, Little Bee. Last night meant a great deal to me. I know it was your first time and you're grappling with different emotions than I am, but trust me, I want you in my bed tonight. Tomorrow. As to how I want you to act, just be my little bee. Mouthy, funny, and sweet. I like it when you tell me off. Most people wouldn't dare. I like everything about you, okay? So I just want you to be you."

I stared at him.

"You're the worst kidnapper in the entire world, you know that? You're supposed to frighten me, keep me chained up, and order me around. Not say such sweet things to me and do what you did last night when we, ah, when we..."

He grinned. "When we what?"

"That's the thing. I don't know. Made love? Had sex? Um, frolicked?"

He barked out a shout of laughter. "*Frolicked*? You mean fucked?"

"I don't use that word."

"It's just a word."

I shook my head.

"I'll get you to say it, Bee."

Gia walked in, interrupting us. "There is a delivery. A large one."

Dante stood. "Your supplies are here." He bent and cupped my face. "You light up my world, Little Bee. Is that what you need to hear?"

"It'll do," I whispered.

He kissed me, hard and deep, leaving me no doubt he meant what he said. "Now, plan today's cake. I want a good one."

He stopped and said something to Gia on his way to the door. I couldn't understand what it was since he spoke so quickly in Italian, but they smiled in my direction and she nodded.

I finished my latte and stood.

Time to start baking.

I was in shock as I looked at the mountain of supplies Dante had ordered.

"How much flour is here?"

"I got three fifty-pound bags."

"Dante, a fifty-pound bag has about two hundred cups in it. One would have been plenty." I held up the sack of icing sugar. "Six of these?"

"I like frosting."

"How much cream cheese did you get?"

"One hundred packages. I got the kind you said you like."

"I would have to bake hundreds of cakes to use all this before it expires," I muttered.

He shrugged. "Use what you need. The rest can be donated."

But I heard him as he walked away. "Or stay and use it all. I'm good with that."

Gia and I sorted the huge pile, filling a pantry in the kitchen where she kept staples. It hadn't been used much, but once we were done, it was full. Everything I'd asked for had been ordered in bulk. And I had discovered one of the boxes upstairs contained my small airbrush set I always used, so I had everything I needed to create the beautiful cakes Dante wanted. I had bought a top-of-the-line one, and I was pleased to see it. I liked how well it worked.

Gia waved, leaving me alone in the kitchen. I dug the phone Dante had given me from my pocket, selected a playlist, and got to work.

I knew how much Dante loved the hummingbird cake, but it took a long time to make and cool, so I went with a simple vanilla one. I would do the hummingbird tomorrow. I tied on one of the new aprons and gathered my ingredients. As I measured and stirred, I began to hum. The kitchen was sun-filled and large. Lots of work spaces. The tile was warm under my bare feet. I could do exactly what I wanted. No MaryJo breathing down my neck, tracking how much time I used on her ovens, yelling at me to work faster, stop humming, or get more cupcakes done for her. None of the attitude to deal with from her children and no customers to attend to. It was tranquil and lovely. And I would never have a more appreciative customer than Dante. How I got here didn't matter. Whatever deal we struck no longer concerned me. I loved it here, and I was going to enjoy every moment. Both in the kitchen and the bedroom.

Although I had a feeling he was the sort of man whose sexual appetite wasn't limited to just one room.

I planned on satisfying all his cravings.

Anywhere he wanted.

DANTE

I carried my laptop down to the main floor, using the other, smaller office off the kitchen. I kept the doors open, and I enjoyed the show. My little bee was busy and had no idea I was watching her. She moved and danced around my kitchen like the sexual magnet she was. I needed to be in her orbit. She hummed and sang as she stirred and mixed. Little clouds of flour and sugar puffed from the mixer, and I imagined I would taste it all on her skin later. The stalker I had become, I snapped a couple of pictures of her, then settled back, enjoying her sweet soprano. Her voice relaxed me, easing the tension in my shoulders. Her joy of baking brought a smile to my lips and did something to my chest. What, I didn't want to question, or perhaps I was too frightened to do so.

My phone rang with an incoming video, and I frowned at Paolo's name. I shut the door to the office and accepted the call.

"Paolo. Good afternoon, brother."

He didn't bother with a greeting, leaning close to the camera. "Where is the girl?"

I crossed my legs, looking indifferent. "I beg your pardon?"

"Don't play games, Dante. You asked me about the cake baker. Carolina said she tried to call her, and her number is disconnected. She asked me to check on her, and her boss informed me she quit. That some man called and did it on her behalf. You. Where is she?"

"With me," I said simply, keeping my face neutral.

He slammed his hand on his desk. "*What*? Why? Are you out of your mind? She's twelve years younger than you!"

"And Amanda is seven years your senior," I snapped.

That startled him. "Dante, what is going on?"

I wasn't prepared for this confrontation. I scrubbed my face and told him a half-truth. "She was in a desperate situation. I offered to help. She's here with me."

"As?"

I frowned. "A guest. An employee."

"Which one?"

"None of your goddamn business which one," I replied, my anger surfacing. "She is safe and happy, and that is all you need to know. None of this should concern you."

"Is she? Safe and happy, I mean?"

I sent him a photo I had just taken. Brianna was concentrating, a smile on her face and some flour on her nose. She looked adorable and content.

"Yes," I said tersely. "Satisfied now?"

"Why, Dante?" he asked again. "Why her?"

"I don't know. There is something about her. We clicked."

"So, she is okay?"

"She is fine. Do you want to talk to her?"

"No, but Carolina might."

"Her phone was a piece of garbage. I got her a new one. I'll send Carolina her number."

"Is she baking in that picture?"

"Yes. She is making me a cake. One of many."

As soon as I said that, I knew I'd fucked up.

"What?" he joked. "Did you kidnap her to make you cakes? Are you holding her for ransom, and she is paying it in baked goods?"

I took too long to answer, and his face went lax. "Dante, what have you done?"

I shook my head. "Nothing. We made a deal, and she came to visit."

"You had better be telling me the truth."

"You are the irresponsible, reckless one, remember?" I deflected. "I don't pull crazy, half-assed stunts."

Until now, I added silently.

"That was years ago."

"She is fine. Everything is good," I repeated.

"It had better be."

"Are you threatening me?" I asked, keeping my voice low.

"I'm warning you. She is a good friend of Carolina's. She made her wedding cake as a favor. Not to fall prey to some whim of yours."

It was on the tip of my tongue to tell him she was not a whim. I had no idea what she was anymore, but I didn't want to talk about it with him. And I didn't want to say anything else that would make him suspicious.

The last thing I needed was for my brother to pay an impromptu visit and bring his wife. If they found out how I had acted, there would be hell to pay. I had never done anything so outrageous before. "Whatever," I said dismissively. "Anything else?"

"Does she know what you do?"

"That I own some art galleries? Yes."

"And?"

"And nothing. This is only temporary."

"I see."

"A couple months. Maybe less."

He narrowed his eyes. "Something is going on." He was too close to home with that statement. Something unexpected was going on, and I had no idea what it was or how to handle it.

"Nothing is going on except I have a houseguest and she is baking me a cake right now. You are reading something into all this that doesn't exist. I'm done with this conversation. I'll forward Carolina the number. Goodbye."

I hung up, seething.

I hadn't counted on my younger brother finding out she was here. At least, not this way. I had no doubt Carolina would call Brianna and ask what was going on. If Paolo discovered I had called Carolina on her honeymoon to pump her for information, he was going to have a fit. If Brianna couldn't convince Carolina all of this was consensual, Paolo would show up here, and things would get messy.

I buried my head in my hands and cursed.

I would have to do some damage control.

Fast.

T headed for the kitchen, my anger still bright. I had texted Carolina the number and received an immediate reply.

> CAROLINA
>
> What is going on? Why is Bri with you in Italy?

My reply had been short.

> ME
>
> Ask her yourself. But give her a while. She is busy.

> CAROLINA
>
> Doing what?

> ME
>
> Baking me a goddamn cake. Later, or I will cancel her phone. I have been waiting all day.

> CAROLINA
>
> Touchy.

I ignored her and went to see Brianna.

In the kitchen, I leaned on the doorframe, simply watching her. She was in her element, ingredients around her, the scent of baked goods heavy in the air. She was tapping her bare toes to the beat of the music, humming along, occasionally singing the words in her pretty voice. I stared at her bare feet, remembering what I had said to her earlier. She was strong and fierce. And that would become more prominent as she grew older. I wondered what a force she would be in a few years. She was already incredible.

I inhaled, the sounds of her voice and the fragrance of sweet vanilla smoothing the rough edges, my anger fading somewhat. She looked up and saw me. Her smile was so bright, it made me catch my breath.

"Oh, hi!"

I chuckled. "How is my industrious little bee faring?"

"Good." She rubbed her cheek absently, leaving a trail of icing on it. "Cakes are in the oven, I have cookies started, and I'm planning tomorrow already."

I went closer, cradling her chin in my hand and bending low, licking the icing from her skin. "Mmm, buttercream. Why is yours so delicious?"

"I add cream cheese to most of my frostings," she replied, her voice breathless. "It makes them smoother, richer, and less sweet. And real vanilla." She dragged a finger through the bowl in front of her and offered it up. "See?"

I held her hand, sliding her finger into my mouth and sucking off the icing. I swirled my tongue around the digit, then kissed the tip as I let it go. She stared at her finger, then me, her dark eyes lit with a different fire than usual.

"That was the second-best thing I tasted today."

"What was the first?"

I leaned closer, our lips barely touching. "Your mouth."

She swallowed, then did something I didn't expect. She dipped her finger into the icing and smeared it on her tongue. She licked her lips, leaving a trail of frosting behind.

"Come and get it, old man."

I grabbed her overall straps and dragged her to me, kissing her until she was breathless. Until my own head was spinning. It was only the timer going off that broke us apart. I stepped back, meeting her gaze. She looked dazed, flushed, and inviting. But she shook her head.

"The cakes," she murmured, brushing past me.

If it had been anything else but cake, I would have told her to leave it. But she had worked hard, and I wanted the damn cake. I had been patient long enough.

She took the pans from the oven and set them on racks to cool. They were golden and smelled incredible. She adjusted the temperature and put two sheets of cookies on the counter, ready to go in.

She tilted her head, studying me. "What's wrong?"

"What makes you think something is wrong?"

She came close and rubbed my forehead. "When you're upset, you get a line between your eyes. It was gone earlier. It's been gone a lot the last few days. But it came back after you saw Winters, and it's back now. What happened? Is he causing you trouble?"

I was surprised at her observation. Most people wouldn't notice something like that. But she had. And she was worried about me. I liked that.

"No." I told her about my brother and his call. Carolina's text.

She listened and slid the cookies into the oven, setting the timer. She turned and leaned on the counter, crossing her arms.

"And you want to make sure I tell her the same version of the story. Not mention the drugging and kidnapping part?"

"Yes. I think we're past that now."

She nodded, then again surprised me. "I have one condition."

I mimicked her stance. "I see. You want another negotiation. Let me hear it."

"I'll tell Carolina the PG version. I don't want her or her father here either."

"Good."

"As long as you tell me why Winters thinks you stole something from him."

My eyebrows shot up. She was being direct.

"You already told me you did. So I want the story."

"Why?"

"I have a feeling it is a big part of what makes you, *you*."

"You really want to know? You want to know something that basically ties you to me forever? Curiosity killed the cat, you know."

"I doubt what you'll tell me is going to endanger my life."

"It would be best if you left it alone."

"It would have been best if you'd never taken me, but that worked out okay, didn't it? At least this time, I have a choice, and I choose to know."

I blinked at her directness.

The timer went off, and she opened the door, sliding out the trays. My mouth watered at the scent of peanut butter cookies. "I want one."

She frowned. "They're hot. Give them a minute, you impatient fool. And don't change the subject."

"Are you telling me if I don't give you my story, you'll tell Carolina the unvarnished truth? You're threatening me, Little Bee?"

She lifted her chin. "Those are the terms."

I was wrong. She was already a force to be reckoned with. I felt a flash of pride for her.

"Tonight, then."

"Okay." She slid a cookie off the tray, holding it out. It began to slip, and she grabbed it, yelping at the heat.

"*Sugar Honey Iced Tea!*" she yelled, waving her fingers.

All my annoyance faded. Laughter took its place. I took her wrist, checking her fingers. I made her hold her hand under the running cold water, still chuckling. I kissed the reddened tips and then kissed her.

"You are fucking hilarious. I have no idea how you make me so happy." I took the cookie, plus two others and walked out of the kitchen, shaking my head. "I'll see you tonight, my angry little bee."

I headed back upstairs, deciding to go for a run. I bit into the cookie, the texture and taste perfect. It was still hot, and I bit back a curse as I chewed, knowing she was right that I needed to wait. But I was an impatient fool—just like she said.

Sugar Honey Iced Tea.

I began to laugh again.

She was brilliant.

Chapter Sixteen

BRIANNA

I stepped back, admiring the cake. I was sure Dante would love it. It resembled a garden, with a variety of piped flowers on top and the sides iced to look like a trellis with more flowers. He loved icing, so I went overboard with the entire thing, hoping that would satisfy his sweet tooth.

He hadn't come back into the kitchen, and I wasn't sure how to take that. I was certain he would come get more cookies, but I had a feeling the call from his brother had set him on edge.

I had cleaned the kitchen as I went and put all the ingredients away. It was tidy, the cake was done, and it was still sunny outside. I wandered to the patio, sitting at the table, staring at the pool. I thought of last night and the terror I had felt as I'd sunk in the dark water. I recalled Dante's offer to teach me how to swim and decided I would take him up on the offer.

My phone buzzed with a text, and I saw Carolina's name.

> **CAROLINA**
>
> Bri—Are you all right?

I sighed and shook my head.

> **ME**
>
> I am fine.

> **CAROLINA**
>
> Why are you with Uncle Dante?

I nibbled my lip as I contemplated what to say. I decided to stick to a basic outline.

> **ME**
>
> He came to ask me to bake him some cakes. I had just been let go from my other job, and MaryJo was threatening to fire me as well. I was upset, and he offered to bring me here and let me find my feet. I mean, summer in Italy—who could resist?

> **CAROLINA**
>
> Are you romantically involved?

ME

That is personal, Carolina.

CAROLINA

OMG you are.

ME

No comment. But I am fine, happy,
and baking.

I attached a picture I had taken of the cake I'd made.

ME

See?

CAROLINA

He is older than you. And grumpy.

ME

And your mother is older than your
father. Dante and I get along well.
He isn't grumpy with me. He is very
sweet, actually.

CAROLINA

TMI

ME

Then don't ask. How is Allan? How
was the honeymoon? Is married life
treating you okay?

That got her off the subject, and she gushed over her new husband and their trip and how much fun they had. Then she asked one more question.

CAROLINA

So I shouldn't be worried?

ME

No, I am really good. Learning to swim, even. Roomba loves it here.

CAROLINA

You brought your cat?

I smirked as I replied.

ME

Dante insisted. They are best buds.

CAROLINA

I am not sure this is the same Dante we are talking about, but as long as you're okay, I'll leave it. The honeymoon was fabulous. I will tell you more later.

ME

Okay, good. I'll see you when I'm back in Canada.

CAROLINA

Which is when?

I swallowed as I replied.

ME

No exact date yet. I'll let you know.

She signed off with a smiley face, and I set the phone down, staring at the water. My Stockholm syndrome must have kicked in big-time, because the thought of going back to Canada made me anxious. I loved it here.

I shook my head. I had lots of time left. I would enjoy it.

I was determined.

DANTE

I came downstairs, my mood slightly improved. The house smelled delicious. Even in my office upstairs I had heard Brianna's voice at times, and I had enjoyed it. The sound of her singing relaxed me. In the kitchen, I saw her cake on the counter, and I stared at it for a moment, taking in all the details.

The flowers, the trellis, the tiny leaves that looked as if they wrapped around the posts. Roses, lilacs, daisies, all sorts of blooms were featured on the cake. Each one was lifelike. Some piped, some molded, all perfect.

She was an artist, using icing as her medium. I had to snap a couple of pictures. I began to chuckle when I saw the small bowl and the note beside it.

Leftovers.
Please don't destroy the cake.

I sampled the contents of the bowl, the buttercream rich and decadent. There were enough crumbs of the cake to make me want to cut a piece and devour it, but I resisted.

I looked out the terrace doors, spying Brianna sitting at the table. She was staring at the water, and I wondered what she was thinking. I took a bottle of white wine from the chiller, grabbed a couple of glasses, and headed outside to join her.

She smiled at me as I sat down. "Found the taste tester?"

"Delicious," I replied, "but how did you know?"

She leaned over and ran her finger along the edge of my mouth. "You missed a bit."

I captured her hand and licked the icing from her finger. "Incredible now."

I loved how the color crept up her cheeks, and she glanced back at the pool. "Would you really teach me how to swim?"

I pushed a glass of wine her way. "Yes."

"Can we start tomorrow?"

"We can start anytime."

"Tomorrow is good."

"I had Gia take out some steaks for dinner. I'll grill."

"I'm getting spoiled," she murmured.

"Good."

"I texted with Carolina, she's fine," she said, surprising me.

"What did you say?"

She pushed her phone my way. "Read it yourself."

I read her texts. "You shut her down quickly."

Brianna shrugged. "What did you expect me to do? Tell her the truth? You're right—we're past that now.

I'm here, and I wasn't lying. I'm fine. I'm happy and I'm baking."

I tugged her chair closer. "I'm glad you're here." I cupped her head and kissed her, ravishing her mouth. "I'm glad you're happy." I kissed her again. "And I'm fucking thrilled you're baking."

"Potty mouth," she mumbled, but she smiled.

We were quiet for a while. That was something else I adored about Brianna. She didn't chatter. Try to fill in silence with unneeded conversation. Unlike many women her age, she was comfortable with the quiet. Being in the moment. She tilted her head back, the sun playing on her dark hair. Unable to resist, I lifted one heavy pigtail. "You have lovely hair."

"It's long and brown. Dull."

"No," I protested. "It has reds and golds in it. The sun highlights the colors. It's very attractive."

"Hmm," she responded, noncommittal.

"Do we need another lesson in front of the mirror, Little Bee?"

Her fast inhale of air made me grin. I had enjoyed our little mirror time. Next time, I'd get her to ride me. I'd enjoy that.

"No, thank you," she said in her prim voice.

I leaned over and kissed her neck, feeling her shiver. "Liar," I whispered into her ear.

I was rewarded with her glare. I loved her fire, especially when it was directed at me. She came to life, and I wanted to stoke her passion.

"I'm going for a swim," she said.

"Are you?" I asked, amused. "Need to cool down?"

She stood, shaking her head, heading upstairs.

I watched her, my amusement growing, knowing the explosion that was going to happen in about five minutes. Maybe less.

I sat back, sipping my wine, and waited.

S he didn't disappoint. She reappeared in front of me, still in her overalls and pigtails. She slammed her hands on her hips, the fire an inferno now as she glared. I assumed she thought she looked tough and furious.

Instead, she looked delectable and sexy. It made me want to grab those straps and haul her to my lap and fuck her. But I wanted to hear her scold me. I'd do nothing to change what she was angry about, but I did like to hear her tell me off.

"Why are all my things in your room?"

"I had Gia move them," I replied calmly.

"I didn't agree. You didn't even ask!"

I rubbed my lip as I regarded her. I was certain she was mentally sharpening that stinger of hers, ready to have a go at me. Her color was high, and she was gearing up for a good argument. One she would lose, but she wanted it.

I stood, towering over her. "It's my home. I told you I wanted you in my bed, and that is where you will be from now on."

"And I have no choice?"

"Sixty days." I reminded her.

"Sixty cakes," she snapped. "Is your memory that bad, old man? I said sixty cakes, not sixty nights of...fornication."

My lips quirked, and I stepped closer so we were almost chest to chest. Her pupils dilated, and her breathing picked up. "It won't only be nights, Little Bee. And I warned you about calling me 'old man.'"

"You're acting like a cantankerous one."

"And you're acting like a brat." I grabbed her straps and dragged her close, pulling her up to my face. The stress of the day had ramped me up, and suddenly, being inside her was what I needed. And I needed it, *her*, now.

"You need a good fucking to remind you who is in charge here."

She gasped as I covered her mouth with mine. I kissed her until she was a shaking mass in my arms. "You are staying with me in my bed," I told her, unsnapping the clasp on her overalls and yanking them down.

"No."

I tore her T-shirt over her head. "You will be with me every night."

"You can't force me."

I kicked off my pants and tugged my shirt over my head. "I beg to differ, little prisoner."

"You mother*plucker*," she hissed, standing so her shoulders were back, her breasts jutting out, the nipples stiff and pink against her pale skin.

"That's fuck-her," I murmured. "And I plan to." I dragged her into my arms and carried us into the pool. She flinched as the cool water surrounded us, and she wrapped her legs around my waist. But she didn't protest, and I knew she wasn't scared. I sat her on the steps and kept kissing her until she was undulating under me, and I felt her heat surrounding my cock, even through the fabric that separated us. I removed the offending material, tearing it from our bodies so we were flush.

"You wanted to know if last night was making love or frolicking, Little Bee? Well, hold on because I am about to *frolic* you so hard, you'll know the difference."

"Bring it on, old man," she whispered in my ear, biting down on the lobe.

I reared back and sank in deep. She was still tight, surrounding me with her heat and honey. She cried out, gripping my back, and I began to thrust in long, powerful strokes. I cupped her perfect ass in my hands, holding her at the right angle so I hit her exactly where I knew she needed to be stroked. She moved with me, whimpering and moaning as I moved. I grunted and growled as the pleasure rolled through my body.

"Feel that, Little Bee? Feel my cock filling you?"

She clutched at my shoulders, her blunt nails digging into my skin.

"You feel so good. So tight. So fucking hot," I hissed.

Lowering my head, I sucked her nipples into my mouth, going back and forth between them. They were hard under my tongue, and she cried out as I licked and bit at them. She gasped as I sank into the water and rolled us so she straddled me, then pulled us up the stairs, the cool air surrounding us as I leaned back. "Want a turn? Want to fuck me for a change?"

She was wild. Straddling me, she attacked my mouth, sucking my tongue and kissing me with abandon. She gripped my shoulders, undulating over me, and I guided her hips, lifting her and snapping my hips hard. I braced my feet on the bottom step and gripped the ledge above my head, watching her. She was a vision in the sun, her breasts bouncing, her head flung back in ecstasy. I had never seen anything as erotic as Brianna lost to passion. The water splashed around us, the ripples never ending. The air was warm, the water warmer, and the heat between us blistering.

She raised her head, her eyes finding mine. The desire in her gaze was incredible. She was stunning.

"Look at you," I praised. "Riding me. Fucking me. Take me, Little Bee. Take all of me."

And she did. Moving and arching, crying out when I slid my hand between us, pressing her clit.

"Come all over me, Little Bee. Drench me with your honey."

Her head fell back, and she cried my name, milking me. Her muscles fluttered, grabbed, and held me, and I fell over the edge, roaring my release into her neck, holding her tight as we both succumbed.

Then she slumped against my chest. Quiet. Still.

I slid down the steps and into the water, the feel of it refreshing around us. She draped her arms around my neck, and we sat, wrapped around each other.

I felt a sense of peace flood me. Being with her was incredible. And unlike other partners, when we were done, I wanted to stay close. I wanted more with her. More kisses, more snuggles, more time. More her. It was an unusual feeling for me, but I was becoming used to unusual when it came to Brianna.

"So, the discussion is settled," I murmured. "My room is our room now." I paused. "I want you with me, Bee. Please."

"Well, since you asked so nicely," she replied, her voice sleepy and content.

I chuckled and pressed a kiss to her head. "Want that swimming lesson now?"

"I need a suit."

"No, we are totally private. Nude swimming is highly encouraged by your kidnapper."

"Hmm," she hummed. "My favorite one."

I hugged her close, her words making me smile.

"Did I wear you out, baby?" I asked softly.

"Your frolicking was very, ah, vigorous."

"Then sleep."

"Just for a minute."

She was out almost immediately, her head on my shoulder, her wet pigtails floating in the water. I marveled at her trust. Despite how we started, she knew that she was safe with me. That I would look after her. From what I'd gleaned of her past, no one ever had before.

I pressed a kiss to her head.

I wouldn't let her down.

Chapter Seventeen

BRIANNA

I peered over my wineglass at Dante. After he had finished his dinner, he ate two large slices of cake, his praise exuberant over both.

"This is the best vanilla cake I have ever tasted."

"I use fresh vanilla I scrape from the pods. The flavor is incredible."

"The icing." He licked his fingers in delight like a child. *"Jesus, it's incredible. Make this one again."*

He had eyed the cake when he was done, trying to decide whether he could eat a third slice, then decided to wait a while. He took some slices to Gia and Mario, who lived toward the back of the property, returning with a large smile.

"They send their compliments."

Now he was gazing at the sunset. He was relaxed and quiet, his leg crossed over his knee.

He was a complex man. Handsome, arrogant, and in control. Tender and achingly wonderful. Funny. I was certain I was one of the few people who saw some of those sides.

He liked to make the decisions, and he was swift with his judgments. Yet he loved it when I challenged him. When I'd gone upstairs to change into my swimsuit, I had been puzzled when I walked into my room and found all my things gone. The closet was empty except for the boxes Dante had brought from my apartment. The bathroom was clean, the bed made, and the room was pristine.

It had only taken me a moment to figure out where my things were, and sure enough, my clothes were now in his closet. My toiletries in his bathroom. A pretty silk robe was draped across the bottom of the bed in a rich red with flowers on it. I had seen it in the shop and admired it, and I knew Dante had bought it for me.

Part of me was thrilled that my things were here. That he wanted me with him. The other part of me was furious. Something like this deserved a conversation at least.

When I confronted him, I expected his pushback, his smirk as he told me what was going to happen.

I hadn't expected his unbridled passion. Or how being angry with him would light a fire in me only he could quench.

The way he commanded my body was unexpected. I had always wondered about sex. My friends talked about it. Carolina went on about it. The few guys I had dated never brought forth anything like what she described. The one attempt I'd had with a man had involved a lot of fumbling, some lackluster kisses, and him asking if I was "*done yet.*"

I experienced none of that with Dante. He knew how to touch me. Even his dirty words did something to me. He gave me the freedom to explore him. I loved the way he took control. Gave me some of it back. Enticed my passion.

Made me feel sexy.

And this afternoon had been beyond anything I could have imagined.

I liked frolicking with him.

Afterward, I had slept for a short time, waking up to his warm gaze and safe embrace. After a sweet kiss, he dumped me in the water, and I had my first lesson. I was quite pleased that I had learned to float.

"Relax, Bee," he encouraged, standing over me, his hand under me, holding me up. "I have you. Breathe and let yourself relax. Find your balance in the water."

"Move your arms and feet a little."

"That's it. You're doing well."

He was patient, talking to me, and then I realized his voice didn't seem as close. I opened my eyes to find him on the other side of the pool and I was on my own.

"You're doing it," he said. "All on your own. Now stand and try it again."

I had, and I was proud of myself.

We made dinner together and ate on the patio. The simple grilled meat and salad was delicious, and I noticed everything here tasted better. I wasn't sure if it was the food or the company.

Or perhaps, both.

I set down my glass and found his eyes on me. Intense, golden, and suddenly serious.

"You were in foster homes all your life," he said.

"Yes."

He studied me, his gaze dark. "Is there anyone I need to pay a visit to for retribution?"

I was startled but shook my head. "No. I was never abused like some kids. I was just ignored. Overlooked all the time. It's lonely growing up that way. Never belonging. Looking for a place."

"You have no family."

"No."

He looked away, serious and strong. "Well, you belong right here. With me."

I had no idea how to respond, so I stayed silent. His words did something to me, though. Lit a small fire within me that healed a little piece of my heart.

"Carolina once told me you were a silent partner in her dad's firm."

"I am. I was his first investor. He lost all my money. I gave him more. He learned and grew, and he holds a large chunk of my wealth. He is brilliant with numbers. I make sure his company always has the cash reserves he needs to take the risks that his clients need him to take to make them money."

"Wow," was all I could say.

He shrugged. "He's my brother."

The silence fell again, and he turned to me.

"I'm a thief," he said shortly.

"Pardon me?"

"I own art galleries. I do appraisals. I know a lot about art. I'm also a thief."

I was shocked. "You steal the art you sell?"

He poured us some more wine and shook his head. "No. I won't go into a great deal of depth, but—" he swirled the wine in his glass "—you should know the man you're involved with."

His words gave me another thrill, but I only nodded.

"I was a bit of a troublemaker when I was young. I had light fingers and a knack for breaking in to anything locked. I loved a challenge. I got into some trouble, and my mother put a stop to my foray into the criminal world. She sent me here to visit my aunt and uncle. My uncle was a collector, and I became obsessed with art.

Paintings, sculptures, any medium. I loved it all. The masters, new artists. Everything in between. He taught me everything he knew. I studied art. I lived and breathed it. I went to university and then spent two years traipsing around Europe, living on whatever job I could find as long as I could visit galleries. I made friends with artists. Gallery owners. I found some backers and opened a little gallery in London. It failed miserably. But I learned. Got more backers. Found a good clientele. One gallery became two, and that became three. I did a lot of consignments, selling pieces often for more than the owner expected. As my reputation grew, so did my fortune. I have a good eye, and I'm a great negotiator."

I rolled my eyes at his droll wink. "Are your aunt and uncle alive?"

"No. I inherited his collection, though. Some of his pieces helped me get a start. I've bought a few of them back just because he loved them."

He took a sip of wine.

"The art world has an underbelly. Several, as a matter of fact. There are collectors such as myself who surround themselves with pieces they love. Share them at times."

"You show your collection?"

"At my gallery, yes. Not all at once, and I admit not every piece, but yes. Very few have ever seen my whole collection or know where I store it. The rumor is a vault in a Central London bank, and I go and look at it on occasion, only keeping a piece or two out at a time."

"Who started that rumor?"

"Me."

I scoffed at his casual confession. I wasn't surprised.

"But it's here. In the open. You have pieces everywhere."

"Some are extremely good forgeries because I know if they disappeared, I would never see them again. This estate is under so much protection, it would make your head spin. Getting into my villa is almost impossible. I allow very few people here. My most valuable pieces are in my galleries under tight security. I like the fact that people can see them, marvel at the beauty. I move them around a lot, so it's harder to plan a theft."

"I see."

"There are, however, collectors without honor. They see something they want, and they decide to have it, no matter who it currently belongs to. A private collector, a museum, whatever. They decide to take it."

"They steal it?"

"Yes."

"Is Winters one of those types of collectors?"

"Yes."

"And you stole it back?"

"My ability to figure out any lock and my light fingers have come in handy. I was approached years ago by someone who ran an organization that helped people who have suffered losses because of people like Winters."

I leaned forward. "You're like a spy?"

He chuckled. "No, I'm just a thief. Our organization is known as the Robin Hood Society."

"Because you rob from the rich and give it back to the rightful owner."

"Yes. But I'm not a hero, Bee. I get paid well for my time and effort."

"Is it dangerous?"

"If I were caught. Or my identity compromised."

"Winters knows?"

"He suspects a lot of people. We've always disliked each other. The business he runs is shady at best. He has a huge collection that he has acquired through dubious sources. He has no boundaries. He takes priceless artifacts that should be in a museum and squirrels them away. He steals paintings that should be with the family that purchased them. He buys forgeries and passes them off as original works of art and sells them to unsuspecting clients. He is the lowest of the low."

"I am surprised you even associate with him."

"He wasn't always such a lowlife. He started out much the way I did. But he took a different road, choosing to lie and cheat rather than learn and build his reputation. He got involved with forgeries and the darker side of the art world. His reputation became tarnished, but he has enough of a hold not to be ostracized completely. Yet. That is coming."

"What did you steal?"

"A small Ming dynasty bowl." He laughed. "I stood beside him with it in my pocket, and he had no idea." He took another sip of wine. "To his own detriment, Winters is a braggart. He had the audacity to show part of his collection to a select group. I was among them. The piece was there, and I recognized it as stolen."

"Why didn't you just report it to the police?"

"Many people who experience losses like that do nothing about it publicly. The insurance rates are off the charts, and knowing their collection is susceptible to theft invites more robberies. But the art world is small, and news gets out. That is why we exist. The services are offered if desired. How, I don't know. All I get are the details and am paid when the job is done. All very hush-hush. They have no idea who the people are who get their valuables back. They deal with the higher-ups. It gives us all a layer of safety."

"How did you do it?" I asked.

"Right under his nose. I got myself invited to another event, and I was provided with a forgery to take with me. I swapped it out when someone else caused a distraction. The original was returned to its rightful owners. He didn't know it was a forgery for ages. When he discovered it, he went crazy and accused a lot of people. Me included since I had seen it. It caused a great stir, and his business and reputation suffered even more. He insisted he had bought it and had no idea it was stolen, but we had proof he was responsible."

"Do you do this a lot?"

"Only when my skills fit the job. I don't break in to someone's home and abscond with a painting or a massive statue. I'm good with sleight of hand and getting into locks." He winked. "Like the one to your apartment. That was a five-second job."

I was about to tell him off when he spoke again.

"And I got the most valuable treasure on earth for my trouble."

"Jerk," I mumbled, trying not to smile.

"Winters focused on me for some reason after the forgery was discovered, so I have been laying low. But stay away from him. I don't trust him, and I hate the fact that he was ever close to you for a moment."

"I have no intention of going anywhere near him. I didn't like him then, and I dislike him even more now."

"Good." He regarded me, his gaze never wavering. "Aside from my brother, one other person, and the society, I've never told anyone else."

"Why are you trusting me?"

"I don't know, but I do. Implicitly. You asked. I want you to know me. To hide this from you would be unfair."

"Why? In sixty days, I'll be gone from your life."

He frowned. "You really think so, Little Bee?"

"Should I think differently?"

Silence hung between us, then he spoke quietly. "Time will tell."

I heard something in his words. The way he murmured them. A promise.

Of what, I wasn't sure. I was afraid to hope.

But I felt it too.

He stood, holding out his hand. "Dance with me."

Without the heels I had worn, I was shorter than when we'd danced at Carolina's wedding. Still, we fit together well. He rested his chin on my head.

"Hum for me, Little Bee. Let me hear your voice."

I did as he asked, and he moved us around the patio. I shut my eyes, melting into him, letting him guide me without question. I lost track of time as I hummed and sang quietly, choosing some older songs I loved and he seemed to enjoy. When I stopped, he looked down at me, his eyes burning.

"How you brighten the night, my lovely lady."

Then he kissed me, and I clung to him, his arms a prison I was happy to be in.

He rested his forehead on mine.

"Come to bed with me."

I didn't object when he swung me into his arms and headed to the stairs. In fact, I snuggled closer, resting my head on his shoulder.

It felt right there. All of this felt right.

And I didn't question it.

Chapter Eighteen

DANTE

If someone had told me I would be ignoring my businesses, eating so much cake that I had to increase my daily runs to twice the length and add more time on the machines in my gym, all while obsessing over a woman who baked those cakes for me and teaching her to swim, I would have wondered what sort of drugs they had taken.

If they added in that I was crazy about her, having the most incredible sex of my life, and found myself smiling most of the day, I would have suggested they sign themselves in to a psychiatric ward.

But here I was. Cheering on a twenty-six-year-old woman who had just dog-paddled her way across the pool on her own.

"That's it, Little Bee. You can do it!" I called, sounding like a pussy.

And I was. For her.

She reached the steps of the pool, standing in the shallow end, flinging her arms up in victory. Her full breasts swayed, the water rolling off her skin, tempting my tongue to follow its path. I should have mentioned the swimming lessons took place in private and suits were not only optional, but not allowed.

My pool. My rules.

Swimming lessons invariably ended in sex. Brianna loved pool sex, and it had become one of my favorites as well.

Every day for the past ten days had been filled with her. Her baking, her laughter, her droll sense of humor. She sang in the kitchen every day. Hummed as she went around the house. I could pinpoint the room she was in simply by the way her voice sounded. I worked from the office downstairs while she baked, but the honest truth was, I watched and listened more than I worked.

I found her endlessly fascinating. Her refusal to swear amused me, and I tried to trick her into it and failed daily.

"Luck," I whispered. "Suck. Duck." I bit down on her lobe. "Just words."

"Uh-huh," she replied, gripping me. "Move, Dante. Cheese and crackers, move."

I held myself over her. "Fuck."

"Fudgsicle."

"Fuuuck," I said, moving just enough to tease her.

"Frack. Frickle. Forgetit."

I started to laugh. Then I gave her a physical demonstration of the word.

I loved her silences. The way she spoke without saying a word. The concentration on her face as she decorated another cake for me. The sheer delight when I would take a second or third piece, announcing that this one was now "my favorite."

They all were, because she made them.

I had never acted like this with a woman. Never said the word please so often. Wanted to make someone smile. I was used to issuing orders, making rapid decisions, expecting people to follow my demands. That didn't work with Brianna, and although I loved her fire, I disliked it when she seemed hurt by my curtness, and for the first time in a very long while, I tried to curb my impatience. Somehow, because it was for her, it seemed easier.

She was my entire focus most days. I smiled as she paddled toward me, pulling her out of the water and planting a kiss to her tempting mouth.

"Good job. We'll start on learning the breaststroke next."

"Okay."

I touched the end of her nose. "But we need to talk."

She frowned. "I don't like the sound of that."

"I have to go to Naples. There is some gallery business I have to handle in person. And I have some business meetings and dinners to attend."

She sat down beside me on the steps, the water glistening on her skin. I was tempted to kiss off the drops, so I did, tonguing them from her shoulder and kissing it. She shivered under my touch, making me grin. She slid closer, her hand on my thigh.

"How long will you be gone?"

"A week."

"Do you want me to keep baking cakes?"

"That's something else we need to talk about. You were right. A cake every day is too much. Gia told me the freezer is getting full, even with the smaller ones you're making. And my pants are getting tight."

She leaned her head on my shoulder and laughed, the sound clear and loud. "I warned you."

"Maybe every other day. And those little ones you showed me that we can polish off easier."

She was quiet for a moment. "And the timeline?" she finally asked.

"We'll discuss that in a while." I sucked in a deep breath. "I want you to come to Naples with me."

She tilted up her head. "Why?"

"I can't go cold turkey on the baked goods, Little Bee."

She rolled her eyes, and I tapped her nose again. "I want you to come to the dinners with me."

"Why?" she asked again.

"You handled Winters so well. Charmed Mario and Gia. Simona. Officer Rossi. Everyone who comes into contact with you adores you. I think you'd be a fabulous companion at these dull dinners."

She furrowed her brow. "Really? But I'd have nothing in common with your art friends."

"They talk about what they love. Art. Their families." I grinned. "Themselves."

"Are the dinners fancy?" she asked, sounding nervous.

"We'll go see Simona and buy you a couple of pretty dresses. And you can wear your sundresses you already have. See some of Naples. It's beautiful. I can show you around."

"Could I see Mount Vesuvius?"

"Yes. I'll take you to Piazza del Plebiscito. Lots of historic and artistic importance there. The Museo di Capodimonte. They have a great park right outside. Plus, the zoo. The city is bursting with things to see. Old and new. Great restaurants."

"You'd have time?"

"I'll make time."

"I'd love that."

"Then come with me." Then because it was her, the word slipped out again easily. "Please."

"I guess I should see some of Italy while I'm here."

Her words bothered me. I wanted to tell her I would show her everything and we had all the time in the world, but I held back. I had set the time limit, and she thought it was still in place.

I wasn't sure how she'd react if I told her I wanted more time with her.

I wasn't sure I was ready to admit it.

"So, that's a yes?"

"Yes."

"Okay, tomorrow is shopping, and we'll be leaving in the afternoon. It's a short drive, and we'll have dinner at a restaurant close to the gallery."

"Okay."

I pulled her to my lap, and she straddled me, most of her shyness gone. Not completely, which I adored, but she was braver. My cock swelled at her closeness, the feel of her his favorite place. "Now," I said, sliding my hand over her back and cupping her ass. "I think we have a victory to celebrate?"

She draped her arms around my neck. "Yes, yes, we do."

"That lap deserves a huge reward, baby. And I have just the trophy for you."

She began to laugh.

That, too, was music to my ears.

BRIANNA

Naples was a wonder. Dante's condo was a mix of contemporary and classic. High ceilings, beautiful wood, an old-fashioned claw-foot tub, but the kitchen and bathroom were modern. It was full of large furniture and antique pieces. There was a wraparound balcony with one side of city views, while the other looked out to the sea. The paintings and other pieces of art were a blend of styles. It had only one bedroom and a small office, but the bed was as big and comfortable as the one in his villa. He'd proved it as soon as we arrived. Twice.

He'd had me bring ingredients to make cookies when I assured him those would be simpler, but still a way to satisfy his sweet tooth. I also brought some of the frozen hummingbird cake with us. He loved that one.

I stared out the balcony at the sea surrounding the city. He had told me Naples was one of the busiest ports, and I could see the massive ships that came and went all day.

The sun was bright this morning. From his office, I could hear his voice speaking Italian to someone on the phone. He was going out for a while, then planned on coming back and taking me out sight-seeing. Later was one of the dinners he had to attend. He assured me it was a small group of his investors, but they were only in town for a few days, so he'd agreed to meet them tonight. Simona had helped me pick out a pretty dress, and I hoped I didn't do anything to embarrass him. I wasn't used to social situations involving investors and art. But somehow, when he was close, I wasn't as shy. I felt bolder with him next to me, as if nothing could hurt or bother me. I liked the feeling.

He promised to take me to his gallery tomorrow and I could look around while he met with his staff.

He joined me on the terrace. "I have to go, but I'll only be a few hours. You plan to go out?"

"No."

"Okay. Tomorrow, you can look around. Lots of wonderful shops around the gallery. You could wander, and I'll meet you for a coffee."

I only nodded, and he sighed, wrapping his arms around me. "You have the card. I want you to use it. It would please me, Little Bee."

"What should I buy?"

He cocked his head. "Why don't you just buy anything you see that you like? Have you ever been able to do that?"

I crossed my arms. "You are completely insane. Again, you prove you are the worst kidnapper in the history of kidnappers. You are going to be kicked out of the club. You don't give the kidnappee a credit card and tell her to go shopping."

He rubbed his chin, looking like he was going to laugh and trying not to. "What should I do?" He waved his hand in the air, moving his fingers like an invitation. "Since you're a kidnapper-behavior expert, how should I be behaving?"

"I would expect someone with your sweet tooth to have me chained to the kitchen and denied anything but the basic necessities and the ingredients to bake. Dressed in rags like Cinderella and locked up at night. Not taken on trips, bought pretty clothes, given a bike, or—"

He cut me off with a wicked smile. "Given as many orgasms as you can handle?" He stepped closer. "I'd happily chain you, Little Bee, but it would be to my bed. I'd deny you the basics and hand-feed you only the best. I prefer you naked, so we can forget about new clothes. And I'll take you anywhere you want to go."

"Um."

"You don't want the orgasms to stop, do you?"

"Oh, ah, no. But I mean it. You're out of the club."

"They're a bunch of pussies anyway. I like the company of my own little club. She is far sweeter than any cake ever made anyway." Then he caught my mouth with his and kissed me until I was dizzy. "I retired from the kidnapping game, Little Bee. I can't get a better hostage."

I shook my head to clear it. "Best out before the shame of being kicked out, then."

He nodded, grinning. He tilted up my chin and kissed me. "I'll see you in a while."

I baked some cookies. Dante was a huge peanut butter fan, but I added chocolate chips and folded in some English toffee bits. They smelled incredible. I went back to the balcony, curling up on a chair in the sun. It felt odd to hear the bustling city again, the sounds of people, cars, voices. I shifted in the chair, shocked at how quickly I'd gotten used to the quiet of the villa and the slow pace of the little town close to it.

The idea of leaving it, leaving him, was never far from my thoughts. I counted the cakes in my head. Twelve. That meant I had forty-eight left. I didn't count the cookies, and I knocked off the trifle I had made one night. The fruit had proven too tempting not to buy when I was in the small town, and I had soaked it in rich Amaretto, making the ladyfingers and using a mascarpone cheese layer with cream. It was incredible, and Dante had dragged me downstairs in the middle of the night to finish it off. He licked some of it off my body, using me like a dish, then we swam in the pool, washing off the sticky.

I had given him my first blow job that night. He propped himself up on his elbows on the top step as I knelt in the water, staring up at him. When I wrapped my hand around him, he smiled.

"What do you want, Little Bee?"

"To taste you."

His eyes widened. "Jesus, yes."

He was gentle and coaxing. I was nervous and wanting to please him. His mouth on me felt so good, I wanted to know if mine was the same for him.

His erection was big, slightly curved, and felt hot and heavy in my hand. I was tentative at first, running my tongue along the length. His low grunt of approval made me brave, and I took him in my mouth, sucking lightly. He had cursed, letting his head fall back. I took as much of him in as I could, and he showed me how to stroke him.

"Play with my balls, Little Bee. Suck me. Use your tongue. Whatever you think I might like, I will."

His praise made me bold, and I took him deeper. Used my tongue to tease him. I played with his balls, rolling them in my hands as he groaned. He put his hand on my head, guiding me but never forcing, never pushing. I pushed myself, gagging more than once, my eyes watering, but I kept going, and soon, he pushed on my shoulders. "Enough, Little Bee. I want to be inside you when I come."

I refused to budge, instead going deeper and faster. He made me come with his mouth; I was going to do the same.

He gripped the top step, arching his back. "I can't…"

And he came. Hot, long spurts hit the back of my throat, and I was triumphant when I lifted my head. He stared at me, his chest heaving.

"You've never done that before?"

"No."

"Fuck me, I chose the right woman to kidnap," he muttered, dragging me into his arms and kissing me.

Then he returned the favor.

The memory made me smile. He'd grinned all day. Every time I'd looked up from the cake I was making, he was watching me. His gaze was heated, his eyes liquid gold. When he came to admire the lemon sponge cake I'd made and decorated to look like a daisy, he'd been effusive, then pinned me against the counter.

"I can't stop thinking about last night," he murmured. "Your sweet mouth wrapped around my cock." He stroked my cheek. "Will you say cock, Brianna?"

"Rooster."

He grinned. "Dick."

"Richard."

"Cock. My massive cock."

I tried not to smile. "I can't say that. I don't have one. But you're right, if I did, it would be massive."

He laughed until he had tears in his eyes. I loved the fact that he was silly with me. Only me. I rose up on my toes, my lips to his ear. "Take me upstairs and frolic me with your massive Richard Rooster, Dante."

He tightened his hands on my hips, and he growled low in his chest. It was a seductive sound, and it made me shiver. He swung me up in his arms, heading for the staircase.

"Brace yourself, Little Bee."

I hugged my knees to my chest, staring at the water that rippled in the distance, the color as blue as the sky. My life had changed so much in a few weeks. I'd gone from exhausted and barely keeping my head above water, to spoiled, cared for, and sitting on a balcony in Italy. Waiting for a stern man who showed me a side no one else saw. One who was as complex as he was simple.

A flutter raced through me as I thought of Dante, and I allowed myself to speak the truth.

"I love him," I whispered to the air around me. How or when it happened, I wasn't sure, but it was there. I felt it with every fiber of my being. I hugged my knees tighter as I let the thought of loving Dante settle into my head. It felt strange because I couldn't recall not loving him now.

How was that possible?

The more pressing question was how he felt about me. I saw the flashes in his eyes, the way he watched me. How he allowed me to see him—the real him. The silly and sweet. The caring and funny. The powerful, sexy man who commanded my body and now my heart.

Did I command his at all, or was I simply a placeholder? An amusing pastime for now...not forever? He had set a timeline, laid out the rules, but he was the one who kept changing them. Our physical connection was intense, and he seemed as swept away as I did by our passion.

But I had no idea if our passion, if *I*, touched his heart.

Or how to figure out if I did.

Chapter Nineteen

DANTE

Brianna was quiet when I got back to the condo. I found her on the terrace, sitting in the sun, staring at the water. Her legs were pulled to her chest, and she looked contemplative. But she smiled when I bent and kissed her, and she followed me to the kitchen. I tried one of her cookies, closing my eyes at the taste of the chocolate, peanut butter, and toffee. Rich, decadent, and chewy.

I kissed her forehead. "Again, the perfect cookie." She smiled at my praise, but something was off in her eyes. I saw a glimmer of darker emotion within them. Uncertainty or worry, perhaps. It occurred to me she was nervous being in the city and being left on her own. And perhaps the dinner later. I wanted to alleviate her nerves, but I wasn't sure how exactly. I decided distraction was the best.

"You ready to go to lunch and do a little sight-seeing?"

"Yes, please."

We wandered the streets around the condo. I pointed out some little shops she might like, and we had lunch in the bright sunshine. The sun showed off the colors in her hair that she wore loose today. She stirred her latte, looking thoughtful. She was quieter than usual, and although I enjoyed the fact that she didn't fill the silence with idle chatter, I wanted to hear her voice.

"What's on your mind, Little Bee? You're lost in thought."

"Oh, nothing really. Just adjusting to the noise again."

"Different noises from Toronto, though."

"Yes," she agreed.

I studied her. "You like it better at the villa?"

Her smile was wide and honest. "Yes. It's so lovely there."

"Well, we'll be back in a few days."

She ate her lunch, and we walked around. I planned an entire day of sight-seeing for her. Today was only around the neighborhood. I pointed to a street. "Don't go past here when you're out. This leads into an older part of the city and the streets twist and turn, and you could get lost and end up in a less than desirable area."

"Okay."

I indicated the other direction. "My gallery is up that way, about a five-minute walk."

"I can't wait to see it."

We strolled, and I bought her a hat to protect her from the sun. She had little patches of freckles on her pale skin, and I didn't want her burned. She paused at a window, looking into a shop, and I followed her gaze to a pretty golden yellow dress. Simple, elegant, and timeless, with short sleeves, a scooped neckline, and a full skirt, and I knew she would look lovely in it. I took her into the shop and made her try it on. It fit her perfectly, and over her objections, I purchased it for her. It would go well with the small item currently tucked into my jacket pocket. When she protested, I lifted her hand to my lips. "I want you to wear it tonight. For me. Please."

She knew I rarely said please. Except to her. Brianna had fast become the exception to every rule in my life, and I wasn't sure how I felt about that fact. I tried not to think on it too much. The implications were too great for me to contemplate too deeply.

I wasn't ready to face the answers I already knew to be the truth.

As I suspected, she agreed to my plea, and I carried the garment bag over my arm, while the fingers of my other hand entwined with hers. I had never liked PDA of any kind, but again, with Brianna, that changed.

She got ready for dinner, and I showered and changed my suit. She walked into the room, her beauty making my throat thick. The dress hugged her curves. Showed off her legs and her pretty collarbone. I had never found collarbones particularly sexy, but I did love hers. She wore makeup, highlighting her dark eyes and full mouth. Her hair was caught up at the back of her neck, with lots of tendrils hanging around her face and over her shoulders.

"You are exquisite," I breathed out.

"I like your suit," she responded, patting my lapels, a light blush on her cheeks.

"I like this too," I added, stroking the warm skin. I led her to the mirror, staring at our reflections. She was the perfect height in front of me, my body dwarfing hers like an avenging angel. Her soft-colored dress was a direct contrast to my black suit.

"What are you doing?" she asked.

"I want to see your expression."

"My expression?"

Her gaze followed my hands as I slipped a necklace around her neck, fastening the clasp and settling the pendant on her clavicle. "Perfect," I murmured.

She stared at the pendant. Traced it with her finger in wonder. "It's—"

"A bee. A perfect little bee for my little bee."

I had seen it as I'd walked to the gallery earlier. It was in the window of the jewelry store that was next to the gallery. I saw it and went inside immediately to get a closer look and purchased it.

She lifted it. Ran her finger over the body and outstretched wings. "It even has a little stinger like yours," I murmured.

"It's so beautiful. Are those crystals?"

I chuckled. "Yellow and black diamonds. The wings are inlaid with mother of pearl. The eyes and stinger are diamonds as well."

Her eyes widened, and I chuckled, pressing a kiss to her head. "Relax. It wasn't overly expensive."

"Your expensive or mine?"

"I wanted you to have it. I want you to enjoy it."

She turned in my arms. "I'll never take it off."

"Good."

The two couples we met with for dinner looked shocked when I introduced Brianna.

"My girlfriend, Brianna. This is George and Irene. Burton and Stacey."

She was nervous but polite, shaking their hands and sitting beside me, her shoulders back and a smile on her face. Stacey complimented Brianna on her necklace, and her fingers drifted to the sparkling bee. "It was a gift from Dante."

"So unique. Do you like bees?"

"Yes," she replied.

"Brianna reminds me of a little bee. Industrious and hardworking," I offered.

"Oh, what do you do?" Irene asked.

Brianna hesitated, and I leaned forward, offering a wide smile. "She's a master chef. A baker. Her creations are highly sought-after in Toronto. Look." I showed some pictures I had taken of the tree she had created for Carolina, as well as some of her creations in my kitchen. "Works of art," I insisted. "And they taste as good as they look."

Everyone commented, making Brianna blush.

"How did you meet?"

"At a wedding. He liked my cake, and he kidnapped me and brought me here," Brianna said. "Drugged me and dragged me on to a plane. Smuggled in my cat, too."

I sputtered into my whiskey.

What the hell was she doing?

For a moment, there was silence, then Stacey spoke up, bewilderment coloring her voice. "Dante kidnapped you...and your cat?"

"Well, catnapped her, really. She is still in shock. She lies on the patio, eating fresh tuna and wondering what she ever did to deserve such inhumane treatment." Brianna sighed dramatically. "I watch her from the lounger in the pool as I drink mimosas and pity us. It is truly awful. No one to rescue us. He is relentless. Demanding cakes and cookies. Ravishing me all the time."

I watched realization dawn on their faces, and they all began to laugh. Irene leaned over.

"Do you want to be rescued?" she asked in a pseudo-whisper. "I could trade places with you."

"No, I could never ask someone to bear this torture. I must endure." She looked at me and winked. "Besides, I like the pool at the villa, and Dante is pretty good as kidnappers go. Easy on the eyes and such. He even makes dinner on occasion."

Again, there was a lot of laughter. George clapped me on the shoulder. "I bet she keeps you on your toes."

"That she does," I agreed. "I never know what she is going to say next." I pulled her close and kissed her head. "You are going to pay for that later, Little Bee."

"I hope so," she whispered. "Highly sought-after? Really?"

"You are," I insisted. "By me."

She laughed and kissed me.

Her supposed joke broke the ice, and it set the tone for the evening. The women wanted to know about her baking, and they all chatted. I spoke to the men at length about the gallery and its direction. I had few investors left since I had bought them out, but I trusted these men, and they trusted me. It was pleasant and easy and was more social than anything. They were rarely in Naples and I was rarely in Canada, so it was good to catch up in person.

Walking home in the dark night, I wrapped my arm around her, nestling her close to my side.

"You were brilliant tonight, Brianna. Gave me a heart attack at first, but you were funny."

"I knew they wouldn't take me seriously. No one ever will, but what a great story. It certainly gets their attention."

"That it does."

Back at the condo, I poured a scotch and tugged off my tie, sitting on the sofa and looking out the glass doors. Brianna joined me, wearing the pretty robe I had bought her, her necklace still glinting at her throat.

I pulled her to my lap so she straddled me. I traced the glittering piece of jewelry.

"I've never had anything so beautiful," she said.

"I want to surround you in beauty."

Our eyes locked, and I saw her emotions clearly. There was more than lust. More than teasing. It was right below the surface, and I wondered if mine reflected the same toward her.

"Thank you for coming with me," I murmured as I slid my hands up her legs, delving under the red silk. I cupped her ass, lifting an eyebrow. "Bare, Little Bee? Was there something you wanted?" I dipped my fingers between her legs, feeling the slick wetness of her desire. "You want more ravishing?"

"Yes," she whispered.

"Here?" I asked, my cock already on board. "You want to ride me?"

She placed her lips by my ear. "I want your cock inside me, Dante. Now."

It was the dirtiest thing I'd ever heard her say.

So I gave her exactly what she wanted.

BRIANNA

I walked around Dante's gallery, transfixed. It was incredible. The natural light made the space bright and beautiful. The gleaming bronzes, statues, and other items were dust-free and shown off to perfection. The paintings hung in ways to draw your eye. All sorts of precious metals, jewels, and other items were stunning. I didn't know how to take it all in. Three floors of beauty that only grew in splendor as you went higher in the building. I slowly perused the walls and display cases, no one bothering me. He had introduced me to his staff, so they knew who I was and left me alone. I put my coat and purse in Dante's office, not taking a chance of hitting anything.

He was different here. The closer we got to the gallery, the more I felt Dante the businessman coming out. He walked faster, his shoulders straight. His suit was cut to perfection, his gait sure. He still held my hand, although he didn't walk as close to me as before. Entering the gallery, I felt the last of my Dante fade away. His voice was cooler, stern. His posture was erect, and I felt the authority rolling off him. He was polite and charming but removed. It reminded me slightly of the first time we met, except even then, he had teased me. He escorted me to his office, set back with glass on the top floor, overlooking the entire gallery. Two security guards were on the doors, and everyone coming in was scanned. I found it a little intimidating, but he assured me the people who commissioned him to sell their art appreciated the extra measures he took.

I played a little game as I went around, trying to pick out which pieces in the gallery were his. Several were marked not for sale, but I knew a few were on loan, while some belonged to him.

On the third floor, I could hear Dante's low timbre, and as I was studying a large bowl, he came out of the office with two of his managers. They shook his hand and went downstairs. He came up beside me. "You like that?"

"It's pretty. A little, ah, fussy for me."

"Not into cloisonné, Little Bee?"

"No."

He indicated a set of vases on another shelf. "What about those?"

I studied them, noting the brilliant colors, inset jewels, and gold. I nodded. "I like those. They're pretty."

"Enameled glass. All done by hand by a master. Not as valuable, though."

"I still like them."

"Then if you were buying something, I would advise you to buy those. You buy what you love, what moves you, not for the value."

"Which do you prefer?"

He laughed low in my ear. "The vases. Because they are mine."

"Is the landscape painting on the stairs yours as well? And the gold and green bowl?"

"Yes."

I felt his arm go around me, pulling me close. He pressed a kiss to my head. "You have a good eye, Brianna. And you know me well."

I smiled up at him, pleased to see my Dante wasn't as far away as I thought.

"Have you looked enough?"

"Yes. I thought I'd go and do a little browsing."

"Okay. I'll need a couple of hours. Don't go too far, and we'll have lunch."

"Where will I meet you?"

"I'll call."

"Okay."

In his office, he helped me tug on my coat and slipped my wallet into the inside pocket, along with my phone. "Keep your eyes open and be vigilant. Pickpockets love tourists."

I lifted one eyebrow. "Spoken from experience, Light-hand Luke?"

He chuckled and pulled me close, kissing me warmly. "You're getting much too mouthy for a prisoner. I'm going to take away some of your privileges."

"I have some?" I asked with a grin.

He smacked my butt. "Go, before I do something totally out of character."

"Such as?"

"Fuck you at my desk as I look into the gallery. Take you hard and fast while people are considering paying a small fortune for a piece of art. Staring up at the window, wondering what's behind it, as I make you come all over my cock."

I blinked and nodded rapidly. "Okay, I'll be going now," I mumbled and walked into the doorframe. I stumbled and righted myself, turning to see him leaning on the desk, his arms and feet crossed, looking at me with so much tenderness and desire I had to swallow.

I ran.

I could hear his laughter follow me right down to the street.

Chapter Twenty

BRIANNA

My meandering started off well enough. I looked around some of the lovely shops adjacent to his gallery. I had a delicious latte while sitting in the morning sun watching people. Then I moved to the little café across the street and had a raspberry gelato. After all, I was in Italy and needed to taste all the wonders it had to offer. A third shop smelled heavenly, and I got a slice of still-warm focaccia studded with rosemary and goat cheese and munched it as I strolled. I browsed through a couple of clothing stores and bought a pair of wide-legged pants that had some incredible embroidery on the bottom from one boutique that carried some more casual-type clothing. The pants were made of linen and in a deep blue, and I thought they would look cute with one of my T-shirts.

A slight change from my overalls. Although I did notice Dante liked to use the straps to haul me close and kiss me anytime he wanted.

Just the thought of his mouth made me warm. I had to shake my head to clear my thoughts.

I found another one-piece bathing suit in the same shop, as well as a new pair of sunglasses I liked. It was always bright here, it seemed, and I was constantly squinting. I had left my pair in the apartment so I needed these. Between the sunglasses and the hat Dante had insisted on buying me, I felt very chic. Then I caught sight of myself in a mirror and chuckled. I looked like a tourist. No one would mistake me for a local. The women here were effortlessly stylish. I was just...me.

I hesitated when I saw a pretty red dress hanging up in the corner. It was flowy and different from anything I had ever worn. The back dipped low and crisscrossed with the red silk. Pretty sleeves and a drapey skirt that would sit mid-calf, I judged, made it elegant but still sexy. The slit in the skirt added to the effect. I bit my lip. I had nowhere to wear it. At least, not right now. I knew I had a couple more dinners to attend with Dante. It seemed a little fancy for dinner, though. I was about to leave when his words came back to me.

"Buy what you want for a change. Let me spoil you," he had said this morning. "Don't look at the price. Just say yes."

Ten minutes later, I walked out the door, the dress in the bag with the pants and bathing suit. It looked nice on, fitting me well, and the color was beautiful. So rich and deep. I loved it, and I hoped I got a chance to wear it.

I walked on, looking in windows and stopping at outside tables. I couldn't recall having the opportunity to simply walk and not worry about time or money— ever. I bought a few little things. Nothing big. Then I saw a shop, the sign worn, and when I peeked in the window, I realized it was an antique store, filled with all sorts of items. I typed the name of the store into my online translator, and it came back "Trinkets and Treasures." I liked the sound of that, so I went in. The light was dim inside, and I slipped off my sunglasses, taking it all in. Furniture, bric-a-brac, fabric, paintings, china, bits of everything were stuffed inside. An elderly gentleman smiled my way, greeting me. *"Buongiorno."*

I smiled and returned his greeting.

"Ah," he said in heavily accented English. "American?"

"Canadian."

"Very good." He indicated the small shop. "I own. You look, and I help."

"Thank you."

I browsed the shelves and walls. There was so much to see. So many different things from what I would find back home, yet a few things so similar it made me smile. A display caught my eye, and I approached an arrangement of what I thought were small swords, only to realize they were ornate old letter openers. Some were simple, some overelaborate. All interesting. One caught my eye, the brass of the blade dull in the light, but gleaming with a sharp edge. It had an intricate handle, and I moved closer to see it.

"You like?"

I nodded. "May I look at it?"

"Of course."

He slid it from the display, holding it out to me, the sharp edge pointed his way. "Very fine piece."

I took it carefully, looking it over. I knew nothing about antiques or letter openers. What caught my attention was the glass on the handle. It reminded me of the enameled glass I had seen in Dante's gallery. Red, green, and gold, with a circular golden piece of glass in the middle that reminded me of Dante's eyes. It was unique and different. Heavy in my hand. I could see him at his desk, slicing open mail with it. The blade was embossed and attractive. The gentleman showed me the small brass stand that came with it, the blade sliding in and the glass on display.

I had no idea if it was real. Or worth anything. But Dante told me to buy what I liked. And I liked this.

"I'll take it, please." I wanted to give it to Dante. I would get money from my own bank account to pay for it, so he wasn't really gifting it to himself. I hoped he would like it.

The owner wrapped it, and I used Dante's card to buy it, carefully tucking the receipt into my wallet so I could repay him the money. I slipped the small bag into my larger one with the clothes I had bought. The owner lifted my hand, kissing my knuckles, and made me laugh. I had no idea what he said, but his smile was wide and his eyes danced.

I left the shop and looked left and right. I was on a corner, and before I could decide, I was swept in the direction of the crowd. It was lunchtime now, and the streets bustled. I kept going, not paying attention to where I was until I noticed the streets were a little quieter and the shops not as well tended. I looked around, feeling nervous. I spotted a sign ahead of a shop with large windows, and I hastened toward it. It appeared to be another gallery of sorts, and I slipped inside, hoping the staff spoke English and could give me directions on how to get back to Dante's.

I shook my head. I should have mentioned to Dante I was hopeless with directions and prone to getting lost.

The gallery was dim, not well lit and welcoming like Dante's. I could hear voices in the back, and I wandered around, peering at the displays. The pieces were different from this morning. A lot of them newer. Not as nice. I peeked at a price tag. Expensive, though, I thought. Some items were locked away, obviously the most desirable. I saw a younger couple exclaiming over a vase, and I moved closer, listening to the staff member speaking to them in disjointed English, assuring them of the worthwhile investment and the rarity of the piece they were evaluating. It looked like a regular vase to me, but again, I knew nothing about antiques. Yet none of the pieces took my breath away the way Dante's had. Even pieces I wasn't as enamored with, I could see the beauty. Few of the pieces here replicated that sensation.

I wandered deeper into the narrow building. I was off the street, yet my nerves still felt taut. I reached into my pocket for my phone, deciding to simply call Dante and admit I was lost, when a voice spoke up.

"Well, if the lamb didn't wander into the lion's den."

I spun on my heel and met the remote eyes of Ramon Winters.

He smiled at my shock, his expression cold and calculating. He stepped closer.

"Hello, my dear."

I reared back. "What-what are you doing here?"

"This is my gallery. One of many."

"Gallery?" I questioned, thinking of the elegance and warmth of Dante's.

He shrugged. "To tourists, it is. They can take home a great work of art from Italy and boast to their friends."

I was like a parrot. "A great work of art?" I said, sarcasm evident in my voice.

He didn't look upset over my reaction. "To each his own." His expression turned darker. "I have four of these galleries in the city. More elsewhere. I make a large amount of money with them."

"And you don't care that you fleece tourists?"

"Fleece?"

"Steal from them."

He laughed, the sound unnerving. "I take their money, they take home something they like. Everyone is happy." He took a step toward me, and I stepped back, realizing I was now against a display case. "Unlike your boyfriend, I don't steal."

"Dante doesn't steal either. He is a reputable businessman. Unlike you."

"Oh, I have a gallery like his too. Perhaps not as snobby. But I'm smarter. I cater to the masses." He looked around. "Where is your protector? I'm surprised he let you darken my door." Then his gaze narrowed, focused on me. "Or perhaps he is unaware you are here. How...*fortuitous*...for me."

His words, spoken in his thick accent, sent a shudder down my spine. My heart rate picked up, and I felt sweat break out on my neck.

"He is waiting. I have to go."

He laughed again, the sound freezing my blood. "I doubt that. Besides, I want to show you something."

"No, thank you." I began to move past him, and he grabbed my upper arm, squeezing it hard enough I felt the pressure acutely, even through the sleeve of my jacket.

"I insist."

I reacted as I always did when panicked. I bolted. Tore my arm from his grip and pushed around him, ignoring the sound of breaking glass as I rushed from the store and outside. Blindly, I turned and ran down the street, my gasps of air loud to my ears. I fumbled for my phone, no idea if I was headed in the right direction when I heard it. My name being shouted by a familiar voice.

Dante.

He was here.

I looked around, frantic, spotting him rushing toward me, pushing people out of the way to get to me. Not looking where I was going, I sprinted toward him, crashing into his chest, almost sobbing in gratitude when his arms came around me. Relief flooded me. I was safe. I was always safe in his arms. Greedily, I inhaled his scent, burrowing myself into him as close as I could get. I whispered his name, needing to feel him. He was safety. Strength. Love.

Home.

His voice was soft in my ear.

"It's okay, Little Bee. I have you."

DANTE

I watched the little red dot move as Brianna shopped. I had a program on her phone that tracked her. It wasn't because I didn't trust her, but I had noticed her lack of awareness and bad direction. If she was lost, I needed to be able to find her. I could request a location, and the app told me exactly where she was. I laughed as she stopped at three different cafés, and I assumed she was snacking. She seemed to be in no hurry, and I was glad. I wanted her to enjoy the city. Naples was beautiful. I was amused as the charges started showing on my card. Coffee, gelato, and something from a bakery appeared on it, followed by small charges for God only knew what. I got busy with another meeting and looked again at the credit card. She made a larger purchase at a boutique, probably a scandalous number to her, but to me, it was nothing. I wondered idly what she'd bought and hoped she would show me later. I glanced at the app, frowning when I saw she was half a dozen blocks away from the gallery. I zeroed in on the locale, surprised she was in Gino's Trinkets and Treasures. I relaxed though, because Gino was a throwback to another era and would take good care of her, being the courteous gentleman he was. She would probably head back this way after.

My phone rang, and I spoke to my manager in London about an acquisition that had come in. We discussed my next trip there, and when I hung up, I looked at the app, my blood freezing when I saw she was farther away, not closer. I tapped to see the location and was on my feet, running before it had completely downloaded.

Of all the spots she could wander into, Winters's gaudy tourist trap was the last place I wanted her. I doubted he was there, but nevertheless, it wasn't where she should be. And the area was getting risky.

I was grateful for my knowledge of the city and my fast pace. I cut through alleys, between buildings, and down the center of a couple of streets, arriving by the house of trash, as I called it, just in time to see Brianna rush out the door and begin to run. Fury tore through me as Winters appeared behind her at the door, shouting. He saw me and ducked back inside, coward that he was.

Brianna saw me, the panic on her face evident. With a burst of speed, she barreled into me, gasping for breath. As soon as my arms went around her, I felt the relief that eased her body.

"Dante," she murmured over and over.

I pulled back, gazing down at her.

"Are you hurt?" I was going to kill him if he had injured her in any way.

"No. Winters—he was there. He was—" She burrowed herself back into me. "He was just vile."

"That's one word," I replied, bending and lifting her into my arms, cradling her to my chest. I turned and hurried away from that street. I knew she was upset when she didn't protest being carried or object to the fact that people would stare. No one even glanced our way. It was Italy, and they were used to odd sights. Once we were far enough away, and her trembling stopped, I set her on her feet and examined her face. Her color had returned, and her eyes were no longer wide and scared. I led her to a café and ordered lattes—her favorite.

"Tell me."

She repeated what had happened, telling me what Winters had said. "I think I broke something trying to get out of there."

"He can send me a bill." I paused, letting her drink her latte. "Why did you go that way, Brianna? I told you to avoid it."

"I'm helpless with directions. I was just wandering, and I got lost in the crowds. I went in there hoping someone spoke English and could tell me how to get back to your gallery." She drew in a fast breath. "To you."

"Right into the spider's lair," I mused.

"I'm sorry."

I ran a finger down her cheek. "As long as you're okay. I think I'll wander with you from now on. At least here."

Her smile was tremulous. "Good idea."

"Home or lunch?"

"You mean the villa?"

Something warmed in my chest that she considered the villa home. "The condo."

"Can we have lunch on the way there? Are you done for the day?"

I waved off her concern. I wasn't leaving her alone again today. "I have a few things to take care of from the condo. I can do that while you relax."

"Dante, if I relax any more, I'll be in a coma."

I threw some money on the table and took her hand. "Humor me."

Chapter Twenty-One

DANTE

We stopped by the gallery and I picked up what I needed, then we had a simple lunch, eating slices of pizza as we headed back to the condo. "Everything tastes so good here," Brianna mused.

"The food here is delicious," I agreed, pleased she seemed okay after her run-in with Winters.

That bastard.

We sat on the terrace when we got back, and I brought us each a cold drink.

"Who are we having dinner with tonight?"

"We're having dinner with an associate who is helping me broker a deal. I expect you to behave. No wild kidnapping stories."

I had little hope she would do so, but I had to say it.

She rolled her eyes and huffed. "As if I would embarrass you."

She ignored my raised eyebrows.

"Now tell me about this *associate* so I can prepare myself."

"He has a lot of contacts in America that I don't have. There is a piece of sculpture I have coveted for years. The owner passed, and his family is open to selling it. I am trying to get it before it goes to auction. Richard is friendly with the family and is acting as an intermediary for me, getting it authenticated and valued. All done very hush-hush as to not alert other collectors who would try to outbid me. If it becomes a free-for-all, the family will simply send it to auction. I'd still fight for it, but this is so much more civilized."

"Oh, very cloak-and-dagger." She hummed a tune, and I laughed at her silliness.

"It's not *Mission: Impossible*, Little Bee. Just a business deal."

"Don't spoil my fun, old man."

"What did you just call me?"

She shrugged. "Slipped out. Now, we're discussing your associate."

I tried not to laugh. She was pushing my buttons. Deliberately.

"Is he married?"

"Several times," I replied.

"Seeing anyone?"

"Not that I know of."

"Children?"

"No idea."

"Hobbies?"

"Collecting art. Selling art. Brokering deals."

She frowned. "It's going to be hard to chat with him, then."

"Richard is not a man you *chat* with. We'll talk business. You can smile at him. Be my arm candy." I kissed the side of her head. "Sweetest arm candy in the world."

That got me another huff and a smile. "Your business is so man-driven. Such an old boys' club."

"At times. I deal with lots of women, but yes, men do tend to have the upper hand."

"Fine. So, his name is Richard."

"Yes. Richard Wiggles."

She froze as she reached for her drink, carefully setting it back on the table. She turned and faced me fully.

"What did you say?"

"Richard Wiggles."

"His name is Richard Wiggles?"

I crossed my arms. "Yes."

A smile tugged on her lips. "And he is a big shot art dealer?"

"According to many, yes."

"Named Richard Wiggles."

"Yes, Little Bee. Is that so hard to grasp?"

She began to laugh. The laugh I loved. Loud, raucous, filled with mirth, some snorts thrown in for good measure and causing her to double over in delight.

I tried not to join her.

"What is so funny?"

"You have a business associate named Richard Wiggles. *Dick* Wiggles. Oh, I can't. I can't, Dante. Don't make me go to this dinner."

I glared at her sternly. "You will go, and you will behave yourself."

"I can't," she gasped.

"It's not that funny."

"It is."

She started to laugh again, and I had to bite back my amusement. It was rather amusing. No one would ever refer to him as Dick to his face, but the name was... funny. He, however, was not. He was always serious. Focused. I wasn't sure I had ever even seen him smile.

"Little Bee," I warned.

Maybe I should leave her at the condo. Except, after what happened today, I didn't want to leave her alone.

"Will you behave?"

She stopped laughing. Wiped her eyes. Drew in a deep breath.

"I'll try."

"He has no sense of humor, Brianna. But he is important, and I need tonight to go well." I ran a hand over my face. "Can you do that?"

She straightened her shoulders. "Yes."

"I'm counting on you."

"No pressure, then."

I shot her a look but left it. I had a feeling tonight was going to be interesting.

She wandered into my den about two hours later as I finished up the paperwork. She was in her robe, her hair damp.

"Nice bath, Little Bee?"

"Yes. Very relaxing."

I noticed a small bag in her hand. "What is that?"

She fidgeted a little, then held it out. "I saw this and thought you would like it."

Curious, I took the bag and opened it. I unwrapped the tissue and stared at the letter opener. It was a fine specimen, beautifully crafted, and the enameled glass on the handle in perfect condition. The brass had a lovely patina on it, and the opener was a great piece. Useful and decorative.

I looked up at Brianna. "You picked this?"

"Yes. It caught my eye. The handle..." she explained, sounding shy. "The golden circle reminded me of your eyes. And you told me this morning you liked that enameling. I thought maybe it would be helpful to you. You could think of me sometimes when you used it."

I slid it into the holder and moved it to the center of the desk. I wrapped my hand around her hip and pulled her closer. "I think of you all the time, my beautiful girl."

"Oh."

I tugged her between my legs. "I love it. Thank you."

"It's not a hunk of junk?"

"No. It's a great piece. I told you that you have a good eye."

She smiled, and I ran my hands up her arms, stopping when she grimaced. "What?" I asked. "What's wrong?"

"Nothing," she replied, trying to sidle away.

I stopped her, closing my legs and trapping her. Frowning, I pulled up the sleeves of her robe, ignoring the way she tried to slap away my hands. When I saw the bruises that were forming on her skin, five distinct fingerprints, I was furious. "He fucking *touched* you. He *marked* you."

"I yanked my arm away. I bruise easily. It's fine."

I met her eyes, hers worried, mine angry. "I will kill him."

She cupped my face. "You won't touch him or go near him. He means nothing. He is nothing but a braggart, just as you said. Do not interact with him, Dante. That's what he wants. He wants to start a war. He wanted to scare me. Don't give him the satisfaction."

"He fucking touched you. I hate that he was close. I hate that he scared you. I want to end him."

She leaned close, resting her forehead on mine. "But you found me. As soon as you held me, I knew I was safe. The marks will be gone in a day or two. I don't want to think about him again. Promise me."

I pulled her close and kissed her. The moment our lips touched, my anger faded. I would never show anything but tenderness to her. Even in our most passionate moments, I would never hurt her or cause her pain. Cupping the back of her head, I slid my tongue into her mouth, tasting her sweetness. Sensing her worry, I gentled my mouth, with long, sensuous passes of my tongue on hers. I pulled her to my lap, and she gasped when she felt me hard between us. I drew back, our eyes locking, my emotions rampant.

"Dante," she whispered.

"I can't stand the thought of you hurt," I confessed. "I need you safe."

"I'm safe with you. I'm always safe with you. I knew it from the first moment."

"I need you."

She pressed her lips to mine. "Have me."

I pulled her back. My pants were pushed down, her robe parted. I slid inside her, and she dropped her head to my shoulder.

"You feel so good," she murmured. "So big and hard inside me."

I slouched down, going deeper. Stroking the inside of her, feeling the way she gripped me. Every time I was with her, it felt like the first time, the wonder and intensity still strong.

We moved and rocked, neither of us talking. Our breathing was heavy, the low groans, grunts, and moans filling the air.

She gripped the back of my neck with a sob, and she came. Tight and wet around me, setting off my own orgasm. I clutched her to me until I was spent, and she slumped against my chest.

"Calmer now?" she whispered.

"I still want to teach him a lesson."

"Please let it go. For me."

I kissed her head. "For you. For now."

After a moment, she sighed. "I guess a shower is needed now."

I stood, taking her with me and yanking up my pants. "I'll join you."

She snuggled closer. "Okay."

The blue dress she wore for dinner had longer sleeves, which covered the marks. I was grateful since as soon as I spied them, my first impulse was to go and find Winters and leave the same marks all over his body. The bruises had grown darker as the day wound down, and my anger burned hotter each time I saw them.

She had her hair down, her makeup was simple, and she wore the necklace I gave her.

She was perfection.

She was quieter than usual, the events of the day no doubt playing on her mind. I held her hand in the car and escorted her into the restaurant.

Richard was already there, looking his usual taciturn self. He rose from his chair, shaking my hand, and I introduced Brianna. She smiled benignly and said hello, sitting beside me.

We ordered drinks and made small talk. Richard kept glancing at Brianna, often asking her direct questions. He talked more than I was used to. She kept her answers short, sipping her wine too quickly. I leaned over, murmuring in her ear.

"Slow down, Little Bee. Everything is fine." I gathered her hand in mine, and she relaxed a little. I didn't want her drunk. I had a feeling that would be a recipe for disaster. The word kidnapped would definitely come up.

"Canadian, are you?" he asked.

"Yes."

"What part?"

"Toronto."

"Such a metropolitan town. I enjoy visiting the city."

"And where are you from, Mr. Wiggles?"

"New York is home now. I grew up in California."

"Big difference," she replied.

"Yes. But I enjoy both."

"Ah." More wine disappeared.

He kept peppering her with questions, and her answers became a little longer. She even laughed at a joke he cracked. I'd never heard him try to be funny. I looked between them, trying not to smile. Richard, it seemed, was enamored with my little bee. I had never heard him make so much small talk. Yet, oddly enough, I felt no animosity from him, no challenge to our relationship, and, surprisingly, no sexual interest in Brianna. Simply honest curiosity.

We ordered dinner, and he and I spoke of the acquisition of the sculpture. "All has checked out, and I have advised the family of a fair price and that you would be an honorable man to deal with. It was a favorite piece of their father's, but none of them is fond of it. But they want to know it goes to someone who would appreciate it the way their father did. I assured them you did."

"I'm grateful to you for that. May I have my lawyers get in touch with the offer? It will match your evaluation."

"I value your trust."

"I'm thankful for your help."

"Have you seen his galleries, Brianna?" Richard asked.

"Two of them," she said.

"The one in London is spectacular. You should take her there, Dante."

I smiled in acknowledgment. "One day."

"His private collection—has he shared those?"

"Some."

"You must mean a great deal to him, then. How long have you been together?"

She frowned. "That's a rather private question, Mr. Wiggles."

He winked at her, and I gaped. I had never seen him wink. Smile. Almost flirt, although he looked at her in a more fatherly way. And he acted as if he was trying to make her...comfortable?

"Mr. Wiggles is my father. Call me by my first name."

She picked up her glass, taking a sip.

He leaned closer. "Dick. My friends call me Dick."

The wine in her mouth sprayed wide across the table, hitting him, the cloth, and everything in between. She stared, wide-eyed, then began to laugh.

"Dick Wiggles," she squeaked.

I shut my eyes.

I should have known it was going too well.

Shame about that sculpture.

Chapter Twenty-Two

DANTE

Brianna stumbled from the bedroom, sitting down heavily in the chair across from me. I sipped my coffee and peered at her over the rim of my cup.

She was a total disaster. Her hair was everywhere, mascara smudged under her eyes, and her face was pale. I had managed to get her dress off last night and slide one of my shirts over her while she attempted to take mine off, trying to be sexy and alluring. She came across as drunk and adorable instead.

"You gonna—hiccup—*ravish me with your big*—hiccup—*rocking Richard*—hiccup—*old man?"*

"I highly doubt that, Little Bee."

"But you are soooo sexy—hiccup—*like a tiger in the—"* she tried snapping her fingers, but it was a lost cause *"— what do you call that?"*

"Jungle?" I offered.

"Yesh. The jungle. Flipping sexiest cat there. I want you."

Then she passed out.

The girl snored when she was drunk. And talked in her sleep. About me, mostly. She groped a lot as well. I should have been annoyed, angry with her behavior. But again, all I felt was amusement and worry about the size of the hangover she would have in the morning.

"Coffee?" I asked. "Some breakfast?"

She lifted her head, opening one bloodshot, bleary eye. "No, thank you." She ran a hand through her chaotic hair. "What happened?"

"After you called Richard Dick Wiggles, sprayed your wine all over him, me, and the table, and dissolved into hysterical giggles, you mean?"

If possible, her face went even whiter. "Oh God. I didn't."

"Oh, you did."

She stared at me in horrified silence. Then she swallowed. "I think I need that coffee now."

I poured a cup and pushed it her way. She took a few sips. "Should I pack my bags now, or can I go back to the villa and get my cat first?"

"Little Bee."

She glanced up, her eyes sorrowful.

"You're not going anywhere."

She played with her coffee cup. "How furious are you?"

"I'm in too much shock to be furious. You spewed wine all over Richard, made fun of his name, and suddenly, you're his best friend." I shook my head, still processing everything that had happened.

"Turns out, Richard has a daughter he is incredibly fond of who went to university in Toronto. You reminded him of her. I waited for an explosion after the wine, and he laughed. *Laughed*. I have never heard the man laugh."

I recalled my shock.

"You have a daughter? I didn't know that."

"There is lots about me you don't know. I don't talk about my private life." He glanced at Brianna, who was frozen in place, equally shocked. He patted her hand.

"Don't worry about it, dear girl. My Daphne gets nervous and blurts things out as well. When she is mad at me, which is often, she comes up with some very, ah, unique variations of my name. I find it quite amusing. I think you two would get on very well."

"Your suit," she whispered.

"Nothing a little water and a dry cleaner can't fix. Now tell me how you two met."

"Oh God, I didn't."

"No, you gave a PG version, which, I have to admit, was much less entertaining. Apparently you found me irresistible, and I was obsessed with you and couldn't leave you behind."

"Oh. Well, that is kinda the truth."

I winked. "I am obsessed, so yes. I don't think you found me too hard to resist at first. But I grew on you."

"Like a fungus," she muttered.

I grinned. *There she was.*

She took another sip of her coffee, waiting.

"After that, the two of you got along like a house on fire. You asked about his daughter, he showed you pictures, you got him to laugh and share stories about her." I shook my head. "I have no idea how, but you charmed Richard. You charm everyone, Little Bee. He adored you. Both of you drank too much wine. We closed down the restaurant. He even insisted on us attending a private showing happening tomorrow night, as his guests. He's already sent the information this morning." I shook my head. "And the sculpture is mine. He called the son last night and told him I was the only person he should sell to. I spoke to him after and called my lawyer. The funds were transferred first thing. The sale is complete."

"So, everything is okay?"

I leaned over, brushing the hair away from her face. "Aside from the headache I'm sure you have, everything is fine. But no more nervous drinking."

"I was trying to be so good. I thought if I didn't talk, I wouldn't say it. I kept sipping my wine so I had something to do. But then he said it. I think it was as if the floodgates opened."

"Pretty much," I replied. "You were off to the races then."

She passed a hand over her head and smiled ruefully. "Sorry."

The movement caused her shirt sleeve to fall. The bruises on her upper arm were a deep, vivid purple this morning. I glared at them, my anger instantly flaring. She followed my gaze, pulling on the sleeve and shaking her head. "It's fine."

"Richard and I had a little chat about Winters as well. He thinks he is the lowest of lows. His reputation in the art world is even worse than I thought. He started out well enough, then veered down a road he should never have been on."

"But you said he had a collection himself."

"He does. And there are some nice pieces in it. But he is unscrupulous in his dealings. How he acquires them. And he wants them for the wrong reasons. For greed. Bragging rights."

She shook her head. "I don't want to talk about him anymore."

I brushed my hand down her cheek. "Are you up for some sight-seeing today, or do I need to take you back to bed?" I grinned. "You want me to ravish you with my *rocking Richard*?"

"Oh God, I am never drinking again."

On that, we could agree.

We spent the next two days acting like tourists. I took her to all the places she wanted to see and others she'd never heard of. Hours passed like minutes, every moment with her a revelation of more Brianna. I couldn't get enough. I wasn't sure I ever would. I loved watching her discover things. The cute V between her brows as she studied a painting or some other piece of art and then the smile as she found the beauty. She became animated, wanting to share what she saw. Her hands moved, she talked fast, and her joy was limitless. There was little we disagreed on. She preferred paintings and loved tapestries. She admitted she wanted to touch the sculptures—to feel the lines. I reminded her that would get us arrested but she could feel up my sculpture anytime she wanted.

That made her laugh.

We ate in little cafés; she baked more cookies. I made love to her in the sunlight. On the terrace, high above the city. In the kitchen as the cookies baked. She showed me the dress she had bought, and I assured her it would be perfect for the function we were attending as Richard's guests.

We danced. She loved to dance as much as I did, although she insisted she had little experience. When I informed her it was all in the leading, she had rolled her eyes. But we fit well, and she followed like a dream, almost floating. In the sun, in the dark of the night, it didn't matter. If she was humming, I caught her in my arms and we spun together, lost in the little bubble we had created.

I had never felt this way. Content. Happy to be with one person. Even in the quiet, I was never bored. I sought her out if she left the room. Found excuses to be in the kitchen, on the terrace, wherever she was.

And I tried not to delve into the reason.

I wasn't ready. I wondered if I ever would be.

She appeared in the room, her hair swept up, her neck exposed, her necklace glinting. I loved the fact that she never took it off. The red dress she had shown me clung to her curves, the skirt swirling around her legs. The sleeves mostly hid the bruises on her arm, and she had covered them up well with makeup. It looked modest and elegant. Until she twirled.

It was backless, the strips of red fabric crisscrossed on her pale skin. I stepped closer, running my finger down her spine. "Beautiful," I murmured, bending to kiss a small cluster of freckles by her shoulder blade. "Part of me is jealous."

She glanced over her shoulder. "Why?"

"Other men will see these little sexy dots. Until now, they were only mine."

She smiled, turned, and lifted up on her toes. "They still are."

I caught her around the waist and kissed her. "You are stunning."

"Thank you."

I crooked my arm. "Let's go. I want to get this over with and bring you home. That dress needs to be on the floor beside our bed."

She looked mischievous. "It might look nice on the floor just inside the door, too." She patted the sofa. "It goes well here."

I laughed and bent, nipping her neck. "Don't tempt me."

"Huh, too much for you, old man? Need to pace yourself?"

That was all the encouragement I needed.

Fifteen minutes later, she'd fixed her hair, my cock was satisfied, and we departed for the event.

Both of us were smiling.

I sensed Brianna's nerves as we strolled into the room. Her grip on my hand was tight, and she was quiet. Much too quiet. I slipped my arm around her waist, kissing her temple. "Relax, Little Bee."

"These people look far too intelligent and rich for me," she muttered.

"Hey." I squeezed her hip. "You're with me. You fit in perfectly."

"Such ego."

I winked. "You know it."

I introduced her to some clients. Other art dealers. Collectors. She was gracious and sweet, and I ignored the surprised glances. I rarely brought a woman to a function. And I certainly never held hands or kept them tucked to my side. But with Brianna, it felt right.

Richard sought us out, once again taciturn and stern-looking. But he kissed Brianna's cheeks and held her hands. "How are you this evening, dear girl?"

"I'm fine."

He leaned closer, dropping his voice. "Were you in trouble?"

She side-eyed me. "A little."

He chuckled, then his expression became serious again. "Mingle. Enjoy. Look at the beautiful art." He winked slyly. "Stay away from the wine."

Then he moved on.

"Why would you not have received an invitation to this?" she asked.

"I did. I turned it down as I had no plans on being here. I had forgotten about it, to be honest." I lifted her hand to my mouth. "But I'm glad you're with me."

"Why are we here?" she asked. "Are we looking at something?"

"A new collection in one of the galleries. This is a private showing. It will open to the public in a few days."

We wandered to the gallery, looking at the displays. It was a private collection on loan of paintings, bronzes, and some pristine examples of silver. I walked beside Brianna, finding her discovery of the pieces as enchanting as the works themselves. I enjoyed seeing her reactions.

We headed back to the main area, walking slowly down the dim hall, our footsteps echoing slightly on the marble floors. I ducked into an alcove, pulling her into my arms and kissing her.

She draped her arms around my neck, spearing her hands into my hair and returning my passion.

"You ready to leave?"

"Isn't that rude?" she whispered, sounding breathless as I peppered kisses along her neck, biting down lightly at the juncture of her shoulder.

"Do you think I care?"

"Ah, but why so impatient to leave?" a snide voice drawled. "So anxious to fuck your little prisoner?"

I stiffened at the voice, my rage instant and bright. I pulled Brianna behind me and faced Winters. He leaned against the arch, looking repugnant.

"How did you get in here?" I asked. I knew he wasn't on the guest list. He was no longer welcome at these events.

He shrugged, not put out. "As a guest of someone else."

"Well, they just attended their last showing. They'll be blackballed for associating with you."

He stood, crossing his arms, his anger rising. "So high and mighty. So full of yourself."

I put my hand on Brianna's hip, and we eased toward the opening. I felt her grip on my arm. Heard her whispered plea for us to leave. I wanted to smash his face in, but I was determined to walk away. For her.

He followed, his tone mocking. "Going so soon? Have you finished casing the joint, as they say over in America? Is that right, little Brianna?"

"I wouldn't know," she snapped. "I'm not from America."

"Watch what you're insinuating," I warned. Out of the corner of my eye, I saw a few people gathered at either end of the corridor. Someone moved past them, approaching us.

"Or what?" he sneered.

"Don't tempt me." The urge to break his face was overwhelming, and I tightened my hand into a fist at my side.

"Your little girlfriend broke something in my gallery the other day."

I dug in my pocket, flipping a coin toward Winters. "*Gallery*. I wouldn't call it that. A junk house, maybe. That should cover whatever forgery she broke. Perhaps if you learned to keep your hands to yourself, she wouldn't have been in such a hurry to leave." I narrowed my eyes, my voice dropping to a dangerous level. "You left marks on her, Winters, which is unacceptable, so really, I think you owe her. And I am happy to collect on her behalf."

Winters ignored the coin that was spinning on the floor. We both knew what an insult I had just tossed out, and my words deepened his anger.

"You took something from me," he accused.

"I took nothing."

"You did. You stole something I coveted. I know it was you. Perhaps I should return the favor. Take your little Brianna. Steal her away and hide her where you can't find her. Discover why you're so obsessed with her. Maybe fu—"

That was all I allowed out of his filthy mouth. With a roar, I lunged, punching him square in the face. He staggered back, his body hitting the wall. Around me were gasps of disbelief. Murmurs of excitement. Nothing got a party started like a fist swinging.

He glared at me, his rage and hatred on full display. He bared his teeth, the blood seeping from his nose. "You thief," he bellowed, pulling back his arm.

It happened so quickly. I crouched into a fighting stance, knowing this was going to get ugly and destructive fast. He rushed forward, his fist drawn. There was another flurry, and Brianna stepped between us.

"Stop!"

"No!" I yelled, diving to move her. But it was too late. His fist swung out, glancing off my arm as I tried to pivot her, and caught her on the side of her face. The momentum tore her from my arms, and she staggered, collapsing to the floor. With a roar, I descended on him, red coloring my world as I pounded him over and over, my fists turning his skin bloody and bruised.

It was a stern voice that stopped me cold.

"Dante." Richard's tenor was loud. "Brianna is hurt. She needs you."

I stopped midswing, my brain kicking in. Richard put his hand on my shoulder. "I will make sure he is taken care of. Go to her."

I wiped my hands, looking down at the sniveling man on the floor. He was curled into a ball and had wet himself. I shook my head. "You come near her again, I will kill you."

Then I turned to my Brianna on the floor, cursing myself. She should have come first, but my temper had taken over.

I crouched next to her, lifting her head. Her right eye was swollen, the skin on her cheek already badly bruised and painful-looking. I cradled her face, contrite and upset. "I'm sorry, Little Bee."

She blinked, trying to smile, the action looking more like a grimace. "You should see the other guy."

I took off my jacket and slipped it around her, gathering her into my arms.

Richard looked up. "My car is waiting. Take her to the hospital."

I walked through the gaping crowd, not speaking. People parted, someone opening the door, another coming to the car and making sure we got in.

"A lot of us have wanted to do that for a long time," he muttered. I wasn't on a first-name basis with him, but I nodded in acknowledgment.

I looked down at Brianna, horrified to see her tears. "Go fast," I instructed the driver.

She was my focus now.

Richard found me pacing the waiting room. My hands were still bloody, and my hair was a mess from me tugging on it.

"How is she?"

She had clung to me, silent tears coursing down her face. Panicked when they said I had to leave the room. Her hands gripped my shirt so hard I thought she was going to tear the seams.

"No," I said. "I'm staying where she can see me."

She never took her eyes off me.

Seeing her that way broke something in me I couldn't explain.

"In pain, but the orbital bone isn't broken, thank God. Her shoulder took the brunt of the fall, but it prevented a concussion. Her face is a mess, and she is going to have trouble seeing for a few days. They are cleaning her up and doing a CT to be sure."

He handed me a towel. "Clean yourself up."

I slipped to the restroom and washed my hands. I hadn't wanted to be too far away from her. I dried my hands and disposed of the towel. He was standing in the same spot when I returned, looking angry.

"I'm sorry—"

He cut me off. "Don't say that. You're not sorry at all, except that Brianna was injured." He huffed out a laugh. "He deserved that beating and more."

I nodded, and he stared straight ahead. "Robin Hood?" he asked so quietly his lips barely moved.

I nodded imperceptibly.

"He isn't going to stop. This will just have escalated the situation."

"I know."

"Brianna is in danger. He will exploit that to his advantage."

My breath caught. I already knew it. I had realized some truths in the car on the way over here. One was that I would do anything to protect the woman in my arms. The second was that I was totally and irrevocably in love with Brianna. When and how, I wasn't sure. Maybe from the first instant. Somehow, I had known it but been unable to admit it. But it was real and permanent. I loved her. Every single thing about her. She brought something to my life I didn't know I was missing. She completed me in ways I couldn't even describe. She was perfect for me. The thought of being without her gutted me.

But I had failed her. And staying here with me was putting her in danger.

Which was why I had to let her go.

Richard's words confirmed it.

I had to get her away from the world Winters existed in. It was the same one as me. She wasn't safe, and short of keeping her a real prisoner, I had to send her away.

I looked at Richard.

"I need another favor."

He nodded. "I know."

Chapter Twenty-Three

BRIANNA

Dante came into the hospital room, looking angry. But his eyes softened as they found me, and he walked right to the edge of the bed, taking my hand. I felt my body relax as soon as he touched me. Whenever he was close, I felt the strength of him. Despite what had happened earlier, I was always safe with him. I shouldn't have stepped between them, but it was instinct. I didn't want Dante hurt, and I was trying to stop a melee from breaking out.

I had failed miserably.

Dante studied me, his expression tormented. "How much pain are you in?"

"They gave me some drugs. I'm okay. Can we leave soon?"

"Your CT came back clear, so yes. You need to take it easy for a couple of days." He gently tucked a strand of hair behind my ear. "And you won't argue with me."

I smiled ruefully. I didn't have the strength to argue. My face felt as if it was on fire, my eye ached, and my shoulder was painful. I glanced to the side, my gaze finding my dress. Or what was left of it. It had torn when I fell, the sleeve ripped and my heel tearing the skirt.

"He ruined my new dress."

"I'll buy you another one," Dante promised. "A hundred of them."

"When can we leave?"

"Soon," he promised. "Lie back and shut your eyes. I won't leave you."

I grasped his hand, feeling vulnerable and worried. He was too calm. Far too in control. Something felt off. "Promise?" I hated that I sounded like a child, but I was feeling worried.

He bent and kissed my head. "Yes."

I shut my eyes and gave in to the weariness I was feeling. The drugs they administered took the edge off the pain but made me tired. Dante's large hand held mine, his thumb stroking over my skin. I dozed, rousing often to find Dante beside me, staring, unmoving, and looking as if the weight of the world were on his shoulders. The doctor came in and spoke with him in Italian, Dante asking a lot of questions. I was too tired to try to keep up, and soon I felt myself being lifted into his arms. "What's happening?" I asked, confused.

"I'm taking you home. Go back to sleep."

I rested my head against his chest. He held me carefully, keeping my bruised face and shoulder untouched. I heard a low conversation, and I recognized the other voice, but I was too weary to try to participate. I was in and out, held in the warmth of Dante's embrace. I felt the motion of a vehicle, heard more talking, and finally inhaled the scent I had come to love. Dante's cologne saturated the bed he laid me on, the sheets soft, the mattress cradling my sore body.

I reached out, and he lifted my head. "Drink."

The water was cool and refreshing, washing away the bitter taste in my mouth. "Don't go."

"I'm not, Little Bee. I'll be right here."

I felt the mattress dip and his warmth settle behind me. "I'll watch over you," he murmured.

I sighed, the sound low and weary. "I love you."

The words slipped out without thought or planning. They were just there, hanging in the air, unexpected.

He pressed his lips to my temple.

"I know."

I woke the next day, the room dim. I was alone, but I knew Dante had been there. I could sense him. The water in the glass was cold, and I sat up, sipping it gratefully. I carefully slipped from the bed and shuffled to the bathroom, looking in the mirror. The left side of my face was bruised, my eye swollen. Purple, red, and black stood out against the pallor of my skin. I had a long scrape from where Winters's ring had dragged along my cheek, cutting into the flesh. I shrugged out of the hospital gown I was still wearing. My shoulder matched my face, mottled with bruises and sore. I touched around my eye and scalp. I had a headache from the general pain, but my scalp wasn't sore to the touch.

"No concussion," Dante said from the doorway. "Your shoulder is going to be a bitch for a while, though."

I met his gaze. He looked exhausted. Resigned. Sad.

"He packed quite a wallop," I agreed.

Dante came forward. "If his fist hadn't glanced off my shoulder first, it would have been much worse. I don't even want to think about the condition of your eyesight if that had happened." He leaned behind me, resting his chin on my head. "Richard wouldn't have been able to stop me from killing him."

"Don't say that."

He shrugged. "It's true. I have never experienced rage like that."

"Where is he?"

Again, he lifted his shoulders. "Richard said he pushed him away and left. Went away to nurse his wounds."

"What now?" I asked, sensing his turmoil.

"Now you go back to bed."

"I want a shower. I want to wash off the hospital smell and—" I swallowed "—him."

He immediately turned on the water, letting it heat. He discarded his clothes, holding out his hand. He drew me into the warm spray, and I winced as it hit my skin. He adjusted the shower heads so none struck my face or shoulder, and he helped me get clean. He insisted I sit while he washed my hair, his fingers gentle as he worked the shampoo and conditioner through my tangles. When we were done, he wrapped me in a towel and took me back to the bedroom. I slipped into a T-shirt and leggings, and he tucked me back into bed, carefully rubbing some cream into my skin. "This will help with the pain and heal the bruises," he explained.

I winced as his finger grazed over the thin cut, the area ultrasensitive. "I'm sorry, Little Bee," he murmured. "I'm trying not to hurt you."

"I know. It'll get better."

He didn't reply.

When he was done, he bent and kissed my head. "Rest a bit."

"I can't stay here all day," I protested, even as I snuggled under the blanket.

"You can, and you will. I'll make us some lunch in a bit, but you're going to rest."

I shut my eyes, not wanting to argue. Not having the strength. He kissed my forehead again, letting out a sigh. I felt his pain with the air he exhaled. It was heavy and deep, but I wasn't sure how to erase it. I was bruised and shaken up, but I would be fine in a few days.

He left the room, and I opened my eyes, staring after his retreating form. I wondered if I had dreamed telling him I loved him last night. I hadn't meant to. I wasn't even sure why the words slipped out. I hadn't planned on telling him. But at some point, I had fallen in love with my captor. He had ceased to be that almost right away and instead became my protector, my friend, and my lover. He gave me the freedom to be me. He delighted in my quirks and encouraged my inquisitiveness. He worried about me—something I hadn't felt my entire life. I felt so safe with him. So enveloped by him all the time. It was as if I had finally found the one thing I had sought all my life.

Dante was my home. And I was his. Somehow I knew that.

I was certain he felt something toward me beside lust. It was there in the intensity of his gaze, the way he responded to me. How he acted. How he devoured my cakes, devoured me. His touch said so much without a word.

I touched the necklace at my throat. They had taken it off in the hospital, but he had put it back on after my shower when I asked. His little bee, he called me.

I *was* his.

And as soon as we were through this glitch, I'd make sure he knew that.

I slept most of the day. Dante made sure I ate and drank, but I would fall asleep again quickly. He was never far away, and if he heard me get up, he was right there.

My head was clearer the next day, and I got dressed and went to the kitchen. He was there, making coffee, frowning. "You should be in bed."

"No, I feel better."

"You're still taking it easy."

I didn't argue. It hurt to lift my arm and my face ached, but the headache was diminished and I felt more alert. We ate breakfast on the terrace, the sunshine warm on my skin.

"Did I hear Richard's voice yesterday?" I asked.

"Yes."

"He was here?"

"Yes. He wanted to see how you were."

"Is there, ah, any fallout from the other night?" I asked, unsure how to form the question.

"If you mean, am I in trouble? No. I've had a lot of associates reach out and say they wish they had taken a swing at him. Richard saw him yesterday coming out of a building. He was walking, so my beating was obviously not too bad."

"What if he presses charges?"

Dante sipped his coffee and shrugged. "He came at me first. And considering you were the one who ended up in the hospital, he is lucky he is breathing this morning."

"You hit him."

"He threatened you. He was basically telling me what he planned to do to you. I wasn't going to let that go."

"But—"

He stopped me with a look, standing and leaning on the table, holding my gaze. "I will defend you to my death, Little Bee. Anything that threatens to harm you will be eliminated. No matter the cost, no matter what I have to do. You come first."

His gaze was forceful. His voice low and furious. Filled with pain. Every inch of him screamed aching and torment. I didn't understand what was going on. What was causing him such agony.

"Dante," I whispered.

He straightened. "Finish your breakfast."

He strode away, his footsteps fast.

Worry set in, nagging at me.

I needed to get him to talk to me. I simply wasn't sure how.

He seemed calmer when he reappeared. We spent a couple of quiet days in the condo. He was never far away physically, yet mentally, I had no idea where he was. I caught him looking at me more than once, his expression unguarded and saturated in despair. Then he would clear his countenance.

He was attentive and concerned. Gentle and kind.

And completely removed. His kisses were brief and perfunctory. His gaze became disconnected. As if he was shutting down.

When I woke up that morning, I was alone. In the dining room, he sat, staring out at the overcast skies. A pot of coffee sat in front of him, and weariness was etched into his skin.

"Hi," I murmured.

He offered me a hollow smile. "Hello, Little Bee. How are you feeling?"

"Better."

He poured me a coffee. "Good. Up for a little trip?"

"A trip?" I asked.

"Yes. It's time to go home."

I shut my eyes in relief. He was right. We needed to get back to the villa. We could get past this there.

"Yes. I want to go to the villa."

Something passed over his face, but he only nodded. "We'll leave after we have breakfast and you pack."

"What about you?"

He flashed me another smile. It didn't reach his eyes. "Already done."

"Been up for a while, old man?" I asked, teasing.

He lifted an eyebrow, and I grinned, trying to get him to lighten up.

"I'll let that pass."

I was disappointed. I had rather hoped he'd at least threaten me a little. Maybe walk me slowly to the bedroom and have his way with me to disprove my words. Then I decided he probably was worried about the short car ride and my reaction to it. I'd show him tonight I was okay. I'd bake him some cupcakes, and he'd reward me. We'd get back on track. My bruises would heal and fade, and he'd get over his worry.

Maybe even address the fact that I'd told him I loved him.

I drank my latte and ate the croissant and fruit. In the bedroom, I packed the things I'd brought plus the new items we'd purchased, stuffing them into the bag. Dante came and picked it up.

"It's a little fuller than when we got here."

He touched my cheek. "Good."

I wore a set of overalls and one of my new shirts. I slipped my feet into sneakers and left my hair down since that helped cover the bruising. I followed him to the car, and he tossed my case into the back.

I studied him, feeling tense. Something was off. He was acting oddly. He was stiff and removed. His touch had been distant. I noticed he didn't hold my hand in the car. He always held my hand. We drove in silence, and I was confused. We seemed to be headed the wrong way. My confusion reached epic proportions when I spied the airport. He guided the car through some gates, and we pulled up to a private terminal.

"Dante, what's going on?"

"I told you, a little trip."

"I thought we were going home to the villa."

He shook his head. "No."

He climbed out and held out his hand. "We're flying."

I let him pull me from the car, and we headed to the plane. "What if I didn't pack the right things?"

"You're fine."

He indicated I was to go up the steps. "You didn't bring the bags."

"They'll get them." I looked over my shoulder and saw a man pulling my bag from the car. He went around to the trunk, no doubt to get Dante's bag, and I turned my head back. I still wasn't used to being looked after that way.

Inside, I glanced around, noting the luxurious interior. It was cream and navy with deep carpets, wide leather seats, and tables. I peeked up at Dante. "Guess I didn't notice this on the way here. I was a little out of it," I said, hoping to make him smile.

He didn't reply, and I was shocked at his expression. His face was stoic, blank. But his eyes were alight with a fire of agony. I felt my legs go weak, and I began to tremble. "Dante?"

He pressed me gently into a seat, buckling me in. I began to slap his hands, panic setting in. Something was terribly wrong. "Stop it. Dante, stop it. What is happening? Why aren't we going home?"

He wrapped his hands around the armrests, leaning over me, caging me in. "You are," he said, his voice hoarse.

He lifted his face and met my eyes. The pain was gone, and his were flat. Cold. Unfeeling.

Behind him, someone else appeared, and I gasped when I saw Richard and the cat kennel he was carrying. Roomba was inside, not looking happy.

Understanding dawned. He was sending me back to Canada. Without him.

I swung my gaze back to Dante. "What are you doing?"

"It's over, Little Bee. Your time is done."

"No," I protested wildly. "I haven't baked you all the cakes. I have to go with you. I'm fine." I tried to push him away, grabbing at the seat belt. But he covered my hand, stopping me.

"You are done," he said, his voice cool. "You've become a liability. A nuisance. We're over. You're going home. Richard will escort you."

Liability. Nuisance.

His words hit me, and I stopped struggling.

"No," I pleaded.

He cupped my face, then pressed his lips to my temple and rested his forehead against mine. He didn't say anything. I gripped his wrists, my nails digging into his skin. "Don't," I choked, barely able to speak.

"Thank you for your time," he said.

My time? He was thanking me for my time? Not my love? Not what we had been?

My time?

I looked up at him, our eyes locking. Tears poured down my face, and I didn't hide the pain I was feeling. It hurt worse than any bruise Winters had left on my body.

"I hate you," I whispered.

He smiled sadly.

"I know."

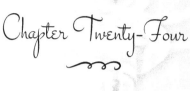

Chapter Twenty-Four

DANTE

I wandered the condo, unable to sit. I drank whatever was handy, the alcohol barely numbing the pain. One night, I drank myself into oblivion and woke up the next day with an upended table, a black eye, and a cut hand. I had no one to blame but myself, and I limited my drinking.

Nothing was keeping me in Naples, but I couldn't stand the thought of going back to the villa.

Brianna had only been here a short time, and she was still everywhere. Her laughter soaked into the walls, her scent on my sheets.

At the villa, she would surround me. Every room, every surface, would have a memory of her etched into it.

Even outside, she would dwell, peering at me around every corner, taunting me with her memory.

I couldn't bear it. Not yet.

I knew she was back in Toronto. Paolo had her. He had met the plane and took her to his house, making sure she had a safe place to recover and find her feet. When I asked how she was, his answer had been brief and to the point.

"How do you think she is?"

"Take care of her," I replied.

His voice had softened. "I will."

Winters's revenge had already started. My gallery in Naples had been broken in to. Or at least, it was attempted. They did a great deal of damage to the outside but, luckily, hadn't made it in. The gallery was closed until I had the exterior fixed. I went to investigate the damage, angry at the sight of my beautiful gallery torched and the glass windows, while still intact, covered in thousands of spider webs of cracks. The canopy was gone, lost to the flames, the beautiful handmade wrought-iron sign covered in soot and warped.

I'd had another run-in with Winters while there. I saw him across the street, his expression smug and satisfied. My anger burning bright over the destruction of my gallery, I stormed over to him, grabbing him by the lapels and glaring down at him.

"Looking at your handiwork, Winters? Gloating?"

"I don't know what you're talking about." His smirk was exultant.

I pulled him closer, the bruises on his face dark and painful-looking. I hoped he was suffering. I certainly was. "I know this was your work. Revenge for humiliating you."

"Where is your little toy?" he asked, his voice menacing. "I still plan on taking her from you."

That was the wrong thing to say. I drew back, punching him in the stomach. He doubled over in pain, falling to the ground.

"You stay away from her. From me. Come near her again, and I will kill you. Do you understand me?" I raged.

A gasp behind me brought me out of my anger. I passed my now-reinjured hand over my head, feeling weary. "Stay away, Winters. That is your last warning."

I didn't want him to know she was gone. I wanted him chasing around, looking for her. Going crazy because he couldn't find her. I knew she was safe and protected. He wouldn't get that satisfaction. I walked away, pushing my way through the crowd that had gathered. I left the gallery and returned to the condo.

I doubled all the security. My villa was protected, and my staff on high alert in my small town. Guards were outside patrolling twenty-four seven.

Another small business I owned in Naples was ransacked, the damage expensive. He was hitting where he thought I would hurt the most—my pocketbook.

But my heart was the worst place he struck. Without my little bee, nothing seemed to matter. But she was safe with Paolo. Winters had no information on her. He wouldn't be able to find her.

Richard told me she had sobbed herself to sleep, and when she woke up, she was angry and defiant, barely talking unless she was expressing her displeasure.

"She called me some odd names," he shared. "Motherplucker. Son of a biscuit eater."

"She doesn't like to swear," I explained. "She prefers colorful expressions she has overheard."

He had chuckled. "Colorful, indeed."

Despite the pain I felt, his words made me smile. My little bee was tough. She'd make it through this. I had put money in her account, and I planned on backing a bakery for her—not that she would know the money was from me. I would have Paolo present her the offer, and I hoped she would accept it. I wanted her to have her dream.

For a brief while, she had been my dream. All the things I had never known I wanted or needed. But I had to let that go to keep her safe. Winters was unhinged enough; he would make good on his threat, and I couldn't risk her being taken. Even once she left Paolo's, I would make sure she was watched.

I sighed and scrubbed my face. I needed to get my act together. I showered and changed, heading to the kitchen to make some coffee. I looked at the calendar. She had only been gone a week, and it felt like forever. I wanted to call and talk to her, but I knew I couldn't. She had to believe she was a passing thing. That we were over, so she could get on with her life. If I called, that plan would be out the window. There was no way I could disguise my anguish.

I got reports from all my people, pleased there was nothing new. No further damage, no fires, nothing even remotely suspicious around my buildings. Sipping my coffee, I wondered what Winters was planning. I could only hope I stayed a step ahead of him.

A knock at the door surprised me, and I was even more shocked to see the police officers waiting outside in the hall. Maybe Winters had decided to press charges.

I opened the door and forced a smile in greeting, hoping to be able to tell my side of the story.

I wasn't smiling for long.

BRIANNA

I stared out the window at the water beating on the glass. The dark skies and rain matched my mood. I leaned back against the headboard, running my fingers through Roomba's fur. She wasn't very pleased with her new accommodations. I wasn't either, but it appeared, for now, we had no choice.

Dante's brother, Paolo, had met the plane. He came on board, looking serious, and for the first time, I saw the resemblance to his brother. Paolo was usually smiling and gregarious, but he was emotionless, informing me I was coming with him. Between him and Richard, I didn't have a chance of running, nor did I have the desire to try. I picked up my cat and followed him.

He was silent on the drive except to tell me I would be staying with him and his wife for the time being. That I was welcome and had full use of the house.

"Carolina is looking forward to seeing you as well," he informed me, injecting a pleased tone into his voice.

I only nodded.

The room he showed me to was spacious and pretty. Light-blue walls with a view of the yard, a nice en suite, a comfortable chair to sit in, even a space in the walk-in closet for Roomba's needs. My suitcases were there, empty. My clothing hung in the closet, my toiletries in the bathroom.

"My wife is not partial to cats," he said quietly. "So she will have to stay in here."

"Of course," I replied. I didn't have plans to leave the room much. I didn't want to bother them. "I'll be out of your hair as soon as possible."

He shook his head. "You are welcome to stay as long as you need to. I have some things to tell you when you're ready." He studied my face, his concerned look reminding me too much of Dante. "How are you feeling?"

"Fine."

He huffed a laugh. "Dante said you would say that."

The sound of his name caused a wave of pain to curl through my chest.

"I'd like to lie down," I lied. "I'm tired."

"Of course. I'll have some food sent up later."

I'd barely left my room since.

There was a knock on the door, and I lifted my head. "Come in."

Carolina came in, carrying a tray. She'd come a couple of times, and conversation had been stilted. She'd been horrified to see my face and confused about my relationship with Dante. But what had happened was still raw, and I couldn't talk about it.

The events leading up to that night still played in my head. The what-ifs.

If I hadn't gotten lost. *If* I hadn't stumbled into Winters's shop. *If* he hadn't grabbed me.

If he hadn't provoked Dante.

Would I still be a liability? A nuisance?

She handed me a coffee and a bagel. "Eat this, please. You are wasting away."

Then she sat down in the chair, looking at me. "Your bruises are fading. And the scar cream I brought you is helping."

"Yes," I said. "Thank you."

"You don't have to thank me. But please, eat."

I had always liked bagels. But I had grown very fond of croissants in Italy, and now the bread seemed heavy. And I liked jam now, not cream cheese. But to please her, I ate it.

"I'm sorry Uncle Dante was such a bastard to you."

Her words startled me. The problem was that until the last minute, he had been anything but. Before I could say anything, she kept talking.

"I know he took you there without permission. My dad told my mom, and she told me the whole story. You must dislike my family."

"No."

"Did he hurt you, Bri?"

I shook my head. "He-he was very kind to me." I looked down, tracing a finger over the blanket. "He was nicer to me than anyone else has been my whole life. He treated me like a queen." I dropped my voice. "Despite how we started, I thought he loved me. I was wrong."

"You love him?"

I could only nod.

"Do you know he has an apartment here for you? All ready for when you want it? And he wants to invest in a bakery for you. He told my dad anything you need or want, you get." She met my eyes. "That doesn't sound like someone who doesn't care."

I leaned my head back, refusing to let her words sink in. "He feels guilty."

She shook her head. "Uncle Dante doesn't feel guilty. I used to think he didn't care about anything, but I was wrong. I think he cared—much more than he let on. I think he still does." She paused. "He's in trouble."

I snapped up my head. "What?"

She leaned forward. "The man who hit you? He's dead."

I gaped. *What?*

"He was found beaten to death. Uncle Dante was arrested under suspicion of murder."

I shook my head. "No. He wouldn't do that."

"Several witnesses saw him beat him. Heard him threaten him."

"He was angry. But he would never kill someone. Not on purpose."

My heart was racing. He wouldn't, would he? Was Dante capable of killing someone? Had Winters provoked him again? Then I mentally shook my head. No. Dante would never. He had too much self-control. They were wrong.

"Where is he?"

"Dad said he was in jail for a few days. They dragged their feet letting him out. But he's in Naples under house arrest. He is considered a flight risk since he has dual citizenship. His passports have been seized. His lawyers are working on proving him innocent."

My bagel was forgotten. "Oh God, Carolina. This can't be happening. He wouldn't do that. He isn't capable." I got off the bed. "I have to talk to your dad. I have to do something."

"What can you do?"

"Call them, tell them they're wrong."

She laughed, not unkindly. "They won't accept his lover as a character reference."

I felt my cheeks darken at her words.

"We were more than that."

"So, you still love him."

"Yes."

"Then let's go see my dad."

Paolo offered me a kind smile. "There is nothing you can do, Brianna. He has lawyers and investigators working on it."

"I could help. Please. Call him."

He shook his head. "He won't allow me to come, so he certainly won't allow you." He looked at Carolina. "I told you what was happening in confidence. You shouldn't have told her."

She tossed her hair, unrepentant. "She loves him, Dad. I think he loves her. She should be there for him."

For a moment, Paolo was quiet. "My brother kidnapped you, Brianna," he began.

"That doesn't matter anymore. He—"

Paolo cut me off. "Let me finish. Dante is level-headed, responsible. For him to do something so unpredictable shocked me. But I saw a change in him while you were there. You made him laugh. He smiled and joked with me when we spoke. He changed when he talked about you. I believe he truly did care."

I felt my chest tighten.

"But?"

"My brother has always insisted he was built for speed, not longevity. None of his relationships lasted. I had thought you might be the one to change him. Despite how you started, he seemed happier."

"He was. We were," I insisted.

"I asked him last night. Directly. I offered to bring you back now that Winters was dead and couldn't hurt you. I suspected that was why he sent you away."

I nodded eagerly. The more I thought about it, the more that made sense. I knew Dante had feelings for me. I knew it as surely as I knew I needed to breathe to live.

"He said no. Without hesitation. That his equilibrium had returned, and he realized he'd been acting foolishly." He met my eyes, his filled with pity. "I'm sorry, but he said it was over. He felt badly for disrupting your life and instructed me to give you whatever you wanted. Purchase a bakery for you. Move you in to whatever condo you wanted. But you are to move forward, the way he plans to once this is over."

I stared at him, his words sinking in.

"He was very blunt, Brianna. I know my brother and when he is telling the truth." He gentled his voice.

"You need to do as he plans to. Think of it as a nice distraction for a while and get on with your life. He has left you in a better place than he found you."

Anger tore through me. "Why? Because now I can live in a nicer apartment? Open a bakery because I was paid like a whore for my time? I was better off in my dingy apartment with my low-paying, nasty boss. At least that was honest. You can tell your brother he can stick his condo and his money up his butt. And he can—" I sucked in a deep breath. "Feck off."

I stormed out of Paolo's office and headed up to my room, Carolina hot on my heels.

She shut the door, staring at me. "Did you mean that?"

"That he can eff off? Yes. I am angry. But not for the reasons your dad thinks."

"Do you believe you meant nothing to him but a whim?"

"No. I meant something. He is still trying to protect me. He always tried to protect me from everything but him." I sat down. "And he was what I needed the most protection from. He stole my heart while barely trying."

Carolina sat beside me. "And broke it."

I turned my head, meeting her eyes. "He dented it and he made me angry, but it's not broken. Dante is unapologetic in his ways. He does what he wants, how he wants, and when he wants. He offers no reasons and seeks no one's permission. For him to be falling all over himself to apologize is total horse pucky. He's the one with the broken heart, not me." I stood and paced. "He's messed with the wrong girl, and I'm going to prove it to him." I stopped in front of her. "I need your help. And your money."

She stood. "You got it."

"Okay, we need to plan this carefully."

DANTE

I paced the condo on an endless loop. I was beginning to go stir-crazy. From the moment I had seen the serious looks on the faces of the police at my door, I'd known I was in deep trouble. I had gone willingly to the station, making sure to contact my lawyer before leaving. The questioning had been endless, and finally, I refused to speak anymore. The new police chief was young, eager, and had a very low opinion of his wealthier citizens. He and his department managed to hold me for three days before I got out, and since then, I had been stuck in this condo.

I had my lawyers on the case. Investigators. On the surface, it didn't look good. There were all the witnesses who saw our fight the night before he disappeared. Heard me threaten him. I had no alibi for when he supposedly went missing later. My hands were a wreck from the fight, as well as the fact that I had the black eye I'd gotten when I'd stumbled around drunk the night I sent Brianna away. According to the police, it showed Winters got in a swing or two before I made good on my threats and beat him to death. What they had was circumstantial, but others had been convicted with less. And all I could do was hope we caught a break in the case.

Thanks to the internet, I could run my businesses easily with Zoom and email, which I did to stay busy when I wasn't on the phone with my team. But I was going out of my mind being stuck in here.

Being without Brianna.

When I'd heard he was dead, my first thought had been relief. She was safe from him now. There was a part of me that rejoiced, that immediately went into planning mode on how to get her back, except I realized he had people still loyal to him. Those who might still want to hurt me, and the best way would be to hurt her.

So, I had to keep her away.

Paolo told me she was safe. Unhappy, but safe. She rarely came out of her room and she wasn't eating much, but she did visit with Carolina. I forbade him to tell Brianna what was happening. I wanted her to have a clean break from me. Knowing her, she would get a crazy idea in her head and show up, demanding to lead the investigation.

I had to admit, the thought made me smile.

My phone rang, and I accepted a video chat with Paolo.

"Hello, brother."

"Any news?" he asked.

"No. They have some leads they are tracking down. I wasn't his only enemy. But it all takes time." I paused. "How is she?"

"Mad as a hornet."

"Why?"

He paused, taking a sip of what I assumed was scotch. "Carolina told her."

"Fuck."

"She wanted to fly back, help. She said you needed her."

Of course she did.

"I hope you convinced her otherwise?" I asked.

"I was very blunt and repeated our conversation from the other night."

"And she was angry?"

"She told me to feck off."

I gaped at him. "She said fuck off?"

He shook his head. "*Feck* off. I think that was as close as she could get." Then he repeated what she had said, and I winced at her words. I hated that she compared herself to a whore. Nothing could be further from the truth.

"But she believed you."

"I think so. Tell me, was I lying?"

"She is better off without me. Don't let her come back here."

"So I *was* lying."

I remained quiet.

"Her passport is in the safe, she has no access to the accounts you set up yet. The phone I gave her has limited usage. She can't go anywhere."

"Good."

"I heard her and Carolina making plans to go shopping. It's colder here, and her clothes aren't warm enough anymore."

I had tossed out most of her things that were old and threadbare. It made sense she needed new ones.

"Make sure she has money."

"I'll give Carolina my card to use. You can repay me."

"Okay. Watch her, though. She is determined."

"I don't think you have to worry. I saw her heartbreak, Dante. She withered in front of me."

I had to shut my eyes at the pain his words caused me.

"She is safe there. Even if this were over, Winters's accusation is making people wonder if I am part of something. That makes me a target. If she were here, she would be a prime way to get to me. This is for the best."

He was silent for a moment.

"For whom, brother?" he asked.

I had no response.

He hung up.

Chapter Twenty-Five

DANTE

The break came when we least expected it. A goon for hire bragged to the wrong people. Showed them the watch he had lifted from Winters's dead body, planning on pawning it for money. It turned out Winters had sold a forgery to an underworld mafia-type guy who disliked being fleeced. When he found out, he confronted Winters.

Winters paid him back with his life.

The goon for hire sang like a canary on his accomplice, and they both ended up dead while in jail two days later. The mafia guy skated away and disappeared.

And I didn't care.

It was over.

I received a grudging apology from the police chief, my passports returned, and the ankle monitoring bracelet removed. My name cleared.

The news made the headlines for a day, and people moved on.

Even Winters's wife did, being spotted with a new man only days after his death.

Being able to leave the condo helped. I could oversee the reconstruction of the front of the gallery, speeding it along. After seeing the extent of the damage to the other business in Naples, I decided to close it, and I made sure the people affected had new jobs at one of my other establishments.

Paolo had been exuberant when I called him with the news.

"Thank God," he exclaimed. "What a relief."

"I know. I can move forward." I paused. "How is she?"

"She and Carolina have been spending a lot of time together. I heard them talking about looking at some buildings for a bakery. She is at Carolina's for a few days since she lives right downtown. Brianna even baked a few desserts here last week. Cookies and a cake."

"What kind of cake?"

"A mockingbird, I think? It was delicious. I was pleased to see her out of her room."

"Hummingbird," I corrected. "One of my favorites."

"Well, she is doing better. I told her I would look at any potential bakery or building. Help her with a business plan."

"Did you tell her the charges were dropped?"

"Yes. She said she was glad that was behind you."

"Ah. Good."

I wasn't sure why her lack of response bothered me so much.

We talked for a few more minutes, and I hung up.

I had to fight down my jealousy. Paolo got to have her cake. Sit with her and help her with her dream.

That was what I wanted for her. Why I was so upset she was doing exactly what I wanted her to do was a mystery. I was proud of her, and yet oddly disappointed.

I called Richard next. He had been in close contact since he left, even offering his own team to help with the investigation. I had assured him I would let him know if they were needed.

"Stupid idiots," he mumbled. "As if you'd beat him to death and leave the body to be found."

I laughed. "You think I'd beat him and dispose of the body, is that what you're saying?"

"Of course. You are far too clever to have left that detail out."

"Thanks for the vote of confidence."

"How is our girl?" he asked, changing the subject.

I told him what my brother had said, and he was quiet for a moment. "So, she is moving on?"

"It appears so. It is for the best."

He didn't reply for a moment. "You don't think you were what was best for her?"

"I wasn't thinking most of the time I was with her. That might have been the problem."

"Or the blessing," he replied. "Sometimes love offers us that."

Then he hung up.

I had no idea what he meant.

A few days later, my phone rang and I answered. "Paolo."

He cut right to the chase. "Brianna is missing."

I stood. "What?"

"She isn't at Carolina's. There was no bakery. No shopping. She left."

"And went where?"

"I have no idea. Carolina refuses to tell me. She won't tell me how long she's been gone. She says I interfered enough."

I began to pace.

"I checked. I have no charges on the credit card. I even looked at the accounts you set up for her. Nothing's been touched."

I sat down, pulling up Brianna's old accounts. "She hasn't taken anything. Where the hell could she go without money?" I stood again and paced. "And why the hell would she go?" A thought occurred to me. "What about the cat?"

"She took the damn cat to Carolina's. It's still there."

"Then she hasn't gone far." Another thought hit me. "Her passport?"

"It's in the safe." I heard him move and the sound of the safe opening. "It's—*fuck*."

"What?"

"It's gone."

"How would she get it?"

"Carolina knows the combination."

I hung up and dialed my goddaughter. She answered with a breezy hello.

"Never mind the sweet shit, Carolina. Where is she?"

"Where is who?"

"You know goddamn well who. Where is Brianna?"

"On a walkabout."

"On a *what*?"

"You wanted her to discover who she is. What she wants. She decided to do that."

"With what?" I yelled. "She has no money, no credit cards. Not even a decent fucking cell phone. Where the hell is she?"

"Why do you care? You sent her away."

"I sent her to be looked after!"

She sighed. "Uncle Dante, I always thought you were a smart man. Brianna isn't a child. She doesn't need to be looked after. She's a grown woman, and she can make her own decisions. She is doing what she wants right now. Spending time in her favorite places. She is clearing her past so she can start her future. Just like you wanted her to." She paused. "And you and Dad aren't the only ones with money, you know."

"Where. Is. She?"

"Think about it."

And she hung up.

All day, I racked my brain. Brianna had mentioned wanting to see more of Canada. But how was she funding it? Later in the afternoon, on a whim, I called my sister-in-law. The puzzle was solved instantly.

"Yes, I loaned her some money," she said when she answered. "I don't want to hear about it. You are being an ass. She is the best thing that ever happened to you."

She hung up.

So I knew Brianna had money. But where would she go? She had told me her favorite place in the world was the villa. That she couldn't imagine loving any spot more. So where—

I stood, grabbing my phone.

Gia answered on the second ring. I didn't have to ask.

I heard my little bee singing in the background.

"I'll be home shortly," I snapped.

I headed to the car, stopping only to grab a few things. I drove like a madman, not caring if the police stopped me.

What the hell was she playing at? Returning to Italy? To my villa? I sent her away. I told her it was over. I fumed all the way there, barely giving the gates the chance to open fully before I was flying down the driveway, the dust on the road swirling behind me.

I opened the front door, striding in and freezing. It hit me like a ton of bricks.

Brianna was in the kitchen, singing, her sweet voice filling the empty house. Filling me. The air was saturated with the scent of cinnamon and sugar. Beckoning. Tempting.

I shook my head to clear it and headed for the kitchen. I stopped in the doorway as memories washed over me. Repeats of the sight in front of me. Brianna, her hair piled up, overalls smeared with icing, her bare feet tapping on the floor as she hummed and stirred. The bruises had faded, the stain gone from her skin—but not from my memory.

Then she looked up, and her gaze met mine. I was lost for a moment. Filled to the brim with echoes of other times just like this one that played in my head. Emotion hit me. She was here. Where she belonged. Then I remembered why I'd sent her away, and I pushed down what I was feeling, determined to remain calm and level-headed. Then she spoke and blew that out of the water.

"Oh hi, Dante."

Hi, Dante.

As if I had been out getting her sugar. Or working in the garden. As if weeks hadn't passed. Pain hadn't been inflicted.

"Hi, Dante?" I questioned. "*Hi, Dante*? What the hell are you doing here, Little Bee?"

She frowned as if I was crazy. "Making a cake."

"What are you doing in Italy?" I spat out.

She sighed, wiping her arm along her head, leaving behind more icing. "You really need to relax. That vein in your head is going to explode if you're not careful. At your age, all this tension isn't a good thing."

At my glare, she waggled her finger. "We had an agreement, Dante. Sixty cakes. I made less than half. I'm here to fulfill my end of the bargain."

"I let you out of the agreement. I provided money for your future. My brother will make sure you have everything you need," I said through clenched teeth.

Jesus, she was pretty. Had she always been this pretty?

She was too thin, though. I didn't like that. She needed to eat some of the cake she was baking.

"Nope," she replied, popping the "p." "My agreement was with you, not your brother."

I edged forward, somehow needing to be closer.

"What are you saying?"

"You want me to take your money. Open a bakery. Live in a decent apartment."

"No. Yes. I mean yes."

I wanted her here with me. But I couldn't ask her to live her life in possible danger.

"Then I need to fulfill my end of the agreement. You get cakes, or I don't take your money. I'll go back to working for MaryJo. My old apartment is still empty. The landlord told me I can move back in anytime."

I had to wrap my hands around the edge of the counter to stop myself from grabbing her.

"Not happening, Little Bee."

"Then I'm here to bake your cakes. Get used to it."

"How long?"

She spread some frosting on the top of a cake, the scent driving me wild. "Hmm? How long what?"

"To bake your cakes."

"As long as it takes," she replied, waving me off as if I were a pesky fly.

"Fine. Bake your cakes. As many a day as you can. Freeze them."

"No. You insisted on fresh cakes. We're sticking to that. And every third day."

"You are trying my patience. I will have you removed."

"Try it. I'll come back. You won't win this time." She crossed her arms. "I'm just as stubborn as you, old man. Now, we can do this the hard way or the easy way."

"What might those be?"

"The easy way is for you to kick me out. I'll keep borrowing money and coming back."

"I'll sell the villa."

"I'll tell Paolo to buy it. You said anything I wanted. I'll come to Naples. London. I know all your addresses."

"If that is what you consider easy, what is the hard way?"

"For you to admit you love me and want me here," she said softly. "As much as I love you and want to be here with you."

I reared back, dumbstruck.

"I know you're worried. We can face it together, Dante. Stop being Robin Hood. Stop avoiding life and live it. With me. You make me whole. You made me feel like I mattered, and I refuse to let you take that from me because you're scared." She lifted her chin.

"I'm not going anywhere, buddy, so get used to it."

She was beautiful in her anger. Her eyes flashed, a veil of tears making them glisten. Her chest rose and fell in agitated pulls of air. Her voice deepened when she was mad, a lower, almost growly edge to it.

She was stunning.

And if I didn't get away, she would be impossible to resist.

"Have it your way," I said. "Bake your cakes. Stay. But it's back to the original agreement. One a day. Then you are gone."

I turned and walked away, everything in me screaming to turn back. To drag her into my arms and tell her she was right. I was scared. I did want her here. In my kitchen. Baking me cakes.

I'd almost made it to the hall when I heard it. She began to sing again, this time a tremor to her voice. I wrapped my hand around the doorknob, voices exploding in my head.

"She is the best thing that ever happened to you."

"For whom, brother?"

"Sometimes love offers us that."

I thought of the peace she gave me. The pure happiness I felt when she was around. The joy I got eating her cakes, listening to her sing. Holding her in my arms as we moved around the patio. The way she made me laugh. She had right from the start.

"...Live it. With me," she said.

"You made me feel like I mattered, and I refuse to let you take that from me because you're scared."

She made me feel as if I mattered too. Dante—the man. Not for what I could do. The money I had. The knowledge I possessed. The power I could wield.

Just my love. That was all she wanted.

No one else could protect her the way I could. I had the resources, security, the house, the time. I could devote all of it to her.

I didn't *have* to send her away.

I didn't *want* to send her away.

I spun on my heel and headed back to the kitchen. She was still standing there, her shoulders hunched. Her voice had dropped, barely a whisper escaping. I cleared my throat. She looked up, the tears on her cheeks slamming into me, breaking me open.

"Your time away hasn't taught you any respect. You referred to my age twice already. We talked about that."

She wiped her eyes on her apron like a child, the action endearing her to me all over again.

"Then stop acting like you're sixty."

"Stop being so damn sexy."

"That is impossible. I know someone who thinks I am."

I nodded. "He does. He thinks you're the most incredible, vexing, stubborn, sexy, wonderful woman he knows. He loves you very much, but he is afraid to admit it. Worried that loving you will put you in danger. Terrified to admit to needing someone. Worried you don't need him the same way."

"I do. I need you more than I can express." More tears coursed down her cheeks. "No one else would put up with my brand of crazy."

"I like your crazy."

"It likes you, old man."

I lifted an eyebrow. "What did you say?"

"Old man," she mouthed.

"You know the rules."

"So you keep repeating. Maybe I need a reminder."

I stepped closer until I was in front of her. Close enough to smell her. The light, alluring scent that clung to her skin that had nothing to do with the sugar she worked with.

"You sass off and call me that, you get fucked, Little Bee. Until I've had my fill. You've been warned."

She tapped her foot. "And I'm waiting."

I had her in my arms in a second.

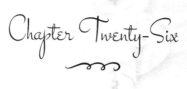

Chapter Twenty-Six

BRIANNA

I was in his arms. Held tight to his chest. Encased in his warmth. His scent. I was home.

I gripped his neck, listening to his heartbeat under my ear. He carried me upstairs, his mouth pressing kisses to my head repeatedly. He lowered me to the bed, hovering over me. "You were supposed to stay away, Little Bee."

"I couldn't."

"I can't give you up again."

"Then don't."

"I love you. I fucking love you so much, I have no idea how to deal with it."

I cupped his face. "I love you too. We'll figure it out. Promise me we'll do it together."

"Always. I'll never let you go."

"Stop worrying about what could happen and instead enjoy what we have now," I urged. "Be with me. Here. Now."

I could see his emotions. They poured from his liquid gold gaze. They dripped inside me, bringing me back to life.

He was struggling. I could see it. He had no idea how to cope with everything. That was what I'd counted on. The reason I'd come.

"I will. I'll try, Bee. But I need you to help me."

"I will. I'm not leaving. No matter what you do."

He shook his head and kissed me. "Good. Now, where is my cat?"

"They wouldn't let me bring her on the plane. I wasn't sure how she'd react to being under it. Carolina is keeping her."

"We'll go get her next week. We can get your stuff, and I'm going to marry you."

"I don't recall you asking."

"I'm not asking. I'm telling you. Next week, we're getting married."

"What if I want to get married here?"

"We can do that too. But I want Paolo there. We'll get married at his house."

"Is this how it's going to be now? You giving orders and me just going along?"

He laughed. "I doubt it, but I'm going to try."

"If you marry me, you can't send me away again."

"I'm never letting you go. I had to protect you, and it was the only way I knew how."

"I'm safer when I'm with you. It's the safest place in the world."

"I know."

Our eyes met and held. The space around us grew hotter, the air pulsating between us. The desire only Dante could make me feel rose and twisted through my body. He was waiting. Wanting me to direct him. I lifted my hand, tracing the lobe of his ear. He shivered at my touch.

"You going to do it, Dante?"

"Do it?" he repeated, his voice low.

I smiled and let my arms fall over my head. "Go on, old man. *Fuck me*."

With a roar, he was on me. His body pressing mine into the mattress. He covered my mouth, kissing me, the action almost bruising in its intensity. He dominated the kiss, ravishing my mouth and my neck with his tongue, lips, and teeth. He muttered and cursed, yanking off my clothes, tearing at his own until we were skin to skin, my soft melting into his hard, his erection pressed between us. He lavished my body with kisses, praises, and caresses. Everywhere he touched left a trail of fire that made me want more. Need closer, beg louder.

When he slammed into me, I swore I saw stars. He rode me like a stallion, hard and fast, not giving an inch. Taking everything I had. Claiming every inch of me. The headboard slammed into the wall over and over, the noise loud. I knocked the lamp off the bedside table, trying to find purchase somewhere. He gripped the pillow so hard, it tore, the material rending like a broken zipper. I was certain the glass in the windows rattled. Finally, I succumbed to the fire building inside, and I came around him, crying and sobbing his name.

He held me tight, groaning through his release. Trembling and spasming until the pleasure passed. Even then, he kept me close, lying down and pulling me to his chest.

"You'll be here when I wake up," he instructed. "We're going to do that again."

I was too exhausted to argue. I wasn't sure I would survive another go-round with him.

"Not sure that is good for your heart. We shouldn't test it," I said primly.

He grinned against my head. "I missed your sass."

"I missed you."

He tilted up my chin, his focus intent on me. "I'm sorry, Little Bee."

"I know."

"Never again."

"Then you're forgiven."

He pulled me back to him and was asleep in seconds.

Wrapped around him, drenched in us, I joined him quickly.

DANTE

I woke, panicked briefly when I realized I was alone.

Had it all been a dream?

But then I saw Brianna's overalls on the floor. I bent and held them up, grimacing at the torn material. I had been in a hurry. A damp towel was beside the clothing, and I knew she must have had a shower. I was shocked I'd slept through it, but given how little sleep I'd had lately, I supposed I shouldn't be.

I slid from the bed, grabbing some pants and sliding them on. I hurried downstairs and found her in the kitchen, her brow furrowed in concentration as she decorated the cake in front of her. She wore my shirt, and her hair was a disaster. She was perfect.

"You were supposed to stay," I said dryly. "Clearly, taking orders is still a hard thing for you."

She shook her head, not looking up. "Something else was hard a while ago. I hope it's abated somewhat. I'm walking a little funny."

I came up behind her, wrapping my arms around her waist and leaning my chin on her shoulder. "It's always hard around you."

"Well, it has to wait. I'm busy, and I don't want this cake to look like it was decorated by a four-year-old high on sugar."

I chuckled and studied the cake. Another masterpiece. The cake looked like a wreath, the flowers piped in different colors, intricate leaves and petals covering the delicious layers. Tiny dewdrops made it look lifelike.

"Hummingbird?" I asked hopefully.

"Yes."

"My favorite."

She put down the icing bag and turned in my arms. "Made for my favorite kidnapper."

"I thought I was the worst kidnapper?"

"You graduated and became the best."

"When did that happen?"

"When you fell in love with me."

I pressed a kiss to her nose. "I think I fell in love with you as soon as you slapped my hands and asked what the h-e-double-hockey-sticks I was doing that close to your cake. Something inside me knew. And I was hooked."

"I am pretty irresistible," she agreed with a mischievous grin.

"You are." I kissed her again. "So, I went from worst to best now?"

"Yes. Best and favorite."

I chuckled. "Favorite husband soon. I prefer that title."

"Not as catchy. I am going to get so much use out of this story. It'll be legend."

"Embellished, of course."

"Well, you'll be much younger. And handsome."

"Little Bee," I warned.

"And none of these defects." She tapped the dimples on my cheeks. "And certainly none of the furrows."

"I didn't have those before you."

"Well, since they make you sexier, you should thank me."

"I should thank you for a lot of things. Like this cake. When do I get to eat it?"

She grinned and wrapped her arms around my neck. "After you eat *me*," she whispered.

"Oh, we are demanding now."

"Get used to it."

"Happily."

Her eyes were soft, melting pools of love I wanted to drown in.

"I love you, Dante."

"I love you, Little Bee. I'll make you happy."

"You already do."

I lifted her to the counter, standing between her legs.

I waggled my eyebrows. "Then let's get busy, Little Bee."

Her laughter was music to my ears.

Epilogue

BRIANNA

I woke up, shivering. Sitting up, I stared in horror around my room. Small, dingy walls. An uncomfortable bed. The air was cold, the sheets rough.

I was in my apartment. Alone.

No dappled sun filtering through the windows. No luxurious bed. No strong arms.

No Dante.

It had all been a dream. The constant buzz I could hear was my alarm, telling me it was time to get up, head to MaryJo's bakery, and begin another long day of endless work.

I put my head down and began to cry.

Suddenly, the mattress dipped, and I felt heat. His heat. His warmth.

"Hey, Little Bee, wake up. Wake up for me."

I startled, opening my eyes, meeting Dante's golden gaze. He pulled me closer, pressing kisses to my head. "I'm here, Little Bee. Right here."

I burrowed into his chest, inhaling his familiar scent. As always, being this close to him calmed me, and I relaxed, letting his proximity soothe me.

"I was back there—in that apartment. Alone. All of this—you—were gone," I gasped.

"It was just a dream, baby. Just a dream."

I shuddered, nestling closer.

"I was only gone a little while. I was just getting coffee and going to come back," he murmured. "I guess being alone in a strange apartment made you disoriented."

I opened my eyes again and looked around. We were in Dante's condo in Toronto. We'd flown here yesterday to get Roomba and our license. We were getting married and then going back to Italy. Somehow, he'd rushed all the paperwork through that we needed to make it happen.

Apparently he was good at rushing stuff through.

He tightened his arms and rocked me a little, the motion soothing the last of the tremors.

"Okay now?"

"Yes."

He eased back and tucked a piece of hair behind my ear. "What brought that on?" he asked, looking concerned.

"I think the different place, the sounds, you weren't beside me. Something about Toronto." I shrugged.

He smiled tenderly. "You already miss the villa."

"Yes, I do. I love it there."

"We'll go home soon. Today, we'll get Roomba and bring her here. I miss that damn lump of fur."

I smiled, pulling my legs up to my chest and resting my chin on them. "I bet she misses you too."

"I'll have to bribe her again not to shit on the carpet in the plane. I wonder if she likes smoked salmon?"

I laughed. "I don't think there's a food she doesn't like."

"There's my smile," he said, kissing the end of my nose. "Come and have coffee. Shake off the nightmare." He paused. "You'll never be without me again, Little Bee. And you'll never go back to living the way you did. Ever. I promise."

"Thank you."

He stood and held out his hand. "Come."

I let him pull me from the bed, and he helped me slip on my robe. We headed to the kitchen, and he glanced over his shoulder. "Paolo said to tell you he still has baking supplies at his house."

I laughed. "Two peas in a pod."

"Mockingbird, he said to me, in case you were interested." He winked. "You can give him whatever kind that is, and I'll take a hummingbird cake."

I rolled my eyes at his teasing. "I think I can manage that."

He slid a coffee my way. "I knew you could."

He waited until I picked up my cup to set a small black box on the table.

I froze, the mug partway to my mouth. I set it down carefully. "What is that?"

He smirked. "A gift."

"For?"

"You, Little Bee. Who else would I buy a gift for? The cat?"

"You are extraordinarily fond of her."

"I'm salmon fond of her. Not expensive-gift fond. That is reserved just for you."

I eyed the box with worry. "How expensive?"

He tapped the box closer. "Wildly. Now, open it."

I took the box, looking at it in my hand. Tracing the leather, admiring the gilt on the top. The tiny little latch. Even the outside was beautiful. I couldn't imagine the inside. I looked up, meeting his eyes.

"Thank you," I breathed. "Whatever this is, I love it. I love you."

His golden gaze gleamed, and he leaned close, grasping the back of my neck and pulling me to his mouth. He kissed me long and slow. "My God, I love you, Brianna, my soon-to-be wife."

"Why?"

"Because most women would open the box. Maybe stare at the inside and decide it was all right. Or not. They wouldn't love it because of the gesture."

"Oh."

He kissed me again. "Don't ever change, Little Bee."

I pushed him away, winking. "Stop. I may have to reassess once I see what is in here."

He laughed loudly. "Okay, then. Open away."

My breath caught at the sight of the ring nestled in the black velvet. Yellow and white gemstones shimmered and glistened in the sun. I pulled it from the mooring, turning it around in the light. Dante leaned forward, taking it from my hand. "Yellow and white diamonds," he explained. "I thought you would like them together. Set in a band with no beginning and no end. Just like us. One second, there was me. Then suddenly, you were there, and it was us." He slid the ring on my finger. "And soon, the whole world will know you are mine."

"It's so beautiful," I managed to choke out. "I've never seen another one like it."

"Each one is an emerald cut. Unique. Like you. But you can wear it even when you're baking. I don't want you to take it off."

He slid to one knee in front of me. "I didn't ask you, Bee. I told you that you were marrying me. But I want you to know I did that because I can't be without you. I need you more than I have ever needed anything in my life. So, marry me, *please*. Be beside me. I will love and protect you with everything in me. Always."

"Yes," I responded, throwing my arms around his neck and launching myself on him. He caught me, falling back, holding me tight and kissing me.

"Can I buy you a ring?" I asked.

"Yes."

"And you'll wear it?"

"I will happily mark myself as taken. Yes."

"Can we go shopping today?"

"After you bake a cake."

"Then let's go!"

T had never dreamed of my wedding when I was a little girl. Never planned the day or even expected to get married. But somehow, Dante created a day filled with every dream I'd never known I had.

The large sunroom was filled with flowers. Candlelight flickered. It was a small gathering. Dante's family and a few friends, including Richard and his daughter. The sun was setting as I walked toward him, wearing a dress I had picked out. Amanda and Carolina had taken me shopping, and when I saw this dress, I was in love. In the softest of yellows with an overlay of lace, it was beautiful, and I knew Dante would go crazy over it. I adored the feminine, flirty look, and when I slipped it on, it fit perfectly. Amanda insisted on having my hair and makeup done, and I was shocked at the pretty woman who looked at me in the reflection in the mirror. Small pearls and glittering beads were woven into my hair that was caught in a loose chignon at the base of my neck. I wore a pair of earrings Dante had given me that morning, and the yellow diamonds glinted in my ears and on my hand. He was tall, stern, and sexy in his tuxedo. Until he saw me. Then he smiled, those dimples I saw so rarely standing out. Or dipping in, actually. He was so handsome, he took my breath away.

He stepped forward, meeting me partway, holding my hand and bringing me with him to the altar. Like a guiding hero, making sure I was where I needed to be.

The stuff of dreams.

Until the vows. They started off well enough. We exchanged traditional vows, then we had wanted to add something personal, and I went first.

"Dante, you gave me a place to call home. You gave me your heart, the greatest gift of all. You make me safe, loved, and seen. I promise to love you forever, and I look forward to our life together." I tried to blink away my tears, but they kept coming. He smiled and wiped my cheek.

"You didn't say anything about making me cakes," he said with a grin.

I knew what he was doing. "I thought that was a given."

"I'd rather you vowed it in church. Made it official."

"This isn't church, Dante. It's your brother's sunroom."

He shrugged. "Still..."

I tried not to giggle. "I promise to make you lots of cakes."

He raised a quizzical eyebrow. "Anytime I want?"

"Yes."

"Good."

"Dante," the minister prompted, sounding impatient.

It was then I saw it. His eyes were bright. He was making light, but his emotions were high. He was struggling to contain himself. He cleared his throat.

"You made me whole, Little Bee. I love you." He folded his hands and nodded.

The minister looked startled. "Is that all?" he whispered.

"Oh." Dante smiled. "Brianna, love of my life, you look stunning. That dress is spectacular."

I tried not to smile as the family tittered.

Dante leaned forward, dropping his voice, but everyone heard him.

"As gorgeous as it is on, I can hardly wait to see how it looks in a pile of lace beside our bed. If we make it that far."

He stood back, proud and unashamed. The minister looked as if he was going to swallow his tongue. Paolo barked out a laugh then covered his mouth when Amanda elbowed him. Carolina giggled and Allan smiled. Even Richard guffawed. I rolled my eyes.

"Forgive him," I said. "At his advanced age, he gets his words mixed up. Speaks out in inappropriate moments."

Dante lifted his eyebrow in warning.

"I love him desperately, but I hope he can keep up. I'd hate to have to trade him in for a better-behaved, younger, more...robust model."

Dante growled and did exactly what I knew he would do. He swept me into his arms in front of everyone and kissed me until I was breathless. Then he stood me upright and waved his hand. "Proceed."

The minister looked confused. "I didn't say to kiss your bride."

I blinked and smiled. "And he's impatient."

Dante laughed, throwing his head back in amusement. "I prefer your words, Little Bee. I'm more about showing than speaking." He winked.

I smiled because I didn't care. I knew he'd whisper his words of love in private. Show me his devotion. That was how he worked.

He lifted my hands and kissed them. He glanced at the minister. "Now?"

The minister had clearly given up. "You are now husband and wife. You may—"

Dante cut him off and kissed me again, cupping my face and smiling. "My wife."

"Yours."

"All my life," he breathed. "You and cake. I'm the luckiest bastard."

Definitely dreamy stuff.

TWO YEARS LATER

DANTE

I stood at the window of my gallery, watching as the customers came and went from the small shop across the street. The Little Bee Bakery was a roaring success.

When Brianna had seen the vacant shop, she'd told me her vision. I wondered how her more North American cakes would go over in Italy, but she insisted the tourists would love them.

"A taste of home, Dante."

So I bought the shop, had it fitted for her, and she opened her doors.

She had been correct. But not only did the tourists love it, so did the locals. Brianna hired and trained several women, and they were all needed to keep up with the demand.

I glanced at my watch, pleased. It was almost afternoon closing time. I'd go get my wife, and we'd go back to the villa. It was a warm day, and I knew she'd love to swim for a bit. She was now completely comfortable in the water. I'd even gotten her on my boat a few times, although the open sea was different from the pool. But baby steps.

My time with Robin Hood ended. I needed to keep Brianna safe, and I didn't want any of the nasty business that occurred with Winters to be repeated. I didn't need the money or the thrill of the hunt anymore. If I saw something suspicious, I did report it in hopes of helping the cause, but that was it. Once he died, the rumors Winters was causing did as well, and I was happy to live in peace. I had a different source of adrenaline now. My wife.

Being married, at least to Brianna, was a wonder. Every day was a new discovery. She still mouthed off, teased me, and made me work for her attention at times, but I loved it. She was a challenge that would never end for me.

She was perfect.

Even when she was calling me old man.

I thought of last week.

I'd heard her in the kitchen, humming away as she baked. I opened the office door so I could hear her better, finding myself humming the tune with her. I knew it but couldn't place it. It went round and round in my head until I thought I would go crazy. Giving up the task I was trying to accomplish, I headed downstairs to ask her.

I walked into the kitchen, the answer solved quickly. She was singing now, softly, with a wide smile on her face. But I heard the words and recognized the tune finally. "Frosty the Snowman"—with a twist.

Frosty, the old man, was a grumpy, grouchy soul

I changed him, you see

'Cause he loved me

And my heart of gold...

She stopped when she saw me.

"Hi," she squeaked.

"Think you're clever?"

She put down the piping bag. "Pretty much."

"You know what happens when you call me old man."

She darted to the right, heading for the patio. I chased her, catching her before she got too far.

She never really tried too hard to get away these days.

And the pool was still her favorite place to frolic.

I grinned, thinking of the amount of water that had been splashed. I turned and let my managers know I was leaving and headed across the street. Inside the bakery, I inhaled the warm aromas of cinnamon and sugar, chocolate, and coffee. I loved coming in here, not only to see my wife, but to snag some treats.

The women behind the counter greeted me, laughing as I grabbed a cookie from the display and headed to the kitchen. The shop was empty now, and they waved as they left, turning the sign on the door to Closed.

I found Brianna working in the kitchen, her brow furrowed in concentration as she piped a design. I studied her for a moment, noting she looked a little tired today. Maybe she needed a break. She had staff she trusted, and I was at her constantly not to work so much. This seemed a good time to bring up the idea of a trip.

I stood behind her, looping my arms around her waist. I kissed her neck, liking the fact that she still shivered at my caresses.

"Hey, Little Bee. Almost done?"

"Yes. I see you were dipping into the profits again."

I reached around her and grabbed some cake scraps on the worktop, munching them. "I have no idea what you're talking about."

She laughed and added a final swirl. "There. Done."

"Special order?"

"The most special. A very picky customer."

She moved away, and I studied the cake. It was a pair of baby booties, yellow and white, the icing mimicking the knit pattern. It was so realistic, even the size. I narrowed my eyes and read the writing.

"Congratulations, Daddy."

I kissed her temple. "Seems a shame to have such a little cake, but it is fabulous, Little Bee. Someone is going to be happy today."

"I hope so."

"Are they picking it up or delivery?"

"We can just take it home," she murmured.

"Home? They're picking it up at the villa?" That was a first, and I wasn't sure I wanted people coming to the villa to pick up a cake. "I can take it to them."

Brianna sighed, her voice patient. "I made it for you."

"But why would I want—*holy shit*."

Everything stopped. She was tired. Extra cuddly these days. She made me a baby bootie cake. Because the baby was mine.

"You're pregnant?"

"Yes."

I pulled her into my arms, joy filling my body. I kissed her repeatedly, running my hands over her stomach in wonder. "How pregnant?"

"About six weeks. The trip to Naples for the weekend."

I grinned at her. "The terrace."

She nodded. "The terrace." She winked. "Not bad for an old man."

I laughed.

"Is everything okay? You're okay?"

"Everything is good. I'm a little tired."

"No more working every day." When she began to protest, I shook my head. "I mean it, Little Bee. You're cutting back. You have great staff, and you can let them run it. Oversee it the way I do the galleries. No more."

"So bossy."

"You love it."

She leaned into me with a yawn. "I do."

"Let's take the cake home and have a nap, then celebrate."

"Is that a euphemism?"

"That's whatever you want it to be, my wife." I kissed her. "Thank you."

She smiled at me, her dark eyes glowing. "I love you."

"I love you."

A YEAR LATER

I stared down into the crib. My daughter slept, a fist in her mouth even as she slumbered. Her dark hair curled on her forehead. Her beautiful eyes were closed, but when open, they were the most stunning combination of Brianna's chocolate and my golden hue. Almost amber with deep brown flecks. We had watched them change in wonder, amazed when they finished.

I was as obsessed with her as I was with my wife. I had immersed myself in Brianna's pregnancy, reading books, learning everything I could. But none of it mattered when Melody was born. All that mattered was her and the immense love I had for my daughter.

I now had two women to protect. And I would —endlessly.

Brianna came beside me, slipping her arm around my waist. "How's our girl?"

"Perfect."

She laughed softly, trailing a finger down Melody's cheek.

"Ready to have another one yet?" I asked.

She peered at me, shaking her head.

"We make beautiful babies. I think we should have three really fast. Let them be close."

"Forget it, old man. I've barely recovered from this one. We just started having sex again."

"Don't say that word in front of Melody."

I loved her name. She was my heart's music. When Brianna had suggested it, it fit her perfectly.

Brianna laughed. "She can't understand us."

"She needs a brother."

"Did she tell you this?"

"In her own unique way, yes."

"I think you misheard her. Your hearing and all."

I put my lips to Brianna's ear. "You trying to rile me up, Little Bee?"

She shivered.

"You want me to prove it to you?" I whispered, grinning. She wanted another baby too. She was playing hard to get. Riling me up so I'd show her who was boss.

"Prove what? That your sperm are still viable?"

She gasped as I swung her into my arms. "I'm going to show you how viable, Little Bee. Twice. Let's hope Melody cooperates. If not, I'll get a nanny in here and kidnap you for a few hours."

She smiled up at me. "It won't be the first time."

I kissed her. "Or the last."

She snuggled against my chest. "Okay. As long as it's you. My favorite kidnapper."

"Damn right."

I carried her to our room, tossing her playfully onto the bed. I hovered over her. "I have you at my mercy now, little prisoner. Trapped in my lair. What will you do?"

She played with my hair, her smile filled with love.

"I'll have to endure. I think I can handle it for a hundred years or so."

"That's a start."

"I love you," she whispered.

I covered her mouth with mine.

"I love you, Little Bee. Always."

Thank you so much for reading MY FAVORITE KIDNAPPER. If you are so inclined, reviews are always welcome by me at your retailer.

This story was written during a difficult time. I wasn't able to find the words for the scheduled manuscript. I had a ridiculous conversation with my PA about the books we were reading. Like Brianna, the idea of this story was unexpected but lovely. As the idea of Dante took root, the words flowed.

If romantic comedy is your favorite trope, Liam and Shelby, from my novel Changing Roles, would be a recommended standalone to read next. It is a story of friends to lovers set in the bright lights of Hollywood.

Enjoy meeting other readers? Lots of fun, with upcoming book talk and giveaways! Check out Melanie Moreland's Minions on Facebook.

Join my newsletter for up-to-date news, sales, book announcements and excerpts (no spam). Click here to sign up Melanie Moreland's newsletter
or visit https://bit.ly/MMorelandNewsletter

Visit my website www.melaniemoreland.com

Enjoy reading! Melanie

IN THE FUTURE - DANTE

My phone rang, and I picked it up, already smiling. Whenever Brianna called me, I smiled.

She was busy at the bakery today with a wedding cake. As usual, she wanted to make sure it was perfect. I had thought she'd be home already, but I knew sometimes things went awry. I had learned to be patient.

"Hey, Little Bee. All done?"

There was silence for a moment before Brianna responded. Her voice was thick, and I knew she'd been crying.

"Dante? I need you."

I was on my feet instantly. "What is it? What is wrong? Where are you?"

"The hospital. It-it's not me. But I need you. Please."

"I'm on my way."

I made sure Melody was good with Gia, and I raced to my car. The dust kicked up behind me as my tires squealed in my haste to get to my wife.

She said it wasn't her. Melody was safe. One of her staff?

Was she lying and it was her, but she didn't want me to freak out? That was something she would do to keep me calm.

If that was it, her plan failed.

I pressed on the gas harder.

She was outside the hospital, sitting on a bench holding a child, speaking to a woman. I jumped from the car, rushing toward her. I dropped to my knees in front of her. "Brianna, my love. What is it? Are you all right?"

She nodded. "I'm fine."

I scanned her from head to foot. She looked fine, other than tired. She had flour on her face and arms. Arms that held a small boy. Thin and sad, he was clinging to her as if she was a lifeline. He had a mop of wild curls on his head. His dark eyes met mine, the sadness and pain in them almost knocking me off my feet. Instinct led, and I kept my voice soft as I spoke to him. "Hey, little guy."

He stared at me, frightened.

"Who is your friend?" I asked Brianna, knowing somehow, whoever this child was, he was part of the mystery and I was going to get to know him better.

"Angelo," she replied.

"Does he speak English?"

"We think so. Italian, for sure."

I switched, speaking directly to him. "Hello, Angelo. I'm Dante." I patted Brianna's leg. "I'm her husband."

He nodded, indicating he understood me.

"Explain," I said quietly to my wife. "Tell me what is happening."

"I always bring extra cake to the children. If they are well enough to eat it, it is a treat for them. Angelo's parents were killed in an accident. He was hurt, but he's healing. I saw him here a few weeks ago, and he smiled at me and held my hand. I couldn't get him out of my mind." She stopped and kissed his head. "He was with a family, but he ran away. I found him in my storage room, behind the sacks of flour. He was sitting in the corner. Alone. I remembered him, and I brought him back. He won't talk to anyone except me. And he won't let go of me." She grabbed my hand. "He has no one, Dante. They are trying to find him another placement." Her voice dropped to a whisper. "A foster."

I met her eyes. The desperation in them shocked me.

"He came to me," she whispered. "He climbed in my lap. He tried to talk. He hasn't talked in weeks." I saw her arms tighten around him. Watched how he burrowed closer, seeking her embrace. "He needs a family."

"Brianna," I breathed out, shocked when I realized what she was asking.

"I can't." She shook her head. "He's been sent back three times. He is too old for the system. I know what happens."

"You can't save everyone."

There was a beat of silence. "But I can save one."

This was the last thing I'd expected. If she had asked me to buy her diamonds, another bakery, a bigger house, it would have been less shocking than this.

A child she had somehow connected with so strongly, she refused to loosen her hold on him.

I glanced at the woman who was watching us in silence. She introduced herself as Margo, Angelo's caseworker. I stood and drew her to the side.

"Do the people he was with know he has been found?"

"Yes. They, ah, don't want him back. They were on the verge of sending him back when he disappeared two days ago."

"Did they notify the police?"

"Yes. But they made no effort to look for him otherwise."

"Why were they sending him back?" I asked, confused. He wasn't a broken toy you returned and got a new one. He was a child. One in obvious need of love and understanding.

"His silence. It unnerves people. He hadn't spoken a word the whole time he was with them. But he spoke to your wife. She got him to eat. She even made him grin." Her smile was kind. "She got further with him than any other person we've seen."

"Dammit," I said quietly. I hadn't expected this. Not in a million years.

"May I have a moment alone with my wife?"

"Of course."

We sat in an office with glass windows. Angelo never took his eyes off Brianna. He didn't protest as she sat him beside Margo.

I knelt in front of her. "Little Bee, I adore your heart, but this?"

"Please," she whispered. "I can't explain it, Dante, but it has to be us. If not, he is going into the system, and he is going to be like me. He will never have a family."

"What about our family?" I asked gently. "Melody?" I placed my hand on the small swell of her tummy. "This little one growing inside you?"

"I can love them all. We are what he needs. I feel it with everything in me."

"Even if that is the case, there are rules. Paperwork. Waiting periods."

"No. I want to take him home today. See how he and Melody get along."

"So, a visit, then."

"We just won't bring him back."

"That's kidnapping, Little Bee."

"You're good at it," she said.

I had to smile. "Not this time."

"You have pull, Dante. Lots of it. The mayor, the police chief. If anyone could do this, it would be you." She pulled at my hand. "I need it to be you."

I couldn't say no to her. I never could.

"Only a visit. And we have to talk."

She smiled. "Once you get to know him, you will love him. You won't want to give him back." She leaned close. "Let me take him home. Even for a few days. Please."

"He has to be told he is a guest. You cannot get his expectations up, Brianna."

"I know. I won't."

I straightened. "I will speak to him."

To my surprise, she didn't argue.

Margo and I changed places, and I spoke in Italian to Angelo.

"You ran from your home."

"Not home," he mumbled. He kicked at the chair leg. "No love."

That made my chest hurt. He said so much with so few words.

"You could come home with us and visit," I said. "Until they find you a home. But you have to talk to us."

He looked longingly at Brianna. "Pretty lady. Kind. Hugs." He met my eyes, his sadness piercing and deep.

He stretched his body up, and I lowered my head, realizing he wanted to say something private. His voice was low and raspy. "My heart doesn't hurt so much when she hugs me."

Then he lapsed into silence and looked away. His shoulders bowed in, and he sighed. Then to my shock, he nestled into my side, a warm weight pressing on my torso. He showed me so much trust in his simple gesture, I was stunned. He used his voice because I asked. His words were few, but he said exactly what he needed to say.

"Dammit," I muttered. I pulled my phone from my pocket. I had favors to call in.

A month later...

"What's that?" Angelo's quiet voice asked.

I smiled down at him. He was perched on my knee while I was at my desk. He traced his little finger over the image on my screen.

"A sculpture I want to buy."

He looked around my office. "Like those?"

"Yes."

"Pretty."

I pressed a kiss to his temple. "It is."

Since he'd come home with us, life had changed. He had changed. We had all changed. It was as if I was seeing things with new eyes. The wonder that shone from his. His words were still limited, but he used them every day. He adored Brianna, worshipped Melody, and for some reason, refused to leave my side. He sought me out whenever he wasn't busy with Melody. She fascinated him, and she seemed equally enthralled. She babbled away at him in her little baby voice, shared her toys, squealed when she saw him in the mornings, and he was endlessly patient with her. His manners were impeccable. He was intelligent, sweet, and loving. Quiet but not silent. Nothing like the boy who was rejected three times.

Brianna insisted he'd been waiting for us. I tended to agree with her but didn't let her know it.

He was picking up English easily. He constantly listened to Brianna and asked me often if he was confused. For a six-year-old, he was amazingly adept. We encouraged him all the time.

Margo had been to visit, shocked at the difference in him. He had been upset when he saw her, thinking he was going to be leaving, but we sat him down and assured him he wasn't going anywhere.

Brianna had combed her fingers through his wild, curly hair, shaking her head. *"Home, my Angelo. You are home with us now."* I hadn't fought her on it. I knew she was right.

He relaxed when Margo left, leaving him behind. I found him later in my office, staring at some of my art. It seemed to relax him, and since then, he'd spent a lot of time with me in here. I enjoyed having him with me.

"Dammit," I muttered as I watched the price go up on the auction. It was getting close to my maximum bid, and I wondered if I should increase it or let it go.

He looked at me with a frown. "Bad?"

"Lots of money."

"So pretty."

Angelo liked pretty.

I called my business manager, instructing him to increase my bid, and ten minutes later, the sculpture was mine.

I grinned in victory, raising my hands. "Yay!" I exclaimed, chuckling when Angelo did the same.

"How about a swim and some ice cream?" I asked. He loved both.

"Yay!" He scooted off my lap, and I heard his little feet thumping down the steps. I knew he'd find Brianna to help him. He'd want Melody in the pool with us. I was teaching him to swim, and he loved it, completely at home in the water. She would splash around with us, safe in my arms.

A moment later, Brianna walked in, smiling. Her bump was getting bigger, and she looked healthy. Happy. I held out my arms, laughing as she curled up on my lap, much like Angelo had been. I pressed a kiss to her temple.

"Hello, Little Bee."

"Hi."

"I was going to take the kids in the pool."

"Margo called. She gave us a glowing recommendation."

"Of course she did. Our boy is talking, eating, and smiling. Given what he has overcome, she must be thrilled with his progress." I kissed her head again. "And it is because of you."

She tilted her head up. "Of us. He loves you, Dante. He trusts you."

"He trusts both of us." I took in a deep breath. "I won't let him down, Brianna. I spoke with the right people, and we are keeping him."

Her eyes filled with tears. "Forever?"

"I have no idea how, but he is part of us now. It was as if he filled a little piece that was missing." I shrugged. "I can't explain it."

"I know. That was how I felt as soon as I saw him. When I found him in the storage room, it was a sign. He knew to come to me. To us. Melody loves him. An instant big brother."

I rubbed her bump. "He'll have two sisters soon. We'll be outnumbered for good."

"At least you'll have one other male."

I chuckled. "Me and my boy."

She smiled as I wiped away the tears from under her eyes. "You really feel that way?"

"Yes. He is mine now as much as Melody is. I asked to fast-track the process and adopt him. There is no family. Not even a distant cousin. This is where he belongs."

Brianna threw her arms around me, kissing me with utter abandon. I kissed her back, groaning at the feeling of her in my arms. The taste of her.

Until little feet headed this way interrupted us. I grinned against her mouth. "Our son is about to burst in here, demanding my attention."

She cupped my face. "To be continued later. I'll get our daughter, and we can swim for a while."

"Perfect."

The sun glistened on the water. Melody splashed, gurgling and happy. She loved the pool, and I laughed as I watched her try out the new floating device that kept her upright, while her arms and hands were free. She was fascinated with the water, staring at it dripping from her hands, then splashing more, squealing in delight. Brianna was beside her, ever watchful. Angelo waited as I blew up his water wings and then jumped into the pool, impatient to be in the water. He dog-paddled over to me and used my knee to launch himself back into the water. I gave him a kickboard so he could kick his way around the pool.

"Shallow end only," I cautioned him.

"Okay, Papa."

I was stunned at his words. I looked over at Brianna, who was observing us with a smile. She caught her lip between her teeth, trying to hold in her emotion. I pointed to her. "Who is that?"

"Mamma."

I nodded, the final proof that he belonged with us right there. He felt it as well.

He looked up at me. "Right?"

"Yes. Right."

He sighed happily. "Home."

He kicked away, leaving me reeling. He was part of us. It had been as easy as breathing. As easy as falling in love with Brianna. It shouldn't happen this way. I doubted it ever did. But he was ours. Our boy. My son.

And what happened next proved it.

He slipped from the board, going under for a second and coming up, sputtering and shaking his head. He glared at the board, reaching for it.

"Dammit," he muttered.

Brianna's head snapped our way. I tried to look shocked and cover up my laughter. I used the word often enough, muttered under my breath. I wasn't surprised he'd picked it up.

Brianna turned her gaze to me. Laser-focused and intense.

I would have to chastise him. Correct him and tell him he couldn't use that word. That "Papa" shouldn't use that word. I shook my head, trying to convey with my eyes what I couldn't say.

He grinned. "Oops. Sorry, Mamma. I meant *fudge-sackle*."

His use of the word, the one Brianna often uttered, was perfect. Highly amusing, drawn out in English with his thick Italian accent.

I began to laugh. Even Brianna chuckled, shaking her head.

"Boys," she admonished.

"You got me in trouble," I whispered to him. "But good save."

He winked at me.

Winked.

Sharing the joke. Knowing what he did. Proving once again, he was ours.

I began to laugh again.

My little man.

Our son.

Acknowledgments

There have been many hands and eyes on this book.

Betas, sensitivity readers, language checkers, editors, proofers, designers—thank you to each and every one of you. You made this project so enjoyable.

Lisa, as usual, thank you for all your work.

Karen—you wanted this one and dove in so fast and did such a good job. Love you.

To my Minions, my Literary Mob, my extra team for this book—Thank you for all your efforts and support. I appreciate and love you all.

All the bloggers and book lovers—thank you for sharing your passion.

And Matthew—you lost me for a while to this one.

Thank you for all your patience and love.
You are the one who holds my heart captive.
Never let go.

Also Available from Moreland Books

BAM - The Beginning (Prequel)

Bentley (Vested Interest #1)

Aiden (Vested Interest #2)

Maddox (Vested Interest #3)

Reid (Vested Interest #4)

Van (Vested Interest #5)

Halton (Vested Interest #6)

Sandy (Vested Interest #7)

Vested Interest/ABC Crossover

A Merry Vested Wedding

ABC Corp Series

My Saving Grace (Vested Interest: ABC Corp #1)

Finding Ronan's Heart (Vested Interest: ABC Corp #2)

Loved By Liam (Vested Interest: ABC Corp #3)

Age of Ava (Vested Interest: ABC Corp #4)

Sunshine & Sammy (Vested Interest: ABC Corp #5)

Unscripted With Mila (Vested Interest: ABC Corp #6)

Men of Hidden Justice

The Boss

Second-In-Command

About the Author

NYT/WSJ/USAT international bestselling author Melanie Moreland, lives a happy and content life in a quiet area of Ontario with her beloved husband of thirty-plus years and their rescue cat, Amber. Nothing means more to her than her friends and family, and she cherishes every moment spent with them.

While seriously addicted to coffee, and highly challenged with all things computer-related and technical, she relishes baking, cooking, and trying new recipes for people to sample. She loves to throw dinner parties, and enjoys traveling, here and abroad, but finds coming home is always the best part of any trip.

Melanie loves stories, especially paired with a good wine, and enjoys skydiving (free falling over a fleck of dust) extreme snowboarding (falling down stairs) and piloting her own helicopter (tripping over her own feet.) She's learned happily ever afters, even bumpy ones, are all in how you tell the story.

Melanie is represented by Flavia Viotti at Bookcase Literary Agency. For any questions regarding subsidiary or translation rights please contact her at flavia@bookcaseagency.com

facebook.com/authormoreland

twitter.com/morelandmelanie

instagram.com/morelandmelanie

bookbub.com/authors/melanie-moreland

Milton Keynes UK
Ingram Content Group UK Ltd.
UKHW021427070324
439104UK00010B/846

9 781990 803358